MURDER AT TANTON TOWERS

Praise for Amy Myers

About the author

Amy Myers has written a wide range of novels, from crime to historical sagas to contemporary romance. She is also well known for her mystery short stories that have been published in *Ellery Queen Mystery Magazine* and many anthologies.

Her traditional and cozy mystery series include the Jack Colby, car detective mysteries, co-written with her husband, American-born car buff James Myers; the Auguste Didier series; the Tom Wasp, Victorian chimney sweep novels; the Marsh and Daughter mysteries; and the Nell Drury mysteries.

amymyers.net

For Sally and Martin French
with my gratitude

Acknowledgements

There is no point having a bright idea unless others see it that way too and put it into practice with their expertise. That the fictitious Tanton Towers came into being is therefore thanks to my wonderful publishers, Severn House, to my equally wonderful agent, Sara Keane of Keane Kataria Literary Agency, and the invaluable Gaye Banyard and Martin and Sally French.

I am doubly glad of their help for *Murder at Tanton Towers* because it has enabled me to fulfil a long overdue duty of care to my late friend Carol Tyler. She left behind her the results of several years' research into a particular painting by the 16th-century artist Lavinia Fontana of Bologna. By that time it was not only me who had become involved with Lavinia. My husband and two American friends, Tom and Marie O'Day, were all roped in. On Carol's behalf they made a frantic dash across Washington DC's busy roads to the National Museum of Women in the Arts, who were at the time holding the first US exhibition of Lavinia Fontana's work. They left with Vera Fortunati's magnificent book on the exhibition, which, together with the file of my friend's research, I brought with me when clearing out her home after her death. They fired me with such enthusiasm that I vowed to myself that by hook or by crook I would introduce Lavinia into one of my novels.

Time passed and none of my novels appeared to be exactly the 'right' one – until I began to plan *Murder at Tanton Towers*. The idea of La Galleria was born and I hope Carol would have approved of Lavinia's role in it. She is very far from being a little-known artist and there is a vast bibliography on Lavinia and her work. The paintings that I have described in this novel's La Galleria are, however, fictitious, as are Tanton Towers and village. Since this is a novel, I have not been able to do full justice to Lavinia Fontana's life and works. Do browse the web if she is a stranger to you, as she once was to me all those years ago. Thank you, Carol.

Amy Myers

ONE

Three cheers for Tanton Towers! Cara Shelley blew it a kiss as she hurried down the slope from the lawn to her café after closing time to clear up the remaining dirty plates and teacups. She loved it to bits. There it stood in all its ridiculous majesty. Towers, spires, turrets, chimneys, gables, red bricks and solid grey ragstone, all put together into a glorious whole.

Yes, she had made the right decision in setting up the Happy Huffkin Café in the old folly in the Towers' gardens, especially as the folly was as weird and exciting as Tanton Towers itself. Everyone, save her daughter Kate, had said she was crazy to undertake the café project. It had all begun with Kate's casual remark while on a school holiday job at the Towers.

'Paper cups and biscuits,' she'd said in disgust. 'Why don't they get real?'

The Happy Huffkin was born and here Cara was installed three years later in a mock castle folly, as happy as her name for the café had predicted. She had become part of the Tanton Towers scenery, so to speak. That she should be so lucky!

Tanton Towers itself gloried in being eccentric. That's exactly why it had been built in the late eighteenth century by the highly eccentric Sir Jeffry Farran, planned as a stately home that paid homage to its ancient classic tradition. Sir Jeffry, however, had attacked the project enthusiastically with more than a dash of his own whimsical fancies.

'Gothic and ghouls,' so a visitor had once remarked to Cara, staring nervously at the gargoyles on the folly who were peering at him from all directions.

Ghouls indeed. Cara considered them as friends and consulted them on a daily basis (silently of course). Tanton Towers was full of friends. Standing on the hillside overlooking the village, this huge wonderful house was a refuge from the woes of the world. Cara had had enough woes of her own.

It was well past the estate's closing time of 5 o'clock and the Towers, including the orangery, had shut its doors half an hour earlier than that so it was at peace now. This was a time of day that Cara loved, the time when the chirping of the birds and the scent from the flower beds and rose garden could be enjoyed to their full, especially in mid-June on days like this. It was then that she could take walks around the woodland area of the Kentish estate which spread down the hillside to the River Mizzle. That was a grand name for what was merely a trickling stream joining another one that had once flowed vigorously through the Syndale valley to meet the Faversham Creek as it made its stately progress to the Kentish coast and the sea.

What must it be like to actually own the Towers' estate? A glorious privilege but a monster worry too, in Cara's view. Max Farran Pryde's family had owned it since Sir Jeffry Farran (no Pryde then) had gleefully built this magnificently weird house and Max and his wife, Alison, now her good friends, oversaw the management of the Towers. Max was formally Professor Farran Pryde and had semi-retired when he inherited the estate. He wasn't exactly a prototype absent-minded professor, but he was certainly a single-minded one, as his beloved gallery of paintings by his favourite artist tended to come first.

There had been no knighthood for him to inherit from Sir Jeffry's descendant Sir Alfred, Max had explained. That was owing to a clash with King Edward VII when Sir Alfred had the temerity to marry a lady on whom His Majesty had his eye firmly fixed. The Pryde had joined the family name early in the nine-teenth century when – horror of horrors – a daughter had been the only child born to Sir Jeffry's son Thomas. Max and Alison's own three offspring were all at large in the world, fluttering back like birds to their home nest from time to time.

And Alison? How to describe Alison? Cara always found that hard. She knew her too well. Alison could reach out to everyone regardless of who and what they were and her smile endeared her to one and all. She had the knack of obeying society's rules but calmly making them immaterial.

'Cara!'

That was *Alison.* No calm about that cry! She could see Alison hurtling down the steps from the Towers' orangery, clearly on her way to the café. Cara was jerked out of complacency. She was used to Alison's summons for help but this one was different. It sounded like real trouble. Alison usually sailed with equanimity through the mini disasters of everyday life. Something was definitely wrong.

'*Cara!*'

Seriously wrong. Alarmed, Cara was already running across the lawn. 'I'm coming!' she shouted, her heart pounding as she ran to meet her.

Max was obviously tucked away as usual out of the reach of daily dramas as there was no sign of him. Typical, Cara thought, exasperation mixed with fondness. Whatever had happened, Alison couldn't cope and Cara wasn't sure she could either.

'What's wrong?' Cara cried out as she reached Alison.

'Come and look. You must.' Alison pulled her towards the steps up to the terrace. 'It's *Daphne.*'

Of course it would be. Cara relaxed. Dramas were always happening to Daphne, often self-induced. 'Is she ill?' she asked. 'Where's Mike? He can usually help.'

Mike Hanson, the Towers' accountant, was Daphne's husband and therefore well acquainted with his wife's 'emergencies'. The last one had been an extra-large spider that had obstinately lodged itself in the bonnet Daphne was just about to place on her head.

A violent shake of Alison's head. 'He's already left. She's *dead*, Cara.'

Daphne? For a moment Cara couldn't take it in. For all her drawbacks, Daphne was the sweetest of women. She really was, albeit that she was the greatest nosy parker in Kent. Plump, in her late forties, and always beaming, Daphne had elected herself as queen of the dancing troupe which only an hour or two earlier had been entertaining the public by dancing on the Tanton Towers' lawn in eighteenth-century dress, accompanied by a keyboard pianist and fiddler on the terrace. No one could beat Daphne at whirling around, dancing the Sir Roger de Coverley, skirts twirling, bonnet askew and ribbons, feathers and flowers merrily flying everywhere.

'*Dead?* Are you sure?' This was all Cara could manage to ask, faced with such a shock. How could Daphne be *dead*? She tried to pull herself together. 'Is Rosalie still here?'

Rosalie Atkins, who looked after entrance fees and the shop, superintending the volunteers, was also the Towers' official first-aider and might be needed. Since it was long past closing time, even stragglers in the gardens would have left by now, so Rosalie would have departed from her post at the gatehouse entrance. It was nearly six o'clock and the dancers too would have long since changed as they departed at or before house closing time. All except Daphne.

'Have you called nine-nine-nine?' she cried out to Alison as they reached the terrace.

'*No!* I don't have my phone. Have you got yours?' Alison gasped. 'She's dead, Cara.'

By now they were on the terrace and close to the orangery entrance. Cara dragged her mobile out of her pocket, thanking her lucky stars she'd charged it that morning.

'Ambulance? Shall I call?'

'Police,' Alison managed to say, pushing Cara ahead of her through the doorway.

Police? What *was* this? Cara could only see June flowers and palm trees in large pots with small tables and chairs dotted between them for elegant tête-à-têtes – elegant in centuries past anyway. Nowadays they were a welcome attraction for toddlers and the elderly. On the wall opposite her two Greek god statues were staring down benignly from their alcoves at what was going on beneath them. There was no sign of Daphne. Had Alison got this wrong? Perhaps Daphne had recovered and departed. But why the need for the police?

Then Cara caught her breath in horror. She could see all too clearly why Alison had panicked. Partly masked by one of the trees, there was something – someone – lying there at the far end of the orangery. Terror-stricken, she rushed to check, hoping against forlorn hope that she was wrong. She wasn't. It was Daphne, still in her flimsy silken dancing dress, rucked up displaying the pantaloons beneath. Her bonnet lay forlornly nearby. Even before Cara reached her, she could see Daphne was dead. Horribly dead. The blue lips and extended tongue were all too clearly visible, as was the awful, hideous bruising on her neck. Unbelievably, horribly, Daphne had been strangled. Murdered.

'Pulse. I'll check,' Cara managed to say bravely, aware that Alison had crept up to stand behind her.

Summoning every ounce of mental strength she had, Cara forced herself to pick up Daphne's outstretched arm to feel for signs of life. There was nothing.

'No heartbeat,' she told Alison, wondering whether those words so strongly and confidently spoken were really hers. She seemed to be in two places at once: her outside self was taking control to help Alison, while inside she was stricken with inability to think what to do next, plunged into such horror.

No heartbeat. Daphne would never infuriate them again. Never would she laugh and joke with them. Never would she be leaping up and down in those whirling dances. In her mind Cara could hear Daphne's excited chatter, even as she looked at the still figure at her feet. Even as she punched 999 into her mobile.

Now that the police had marched in and taken over, relief began to give way to apprehension as Cara awaited the next stage. Alison, bless her, had taken on the task of accompanying the police to give Mike Hanson the dreadful news about his wife's death. He had already left before the grounds closed. He and Daphne lived in Tanton village bordering the river beneath the Towers and Daphne usually either walked or was driven home down Church Road. Today she had done neither. Given the shocking news, Mike had insisted on returning with Alison who had taken him to the Towers' family wing, where he had collapsed. Irritating though Daphne could be, it had seemed a stable marriage and how on earth was Mike going to cope with this atrocity?

Cara was waiting in the Snug, as it was affectionately known. Just inside the Towers' front entrance, it served as an entry point, general gathering place and dumping ground for staff or visitors. Now it was serving as the waiting room for unfortunates who had been instructed to await interrogation by Those Who Must Be Obeyed. At the moment its sole candidate was Cara.

Professor Max had promptly realized that the enchantments of history and art (his two great passions) enjoyed when he was tucked away in his study on the top floor had to be abandoned. Now he was efficiently obeying police orders to assemble all remaining inside and outside staff in the imposing Library leading off the Towers' main hall. But Cara was stuck here in the Snug, and the longer she waited, the more she fidgeted. The unknown was hard to bear.

The police's official arrival at Tanton Towers seemed to proclaim loudly that this was no longer the Towers' territory; it was theirs for the duration. But how to define duration, she wondered. How long would the police investigation take? How long before Tanton Towers was itself again? How long before the memory of Daphne's terrible death could be laid to gentle rest?

'Keep outside the tape please,' a young constable had ordered as he directed Cara here. It had been an ominous sign of things to come.

The crime scene cordon seemed to take in not just the orangery, terrace and much of the lawn, but also the dining and drawing rooms in the public part of the Towers, which also included the Hall, the Library and the Snug. The room not far from the orangery where the dancers changed on their way to perform on the lawn was within the cordon. Daphne, however, had apparently either not yet changed or had decided to go home in costume, which in one of her skittish moods she sometimes did. What had taken her to the orangery this afternoon, Cara wondered.

Before coming to the Snug, Cara had been asked to escort one of the constables to her Happy Huffkin Café in order to establish – presumably – whether a murderer could have used the folly as a hiding place. She'd explained the unlikelihood of her assistant, dear Sammy Jones, or herself or any remaining visitors peacefully taking tea and huffkins murdering anyone. The policeman had not seemed convinced even though Sammy had offered him a free huffkin as a goodwill gesture. Like scones, huffkins didn't take kindly to being kept for long, but nevertheless for Sammy, a baker's son, the gift of a huffkin, a Kentish speciality, was a privilege.

She wondered how many staff were gathering in the Library, presumably awaiting instructions of some sort. There wouldn't be many still here after closing time but the senior staff tended to stay later to chew over the day's events with each other. Robert Broome, the librarian and historian, had a habit of leaving the Archives Room at five o'clock promptly, all visitors having left the house half an hour earlier, so that he could browse in peace in the Library. Wedded to his job and to Tanton Towers itself, he had once confided in her that he had plans to write a book about the Towers. Admirable, though she doubted whether it would be a barrel of laughs. He was extremely serious about his role.

Rosalie might still be in the house, Cara realized. By the time she had discussed the day's takings with Dan Dickson, the Towers' business manager, she was usually here till about six or even six thirty, as was Dan himself, who prided himself on superintending the switch from daytime to overnight security.

Keeley Martin, the snappy young housekeeper (or Miss Clip-Clop as Cara privately named her, after the ridiculously high heels she favoured for work) who was responsible for the overall state of the Towers' public areas, might still have been around, as would Ewan Chapman, the enthusiastic and bouncy guided tours and events organizer. The volunteers would have already left, but some other staff members such as the grounds manager might still be here. And there might be a security guard or two already arriving for duty.

Depending on when Daphne died, any of them could in theory have had access to the orangery and murdered her – even now Cara couldn't believe that word. *Murdered.* At Tanton? It still seemed impossible. Was Daphne's murderer still here? After all, a visitor might have killed her if they had hidden somewhere inside at closing time. That passing thought gave Cara a crumb of comfort, because everyone who worked at Tanton was a friend – weren't they? Surely the warm greetings, willingness to share problems and generally help out that she'd always experienced didn't mask a murderer?

'You can always rely on our help,' Alison and Max had assured her when she first opened the Happy Huffkin Café, which fully deserved the name 'happy'. 'Every one of us will give you a hand if you need it.'

That, Cara had found, was true, although it hadn't taken long before she seemed to have gained a reputation amongst the staff for being the first port of call if problems arose. And today, she thought, was no exception, save that for once she was outside her comfort zone with a vengeance.

'Have you seen Alison, Cara?' Max himself suddenly appeared in the doorway, looking very shaken. He must be about five foot

ten and Alison was only an inch or two shorter than he was, so
being reasonably matched in size and build, Cara had mentally
and irreverently labelled them Tweedledum and Tweedledee. Not
today.

'She's probably still with Mike in your living room.' The
family wing branched out on the far side of the Towers – that's
if Tanton could be described as having 'sides', given its uneven
architecture with turrets and towers popping up all over the
place. It was shielded by a garden-cum-yard from the former
Not-To-Be-Seen servants' wing, which branched out not far
away, and which was shielded in its turn away from the Towers'
orangery for the same reason. In this complicated arrangement,
Sir Jeffry, who had insisted on his wishes being obeyed in every
respect by the architects of the Towers, proved himself a far
from ideal designer, having paid no heed to the fashion of
Palladian symmetry but too much to the new move towards
non-conformity.

'I'll join them when I can.' Max paused. 'What's behind this,
Cara? Any idea?'

This was a plea for help, she recognized. But for once she
had no answers save, 'Not yet. But I'll try.'

Where did that come from, she wondered. Looking at his
strained face, and remembering Alison's state, she knew the
answer to that. It was because for Max and Alison – and the
Towers itself – she was going to do her best to find out what
was 'behind this', as Max put it. In addition to the sheer awfulness of Daphne's death, it had cast shadows on the place that
meant so much to her. She had been happy here, so now she was
going to do her utmost to help – although that might mean
working out her own path to the truth. That's what happiness
demanded of you so, scary though it was, she'd find it. Somehow.
Even though the path ahead looked formidable.

TWO

M ax Farran Pryde paced around the Library, far from the placid person he always considered himself. People were coming and going in what was more a huge palace than a place of study, all looking as agitated as he felt. He couldn't leave because it had been deemed the meeting room for staff, but where was Alison? She must still be with Mike Hanson, who would need someone to talk to, but Max too had his fears.

That meant facing Mike. What on earth could he say to him? Poor fellow, he'd lost his wife in ghastly circumstances and no wonder Alison was with him. He'd do his best but in front of Mike he couldn't reveal his own concern at the frightful news about Daphne Hanson. She was a good woman and he could see no earthly reason why anyone would want to kill her. Unless, he reasoned, she'd got in someone's way. Could it be that someone had his eyes on Max's very special territory: his Lavinia Fontana art collection?

Not even Alison appreciated quite how important this collection displayed in La Galleria, the long gallery on the second floor, was to him. His specialist subject was classical history, but his private passion was Lavinia, as he thought of her. The sixteenth-century artist Lavinia Fontana of Bologna was the first woman painter of note and, whether one gazed at her portraits or at her religious paintings, there was depth, quality and an understanding of character and life itself within them.

'I know all about your secret life,' Alison often joked. 'Lavinia's your true love.'

She had a point, Max had admitted. Lavinia was indeed a refuge from the problems of the day. Her paintings were valuable – some *very* valuable. His predecessors at Tanton had begun the collection and it had been his honour to add several to it. One or two of them were 'school of Fontana', but her hand could surely be seen in them. And two in the collection intrigued him. One was a superb painting, but its subject was an unusual one for Lavinia. Would a sixteenth-century highly respected portrait painter, wife and mother choose a subject who definitely looked on the shady side of the law, a bearded rough-looking man who hardly seemed as if he had been born into the aristocracy in Bologna or anywhere else? Even more interesting was one of Lavinia's self-portraits, although it had an appeal quite different to the other self-portraits he'd seen of her, including one he owned himself. This was a woman with a fire and energy that had long fascinated him. This was no stay-at-home daughter and wife.

Above even these two paintings, however, was his own favourite, the jewel in the collection, Lavinia's portrait of Queen Elizabeth I of England, which he was convinced was genuine. Here was a lady who had gloried in victory over the arch enemy Spain, who had rid herself of those who sought to dethrone her, and who had the courage of a lion. A remarkable painting, so remarkable that he had carried out his own research into how this could possibly be genuine.

Nevertheless, Max was gripped with fear. Suppose art thieves had their eye on his collection? Suppose Daphne Hanson had come across a plan to steal one or more of the paintings? Could that be a reason for her death? No, Lavinia Fontana was a well-known artist but hardly Leonardo da Vinci when it came to market value. Anyway, that could make one of the Towers' staff a murderer, given that the volunteers would have disappeared as soon as the Towers closed and poor Daphne had, if he understood correctly from the pathologist, not died until about 5.30. Surely it was not possible that a staff member had killed her? Not at Tanton Towers. Its staff had become friends to Alison and himself, which meant that Daphne's death must surely have been the work of a visitor who had hidden away with murder in mind.

Thus comforted, at least temporarily, Max put his fears aside. Alison – and even more Mike – needed his help now. And they would have it.

Cara was becoming even more restless. Everyone seemed to have a job but her, yet she was under police instructions to stay right where she was in the Snug. How was Sammy getting on at the café? Had the police ordered him to stay here or had he gone home? Ludicrous though it was to think of Sammy as a murderer, they might not see it that way, even though she and he had been together at the time Daphne must have been murdered. Well, both at the Happy Huffkin anyway. He had been tucked away in the tiny kitchen at the rear of the folly while she was clearing the last of the debris. Hopefully he was still tucked away there clearing up, although perhaps terrified that he was going to be dragged off to prison. No, she comforted herself, he was too placid for that.

She was worried about Max though. He'd jump to the conclusion that someone was after his beloved art collection. Even if his terror that someone was going to pinch all those old paintings was justified, that couldn't be the case today. How would Daphne come into that? What art thief would have chosen a day and time when to the outside eye visitors could still be around – unless of course the thief was one of them? Difficult, given that only guided tours were permitted. And anyway, Max must realize that breaking away from a group to steal a painting or two was hardly the modern method of art theft.

Forget Max, think about Daphne, Cara instructed herself. Concentrate on the victim. Immediately she began to feel sick as the image of Daphne on the floor of the orangery rushed back to her. That awful sight. Why would anyone want to murder her? And why here? She tried to think it through. Daphne had lived so close to the Towers, danced here regularly with the Tanton Whirlers dance troupe (privately referred to as the Twerps), and she and Mike had known the Towers for years. Daphne prided herself on knowing more about the Towers than the family who had lived here for two and half centuries. It was Daphne who loved its every corner and who was interested in every bit of its history including the cellars, especially the cellar whose entry point was inconveniently in the corner of the orangery – near which, Cara thought uneasily, Daphne's body had been lying.

'It's the end of the tunnel!' Daphne had squealed excitedly to any newcomers to Tanton – such as Cara when she first opened the café here. Daphne prided herself on knowing every secret about the Towers that there was to expose and had elected to show Cara some of its hidden glories. When they had reached the cellar, Daphne proudly revealed the carefully disguised door to the tunnel.

'It was a *smugglers'* tunnel,' Daphne had continued excitedly to Cara, 'built especially for dear Sir Jeffry who built the whole of Tanton Towers. That would be in 1784. Wasn't he a naughty man? A perfect passion for drink.' A pause and a giggle. 'I don't mean brandy smuggled in. It could probably be *tea.*'

Cara remembered this story well, partly because it had fascinated her and partly because Ewan Chapman's great plan as events manager was to open the tunnel to visitors and to have a grand open day in August to launch it. That was only a month or two away now. All the restoration work had been carried out and passed by the relevant authorities. It still needed attention to make it less bleak and Ewan was working on that now. It wasn't her scene, although she could see its attractions for visitors. When he had taken her a short way into it, she'd found it claustrophobic and – frankly – dull, although that aspect was going to be fixed. Nevertheless, being enclosed in what would seem an endless trek didn't appeal to her, despite its being an excursion into history.

Sir Jeffry Farran had indeed been of a mischievous nature. According to a combination of family hearsay and hints in the Archives, so Max had told her, he gloried in defying the current tax burdens by encouraging smuggled goods from the continent, but on the other hand had no wish to have personal contact with smugglers, no matter how glorious the goods that they brought were. Consequently, his ill-gotten gains were brought up from the river bank to a remote storage cabin halfway up the hill, where any business transactions were concluded. Sir Jeffry had ensured that a secret tunnel ran from the cabin to the cellar under the orangery in order that the goods could then be conveyed along it by the smugglers to be enjoyed by the Towers' occupants. What happened to the goods then was not known, but Daphne was convinced that they were rapidly consumed chiefly by Sir Jeffry although perhaps his wife was the lucky recipient of the smuggled tea.

'Just imagine,' Daphne had squealed, 'poor Sir Jeffry could have died of shock.'

'And why was that?' Cara remembered herself dutifully asking.

Another of Daphne's giggles followed. 'On his wedding day to his second wife, he saw the ghost of his first wife materialize to curse them. I'm writing a history book about the Towers, and so I *discovered* that. Isn't it fun?'

A book? As archivist, it made sense for Robert to be writing a book about the Towers, but Daphne? What was this all about, Cara had wondered, aghast.

That brought her back to the present day and the present horror. Time was passing and nothing was happening. She had obviously been forgotten. She remained mutinous for another twenty minutes when at long last in marched Detective Chief Inspector Andrew Mitchem, as he announced himself.

Should she laugh or cry? This was the last straw. Cara really could have wept. His face was all too familiar and it didn't bode well for co-operation. He was tallish, fortyish and looked like a Greek god who'd been battered by a storm or two. She had seen him from time to time at her café where they had disagreed more or less politely (at first) over whether a huffkin should be filled with a cherry popped into the traditional hole probably first made by the baker's thumb. To Cara, it was obvious that the cherry was vital for a true huffkin (at least during the summer) as the recipe was dreamed up way back to serve to cherry pickers in the nearby orchards. The ignorant DCI Mitchem had argued that jam and cream were just as good. Nonsense. That was an inferior substitute, she argued. One couldn't run a café in Kent without having an opinion on this important matter. He had even suggested she could omit the jam and cream and provide a sausage. A *sausage*? How could that blend with the delicate appeal of a baked huffkin?

'*You're* the DCI?' she asked aghast.

Inspector Mitchem seemed to be eyeing her like a matador sizing up his target. 'I have that honour,' he said, poker-faced. 'We have met before, I believe.'

'Have we?' She tried to sound casual. 'Yes, I think we have.'

The last time she'd seen him, the argument had deepened into her refusing to serve him a huffkin at all if he didn't honour the cherry tradition. He had duly eaten the huffkin save for the cherry left ostentatiously on the side of the plate.

'I suggest we move to a more suitable room,' Poker-face now remarked, holding the folly door open for her.

Right. March on, Cara decided, as she swept through, then

followed him as he led the way to a small room on the far side
of the great hall. In Victorian times it had been the butler's room,
near the entrance to the servants' wing but handy to attend the
current lord of Tanton manor.

Once established in what was in its way a comfortable and
pleasant room with its prints of the Towers' gardens, Cara pulled
herself together. She would play Detective Chief Inspector
Andrew Mitchem's game by ignoring his mention of their
previous encounters and concentrate on what was far more important: Alison.

'Have you interviewed Mrs Farran Pryde?' she asked, much
concerned. Alison might seem resilient, but she wasn't.

'No.'

'Go easy when you do,' Cara pleaded. 'This whole ghastly
business is tough on her.'

He studied her for a moment. 'Ms Shelley, is that right? You
found the body.'

So he was playing the ignoring game too. 'Yes and no,' she
said crossly. 'And in case you ask, I'm *not* related to the poet.
Furthermore, it wasn't me who found Daphne. That was Alison
and she came to summon me about ten to six, because she knew
I would have my phone with me and she didn't.' This might be
getting off on the wrong foot, but this man deserved it. Too late,
she realized she was being childish. Not advisable, so she'd
steady up.

'Tell me about that. Did you touch the body? Touch anything?'
Gimlet eyes bored into hers.

'No.' Then she remembered. 'Yes, I tried for a pulse.' That
brought the memory back too fast and she desperately tried not
to retch.

Perhaps he saw that. 'Good,' he said more gently. 'Tell me
why Mrs Hanson might have been there still dressed in historical
costume, plus I need to know of anyone you think might have
been around after closing time other than the senior staff.'

Cara tried to deal with this. 'Daphne would probably not have
walked home in costume, and her husband Mike had already left.
She would usually have changed with the rest of the dancers but
she must have delayed it for some reason or been killed – ' she
said with some effort – 'before she could do so. She must have

had some plan as the dancers would have finished about four o'clock, changed and left by the time the house closes at four thirty.' Then she remembered one exception. 'One of them sometimes stays later, as did Daphne.'

'Who's that?'

'Simon Harris. He's a semi-retired solicitor, crazy about Tanton Towers and particularly its history. He sometimes pokes around a bit afterwards until the senior staff have left.' In the way that the oddest things pop into the mind at the most inappropriate moments, it occurred to Cara that he too might be planning to write a book. It seemed to be the fashion nowadays.

'Which I'm told is always before six thirty,' DCI Mitchem picked up, 'when the house security systems come into force for the night, unless you have the magic code. The security guards arrive just before that, but Daphne Hanson was killed about five thirty.'

This was all going too fast, Cara thought. This man had a knack of putting you at your ease too quickly and the ramifications of what you'd said only became apparent afterwards. 'I can't imagine any of us having any reason to murder Daphne,' she said firmly.

'But she died nevertheless. Casual intruder?'

'Unlikely.' With all the security Tanton had that was true, even if the full system wouldn't have come into force until after Daphne had died.

He changed tack. 'You run that café. Can you see the orangery from where you work?'

'Only the steps up to the terrace, its door and exterior. It's hard to see much and usually the door's locked at four thirty. The staff – and I – have keys though. And before you ask, I didn't notice anyone crossing the lawn and go inside – but then I was busy dashing around.'

He contemplated her for a moment. A ploy, she wondered uneasily.

'You obviously know the house well. Anything worth stealing in the orangery? It makes a quick route into the house, doesn't it?'

'No. It only leads to the formal dining room.' She was aware her stomach was beginning to play up again and hastily directed her thoughts elsewhere. At least, she thought, Max could be reassured that no one was after his beloved Lavinia Fontana paintings.

'Enemies?'

Cara shook her head. 'We all liked Daphne, even if she was a pain in the neck at times.' The sheer awfulness of what she'd just said struck her and to her horror she felt angry tears looming. 'Sorry,' she managed to blurt out.

He brushed this aside. 'Take your time. Why was Mrs Hanson so difficult to get along with?'

Cara considered this carefully. It seemed much easier to speak to him now, perhaps because she had pushed huffkins off her mental agenda. 'Daphne always took something a stage further than your sixth sense would advise.'

It seemed to her he almost smiled. But his answer was neutral. 'Such as?'

'If you said you'd been to the doctor, she'd always ask why.' She concentrated, thinking this through. 'Daphne asked Max once why his father had put a huge poster over the panelling in his bedroom. Max hadn't wanted to tell her that he'd put it there himself so that his aged father would forget the small cupboard where he kept his booze. She had gone on pressing Max until he lost his temper and had marched her upstairs to show her.'

'Does he often lose his temper?'

'*No!*' This man lured you into the snare and then snapped it shut, she thought furiously. The very idea of Max as a murderer was preposterous.

No reaction. 'How did you come to run a café here?' he asked. 'Are you related to the family?' he asked.

That made her laugh. 'Good grief, no. The Farrans go back to the year dot, way before this place was built and the Prydes nearly as long. I can only trace my family back to a pub in the East End of London.'

'Is that your husband who works in the café with you?'

Now he was going too far. 'I don't have a husband,' Cara replied shortly. 'My private life is just that. Private.' Coming to Tanton had begun a new chapter in her life and it was going to stay that way.

'My apologies. It seems to be the same man working with you every time I come.'

'You're out of date, Mr Inspector,' she retorted. 'We ladies don't need husbands protecting us. We just need good staff. You saw Sammy Jones, my assistant. I run my own business.'

'Tell me why you're so defensive.'

Cara gritted her teeth. Defensive? That was ridiculous. He was trying to rile her. That was his technique – just as he'd used it over the huffkins. 'I told you. Because of Alison. I'm fond of her. I'm fond of Max. I'm fond of them all. That enough for you? And, incidentally, just for the record, I'm not fond of coming across dead bodies of people I knew and liked either.'

He just waited until she'd finished, made no comment and instead asked, 'Did you talk to Daphne Hanson today?'

'No. I saw her from a distance while they pranced around. I have a café to run.'

'Pranced? You don't approve?'

'Of course I do,' she answered wearily. 'The group's dancing is great whether it's the cotillion or Strip the Willow. They wear Georgian costumes and they have fun. Everyone had lots of fun in the eighteenth century. That's what we all try to have here at Tanton Towers. But now it's been ruined.'

A silence. A neutral one, but not unfriendly, she thought, regretting her outburst.

'There are a lot of people gathered in the Library,' he continued. 'More than those whom I gather to be the senior staff. Would some staff have usually stayed on?'

'Yes, including the grounds staff, but they don't have access to the building if it's locked. And by "stayed on", do you mean just to murder Daphne or until her body was found?'

She thought for a moment he was going to give her a pat on the back as he rose to his feet, but apparently not, because he decided on the male trick of looming over her and ignoring her smart-aleck reply. Well, almost looming. Then he strolled over to the window and stared out at the garden. *Really* annoying.

'You – no, Mrs Farran Pryde found her at about ten minutes to six, you say, and came to fetch you. Exactly how long was it before you were both there with the body?' he asked, now choosing to stroll back to regain his seat and piercing gaze.

Should she say that she had had something else other than her watch on her mind at that point? No. This was too serious for games. 'My guess is that we were both in the orangery about three minutes later.'

'As I told you, the pathologist estimates very roughly that Mrs Hanson died not long before that, about five thirty. Had all the visitors gone by then?'

'And as I told *you*,' she said firmly, 'closing time for the house is four thirty. The grounds close at five, but there are sometimes visitors left hanging on to their cups of tea.'

'Tonight?'

'Not as many as usual. Two couples I think. The last one left the café about quarter past five – and,' she added, 'I saw them heading for the gatehouse exit, not dashing back to the orangery.'

'*Back* to the orangery?'

'Sorry.' Cara pulled herself together. What a difference a word can make. 'They had come through the door from the dining room into the orangery where the guided tour ends.'

'So, when did the last group emerge today? Four thirty when the house closed?'

Cara racked her memory. 'Yes. Sometimes they dither to talk to the guides, but they were prompt today. Then we had a rush for those who wanted a quick cuppa before they left. So it could have been one of those who stayed on after five o'clock.' *Damn*. Of course it couldn't. She'd gone wrong. Too late because he immediately replied.

'It's possible in theory if the pathologist is adrift with his estimate of five thirty. You said you couldn't see what was happening inside the orangery and from what you say there could have been at least one person other than the senior staff still in the building.'

Due credit to him, Cara supposed. He wasn't making capital out of her slip, but she wouldn't want to push it. Trust him to hit on the weak point.

'You'll have to ask the dancers.' She was ducking out of this one, remembering the wrangles between Simon Harris and Daphne about who led the Sir Roger de Coverley or who had whom as a partner. Daphne had led the Tanton Whirlers but it was common knowledge that Simon had his eyes on this cherished position. And yet surely theirs were everyday wrangles, not the sort that brought about catastrophes like murder.

Surprisingly, he let it go. 'I'll need a list of the dancers, and a complete one of the staff. I realize that this can't be in your official remit, but I'd be grateful if you could arrange for me to have both.'

'Easy. I'll ask Dan Dickson to give you them tomorrow. He's manager here.'

'Tonight please.'

Cara surrendered. So much for her quiet evening at home watching TV. She'd get her revenge though.

'Have you checked the smugglers' tunnel?' she asked innocently.

'*What?*'

Cara managed a look of dismay. 'It ends in the cellar not far from where she was lying.'

DCI Mitchem looked relieved. 'We checked that stairway. Nothing relevant.'

'That's the cellar. The tunnel opens there and runs down the hill to an old cabin.' She tried not to sound smug.

He looked rattled. Good. 'Is it usable?' he asked.

'On occasion,' she said loftily.

'Is that where you banish villains who put sausages in huffkins?'

Game, set and match to him, Cara conceded, fuming. It was a good job that, as somebody once observed, tomorrow was another day. Battle had clearly been declared.

THREE

'*Here Comes The Sun . . .*' Cara woke up with the Beatles song on her mind, remembering her grandmother dancing round the room as she sang it. Well, Grannie would have got it wrong today. Yesterday's tomorrow had arrived but the sun wasn't obliging. Far from it. The clouds had darkened over the Towers with Daphne's murder presenting a stark reality. The image of her dancing grandmother reminded her all too vividly of Daphne in the Sir Roger de Coverley. It was her job, Cara vowed, to get rid of those clouds.

Don't be daft, the more practical side of her whispered as she showered. What could you do that Kent Police and the Serious Crime Directorate can't do much more efficiently? It was all very well to pretend she could beat DCI Andrew Mitchem at his own game, but reality suggested otherwise.

Twenty-five minutes later, she changed her mind. Perhaps she could at least try to find out exactly what had happened yesterday. Cara eyed her healthy breakfast of wheats and fruit dubiously – especially since she'd put a few cherries on the table. They reminded her uncomfortably of the said DCI's views. He couldn't be Kentish-born or he would understand that cherries went with huffkins like cider with apples. Well, cherries were still grown in Kent and there were still some hop gardens, with which Tanton had once been surrounded. Now there was a resurgence in Kent's ancient crops and the Happy Huffkin Café was going to play its part – with or without DCI Mitchem's patronage.

That was another reminder that there was work to do. It was time to eat, clear up and climb the hill to the Towers. Although their working week ran from Wednesday to Sunday, and today was Thursday, the Towers would be closed. Hard though it had been to think of such practical things last night, she'd had to cut down on the usual supplies of lunchtime sandwiches and cakes ordered in the village from Virginia Harding. Virginia was a relative of Sammy's, widowed, in her forties and indispensable.

Cara's own cooking skills were improving, partly because of her passion for cookery books of the past, but chiefly under Sammy's direction. Nevertheless they were far from perfect and some food would have to be provided for police and such staff as were there – with or without huffkins.

Huffkins didn't make life easy for cooking in cafés. To do them justice they should be fresh and warm so by the time dough had been prepared, kneaded and proven with cooking time added, Sammy was unlikely to insist on them today – even though Max's parents had added the blessings of electricity to the folly years ago. Anyway, judging how many to bake was a constant challenge – and with troublemakers like DCI Mitchem around it was an even greater one.

Cara congratulated herself that although her fifteenth-century cottage at one end of Tanton village wasn't the biggest house around, it was the most interesting. Its position was an advantage because she could feel part of the village and yet set apart from it, which was useful, because the village was tucked below the hillside and had a weird atmosphere at times. Not only was Horace, the less fortunate of the twin sons born to Sir Jeffry, said to haunt it but when her imagination set to work it seemed to be telling her that other evil spirits had decided to cast their shadow over it. That was another reason that the majestic Tanton Towers, rising above it, was such a glorious sight, both a refuge and a fortress.

As was her cottage. Cara laughed at herself for such stupid thoughts, but nevertheless they were true in a way. Supporting one wall of the narrow room upstairs which she grandly termed her study was a fifteenth-century ship's beam. You, she informed the beam every so often, represent history. Inherited from her grandmother, the cottage was hardly a Tanton Towers but to her it was every bit as important as the Towers was to Max and Alison. Cara had been in luck, for she had come here with her daughter not long after that heel Kate's father had abandoned her. The heel was never mentioned between them and seldom thought about, at least by Cara. She did sometimes wonder whether he ever did make that round-the-world trip, living a while in every country, or whether he had stopped off in Paris and could still be found in Harry's Bar telling everyone of his plans for a better world.

Would he be surprised that the results of that night had resulted in her lovely Kate, now fledging her wings at Cambridge University? Perhaps. Would he care? No. His mission hadn't included offspring. Nor did it include wondering what had happened to Cara Shelley, who had had to cut short her college course on management and with Kate to look after had to take any job she could get – although blessedly she had eventually found one in a local farm shop.

Enough of rear-mirror gazing. Tanton Towers needed her. However efficient the police were, Cara thought smugly, they lacked one thing: local knowledge. That sounded so dull, but it was vital. She wouldn't get in their way but would squirrel around gathering nuts of information, which she would keep to herself until they were needed. She had a job to do *now* and not just the Happy Huffkin Café. That too had a role, of course. She could be the observer who wasn't observed. Those who wait at table often wear a cloak of invisibility.

'Top of the morning to you,' she called out to Sammy as normal as she reached the café, realizing too late that nothing was normal. Alison had asked anxiously last night whether she'd be coming in this morning and had been much relieved to see her, when Cara had called in on her way to the Happy Huffkin.

'Good policy to feed the brutes,' Cara had cheerfully explained. Alison looked startled, but then perhaps she still hadn't had the privilege of feeding Andrew Mitchem. Besides, there would also be journalists around plus a mob of sightseers, judging by the amount of TV coverage, but hopefully they'd be outside the gates. It was natural enough, but it made Cara feel like a caged lion.

That was the reason that this morning she had climbed the hillside to the woodland entrance to the Towers, close to where the smugglers' tunnel ran. Using that footpath was quicker and usually more calming than driving or walking up Church Road from the village. Certainly it was today. There were going to be challenges enough without running the gauntlet at the gatehouse.

Now she was here it was deep-breath time. She took one just as Sammy appeared at the folly's front doorway.

The architecture of the folly was peculiar even by 'normal' folly standards. All of them were weird but this one must surely beat them all. Sir Jeffry had let fly with his imagination. It had, Max had told her, been built as a rival to Severndroog Castle folly in Greater London, which was built the same year. Its Gothic windows and castellated roof looked reasonably normal – apart from those gargoyles scowling or grinning merrily at visitors and staff alike. Who therefore would expect to walk round either side and find themselves apparently in one of two ruined small Greek stone temples, both of them crumpling with age and with greenery creeping round the pillars? Both had splendid views with a telescope placed conveniently for the viewer to contemplate the wonderful sight over the woodlands down to the dried-up River Mizzle on one side and provide on the other a useful tool for Sir Jeffry to note all the horses and carriages on their way to visit the Towers – giving him ample warning of unwelcome visitors such as the Revenue.

Today, Cara had to concentrate on more practical concerns. Sammy's kitchen, at the rear of the main folly and full of coffee and tea machines as well as the ovens and microwaves, was the operational centre for the café. That was where she was heading with her contribution of cherries.

'Morning,' Sammy grunted. 'No sandwiches.'

'By midday,' Cara whipped back, well used to joining Sammy's economy with words.

Sammy didn't believe in throwing words around lightly. He couldn't be more than forty-odd she reckoned, roughly her own age, but somehow one never thought of age in connection with Sammy. He was just *there*. Ageless, lean, medium height, old cap on head, wrinkled from the sun and above all placid. She could dance round the folly in Josephine Baker's famous 1920s banana costume and he wouldn't even react.

'Yesterday's leftovers?' she continued the ritual, asked as he emptied the bag and grunted.

'Birds. Or trashed.'

'Ready for huffkins?'

Superfluous to ask really. She could see the dough was rising.

'Yer.'

He had a defiant look in his eye as he uttered this traditional

Kentish form of 'it's here' as she remembered too late that it
had been agreed that huffkins weren't necessary today.

One didn't argue with Sammy. Usually she and he could cope
alone with the café, but in school holidays and at weekends not
only Virginia but her niece, the lovely Lucy Parkin, would join
them. She wowed the visitors with her charm and other volunteers
at the Towers could always be roped in if need be.

'What's happening at the Towers?' she asked patiently.

'Rozzers. Hordes.' Sammy actually stopped work. 'Best get
there, Cara.'

Even given Sammy's usual economy with words, this situation
didn't look good. Another deep breath. Should she head for the
family wing again? No. Anyway she couldn't duck under that
cordon, which was the quickest way there. DCI Mitchem wouldn't
approve of that. Resisting the temptation to do it for that reason,
she headed for the Haven, the small room on her nearest corner
of the building, the western side. Here discarded boots and shoes
could be found, plus umbrellas and raincoats, and it was also her
quickest way into the Towers' main building – if it was open.
Today it wasn't, so she was forced to rush past it to the Towers'
front entrance, with only the smell of roses from the rose garden
calming her. To her surprise, the massive door was open but
unguarded, and once she was inside everything seemed reasonably quiet. No one appeared to be around but, hearing movement
in the Snug, she opened the door and tentatively went inside.

To her amazement Mike Hanson was there. *Mike?* Why would
he of all people be here? Poor man. He must be distraught. He
was standing by the window, staring out despite her entrance.
When he turned around, his arms were folded, perhaps defensively, she thought, and he looked completely shattered.

'Want company?' she asked gently.

He looked up and nodded. She liked Mike. They had never
been close friends but she was so used to waving at him if they
were using the grand staircase in the Hall and chatting at meetings. His office was on the second floor near Max's art gallery
and the Archives Room, so she was even more surprised to see
him here waiting just like anyone else, especially after yesterday's
tragedy.

Mike must have been really good-looking in his younger days

with his rugged classical features, she thought, and he still was, although one never appreciated it because in Daphne's company he had been so much the silent partner. Now he looked the stricken one. Strange how one could know some people for years, then see them in a different situation and realize one didn't know them at all. Often quite little things surprised you, but sometimes they were major. As was this murder. Mike as well as Daphne was a victim.

Cara sat at his side for a few minutes but it was he who broke the silence. 'Why?' he asked helplessly.

'I don't know, but . . .' She hesitated. She'd been going to say on impulse 'I'll do my best to find out,' but were they just words? She would try anyway.

But then he began to talk. She thought for a moment he was going to break down, but he didn't. On the contrary. 'They'll think I did it,' he said flatly. 'The husband. It's always the husband.'

Cara knew what he must be thinking: that he seemed the patient husband of a loquacious woman who innocently enough had a way of finding out more and more about everybody and everything.

'Not in this case,' Cara said reassuringly.

'There's Simon Harris,' he blurted out. 'Could he have done this?'

Just what she had been thinking. Mike was right. Simon and Daphne had always been at odds. He was probably in his late fifties, and the lead gentleman in the Tanton Whirlers, thus his ambitions to take over Daphne's role as *the* leader of the troupe. Its reputation was good so the role of leader carried prestige. Simon had been at daggers drawn with Daphne, who had her own ideas of what dances they should learn, what bookings they should accept and what musicians they required.

'Surely he wouldn't . . .' Cara cut off her instinctive reply. Daphne had been throttled and in a relatively public place. That meant it had been a spur-of-the-moment attack. And Simon was not known for his patience.

'Who knows?' Mike said wearily.

As did Cara, he and Daphne lived in Tanton village but at the other end from Cara's cottage and so she saw more of them here than in the village. The dancers did not perform every day the Towers was open and so she saw more of Mike than she did Daphne. As the Towers' accountant, Mike was steady and methodical, which sometimes exasperated Alison. She had to push her own ideas on how to spend the money available (if there was any) both to get Mike's co-operation and Dan Dickson's as business manager. The Italian garden innovation had taken Alison two years to get past Mike's scrutiny and the woodland tree house for children was still up against Mike's opposition despite Ewan Chapman's efforts as events manager. It was taking Alison ages to persuade Mike that Ewan's plan for the grand open day for the smugglers' tunnel should take place before the season was over.

Today these seemed unimportant far-off matters as Cara sat with Mike. Silent company was surely the best policy for a friend in such circumstances, at least for a short while. Mike and Daphne had seemed a well-balanced couple, but who knows what went on behind closed doors.

'I heard you'd already left when it happened,' Cara said awkwardly at last, judging the moment had come to speak but then kicking herself for bringing up this tender subject at all. 'Something odd must have occurred for her to be there in the orangery.'

She thought he wasn't going to answer her but at last he did. 'Yes, I'd long gone. I had a chat with Rosalie at the gatehouse. Good alibi, isn't it?' he added bitterly.

Just for a moment, Cara saw that other Mike. The Mike driven beyond endurance by a dictatorial wife, and perhaps now struggling with a guilty relief without Daphne.

Without Daphne. Ewan Chapman, tucked away in his first-floor office, wrestled with his conscience. He could hardly take it in that Daphne Hanson was no longer a menace to him. He grinned as he remembered her plump figure dancing away. She'd been amusing and nice enough in her own way, although there was an enormous 'but'. He was thirty now and, having worked at the Towers for six years, he supposed it was time that he got married and started having kids. That took money, but thanks to Daphne he had had to temporarily keep mum about his hopes of having the smugglers' tunnel open this season simply because she had demanded her right to lead the tours through it herself. Now he could go ahead with his plans for that grand opening in August without interference. She would not be hogging the limelight.

'I am the tunnel's *historian*,' she would point out, hurt that anyone could see the matter differently.

No way could she do justice to that tunnel. She was no more a historian than Hans Christian Andersen, whereas for him it would be the fun part of his job, the plum in the pudding, the item that would bring TV interviews and so on featuring *him*, Ewan Chapman. It was high time his career had a wider stage. Daphne had kicked up such a fuss over that tunnel that he'd had to invent reasons why her daft ideas weren't practical – even though some of them had been.

'Such fun those smugglers had,' Ewan had heard her trilling away to Alison. 'We can all dress up like smugglers and carry a cask or two. Perhaps even drink some swag.'

Luckily even Alison had seen sense over that. There was no doubt that life and work at Tanton Towers would be a great deal easier now. Daphne had had this stupid idea of writing a book on the Towers and its history, based as far as he could see entirely on its smuggling connections. Pity about her awful end, but without her hogging the limelight Tanton Towers could be the basis of a money-maker for him and fun as well. They were a decent lot here and they all got on pretty well together. Life could continue smoothly now. The grand opening was make or break time for him – and it would be *make*. Without Daphne.

Without Daphne. Alone in his beloved Archives Room, Robert Broome breathed a sigh of relief. Dreadful though her death was, his tranquil life at Tanton Towers could now continue. Nevertheless, he was nervous. Could the police possibly think that he was responsible for this awful crime? As historian in charge of the valuable records and artefacts of Tanton Towers, he relished his position. He'd taken his post over at the comparatively young age of thirty-two when his predecessor had vanished from the scene after a walking holiday in the Pyrenees on which he had died. Robert had been duly upgraded from being a part-time freelance to the prestige of being Tanton Towers' record keeper. That had been five years ago and he had been happy ever since.

As one of a splendid team, he had a role here and was proud of
it. He was respected for it too, especially by Max and Alison.
Disagreements between the staff were rare and quickly solved.
They were all *friends*.

'Hi, Robbie,' Alison would greet him and Max frequently
asked his advice or discussed some small point of Bologna's
history or English eighteenth-century rural life.

Every so often it occurred to Robert that at nearing forty years
of age it might be time he married and settled down – an idea
that both attracted and depressed him. When his fiancée jilted
him a year before he came to Tanton Towers, he had taken it as
a sign that he could consider remaining a bachelor and continue
the job he loved. It was fulfilling. Or had been. Then Daphne
had come along. A delightful lady normally, but so inquisitive.
He had returned to the Archives Room recently to find her poking
around his shelves of valuable and fragile books and files.
Regardless of his annoyance, she then actually disarranged some
of them and left others lying around.

'I'm going to write a book,' she had announced, as though
that were any excuse.

He had been aghast. 'What sort of book?' he had asked. Was
she capable of doing justice to the wonderful subject of the
Towers' history? Could she write a book as good as the one he
planned to write himself? Would hers just be tales of those smugglers about whom she was so enthusiastic? But she put a finger
to her lips and assured him that her lips were sealed.

He remembered that just as he remembered her chattering
endlessly on about Sir Jeffry Farran.

'Dear, dear Sir Jeffry – such an *interesting* gentleman,' Daphne
had cooed at him, 'until he was cursed by his wife on his wedding
day. No, no, of course, silly me. I mean his *second* wedding day.
Such fun, dear Robert, he almost died of shock when the ghost
of his first wife turned up to curse the marriage.'

Legends, Robert thought in disgust. It was *facts* that needed
recording. That was his mission. And now he would have a clear
field ahead – without Daphne.

Without Daphne. Dan Dickson couldn't resist a dance of his own.
Mental of course. A man of his build and age couldn't very well

resort to capering around like the Tanton Twerps. Daphne had been a dear old stick really, but a pain in the neck nevertheless. Always in the way. His job for the past seven years had been manager of Tanton Towers' public rooms, tours and its general daily operations. It was he who pulled the whole caboodle together so successfully. That was quite a task though luckily Rosalie was pretty good at organizing entrance money and shop income for Mike Hanson's perusal and Keeley Martin, that sexy young housekeeper, was also quite competent. Everyone at the Towers worked well together too. And that, Dan congratulated himself, was thanks to himself. Alison and Max fully appreciated that.

'Nothing antique about you, Dan,' Max had observed last week.

Antiques were his own specialty, of course, and Dan flattered himself that his two books on the subject were staple reading for half of the United Kingdom.

But there had definitely been one fly in the ointment. Daphne. She had upset Ewan – not that he didn't need putting in his place from time to time. She'd upset Robert – not hard to do that, and she'd upset Rosalie – very hard to do that. Keeley simply ignored her. And then Daphne had upset the apple cart with talk of this book she wanted to write about Tanton. She pretended she only wanted to write about smugglers, but there was more to it. Dan was sure of that. She'd been poking around everywhere, clearly bent on trespassing on to his field of the Tanton antiques. His territory. Her writing about that? Never. He had a new book of his own in mind.

Now he could breathe again. Without Daphne.

Without Daphne. At last he had some freedom. Simon Harris breathed a sigh of relief. Without her presence the Tanton Whirlers dance troupe could really go places, travel far and wide – well, if he was in charge it would – and there was no doubt now that he would be. And, what's more, his other plans for Tanton Towers could take a giant leap forward – he could continue writing his book about the Towers unimpeded. Daphne's ridiculous ideas about the Towers weren't worth even considering, and he would be able to have a free hand once Professor Farran Pryde and his wife were no longer forced to listen to her.

FOUR

Where was everyone? Cara gazed around the Great Hall, bemused. Still no sign of the police here, so either they were very hard at work or had just packed up for the day. One or two had dropped into the café for coffee, but otherwise they had vanished. It was Alison she wanted to see, but with no trace of her either, she made her way to the family wing.

The family wing was a place to relax, even on a day like this with the shadow of murder hanging over them. The main comfort zone was their living room, a mix of Victorian, twentieth-century style and a hint of something more modern. Somehow it all worked, gazed down upon approvingly by a Laura Knight portrait, several Cornish fishing village scenes and a Lavinia Fontana painting that even Max couldn't squeeze into his main collection. The effect was such that Cara felt like Peter Pan swooping into the Darling family's hitherto placid existence. Alison and Max's dog – called Jeffry of course – was a dead ringer for Nana in Cara's opinion.

'Is Alison around?' she asked hopefully, finding Max alone in the living room. Alison was often in the kitchen at this time preparing a snack lunch, but this was no ordinary morning, of course.

Max looked up from his newspaper and looked vaguely around the otherwise empty room as though he expected Alison to pop up like toast from the toaster. 'No. She was surrounded by police last time I saw her.' He managed a grin. 'That sounds serious, but I doubt if the police see her as a murderer.'

Cara managed a grin too. Alison of all people could be ruled out. 'Have you been summoned to the presence?'

'Not yet.' This roused Max into action. 'I must say that some-what annoys me. After all, I've told them why that poor woman was killed.'

What on earth did he mean? Cara blinked. 'You *know* who it was?'

In her view Max as a sleuth was as unlikely as Max as a murderer. He and the criminal life were far apart. Max lived in his own world, peopled by his beloved Lavinia Fontana in the evenings and holidays. Even if he wasn't with his precious collection, he was probably thinking of her. Alison was the only person who was exempt from this routine. By day, when not occupied with giving the occasional outside lecture on medieval history, he would be musing, despite shapes who passed him by unnoticed – staff, visitors, even his family on occasion, including his three offspring. One of them was an ambassador somewhere, one a geologist in the depths of South America and the other a primary school teacher in the north of England. Cara had met them all fleetingly.

Max was surely just exaggerating, she assumed. How could he possibly have solved the crime so quickly? Although perhaps he had.

'Of course I know,' Max answered her question.

Then she relaxed. This must have something to do with Lavinia and that could be dealt with. 'Have the police sealed La Galleria off?' she asked tentatively. She used Max's name for his beloved gallery, because the name came naturally to him and thus to everyone else. Until about three years ago La Galleria had not existed in its present form. Most of the collection was there but none of the second floor had been open to the public. Much of it had been storage. Max together with the Archives Room had worked from the first floor with just one room displaying Lavinia Fontana's work to the public. And then the Great Change had taken place, with the happy trio of Lavinia, Max and Archives moving up to the second floor. La Galleria was born and so Sir Jeffry's study was now housing the archives. Obviously Max was assuming that Daphne's murder could only have one explanation. A dastardly criminal was after his collection.

Max looked surprised. 'No, but nevertheless I do know why that poor woman was killed. Someone on one of the guided tours must have been making plans to steal one of my paintings and Daphne suspected it. She was interested in Lavinia's work. The villain was after Lavinia's priceless depiction of Queen Elizabeth I of England.'

So that was it. Cara wasn't particularly interested in art but she had had little choice in getting to know a great deal about Lavinia Fontana during her time here. Lavinia had become a part of all of their lives in one way or another. From Lavinia Fontana's self-portraits – particularly one of them – she had learnt that Lavinia was graceful, calm, interesting and with very knowing eyes. She was, Cara had decided, someone she would have liked to have met, not that her own life in any way resembled Lavinia's. Lavinia had carefully planned hers with the help of her father Prospero, a prominent painter himself, who had lovingly trained her and with whom she remained living and working even when she married. Her rich husband, who was also an artist, had simply moved in to help with the family business. For a woman painter to gain respectability in sixteenth-century Bologna, marriage had been essential, so the gallant Lavinia made time to present her husband with eleven children, despite her rocketing prestige with her religious paintings, portraits of local dignitaries and self-portraits. Her fame quickly spread, not just in Bologna, and she was invited by the Pope early in the seventeenth century to move to Rome, where she remained until her death ten years later. Quite a lady!

How to put this diplomatically, Cara pondered, taking a deep breath. 'There must be a huge market for her work,' she began tactfully. From what she could tell from the internet, there was, but it wouldn't compare with that for a Rubens or Rembrandt, or – in her admittedly limited view – be one for which murder would therefore be committed at Tanton Towers. Max had to be humoured, however. She and Alison did that all the time, regardless of the fact that if art thieves were prowling around Tanton Towers there were far more valuable items around. Take the Gainsborough in the Library for instance, or the Reynolds in the Drawing Room, not to mention Alison's favourite, a Constable sketch. Dan Dickson kept an eagle eye open during the tours.

'But,' Cara continued, 'is there a market for her work that would make it worthwhile for gangs to steal them?' A mental pat on the back for diplomacy.

Max looked astounded. 'Of course there is, although it would be easy enough for the police to track them down.'

Cara had her doubts about this. Max hadn't thought it through. When for instance would this robbery have taken place? Would it still take place? How on earth did Daphne get involved? Why did the security system fail? And had anything yet been stolen? The answer to the latter would be no. On top of Daphne's death that would have caused pandemonium.

'Ah, there you are, Cara.' Alison had come into the dining room and she looked strained to say the least. 'Thanks for keeping Max calm.'

'How can I keep *you* calm?' Cara asked, concerned.

Alison shrugged. 'Calm? I feel as if I'd been hit by a tsunami, my stomach is heaving so much. I know they have to be here, but all these police around are unnerving me. The DCI suggests we formally open again next week. Wednesday as usual – if there is a usual anymore.'

Not till then? Cara was dismayed. It seemed like forever. 'Is that because by then they expect to have solved the case?'

'Hard to tell from Detective Chief Inspector Mitchem's poker face. He wants to see you, by the way.'

Cara bristled. 'What does he have in mind? Handcuffs?'

'Not yet.' Alison grimaced. 'He was grilling me about times, openings, guided tours and so on. I told him Ewan and Dan are the ones to talk to for that, and Rosalie of course since at the gatehouse she sees people trotting to and forth.'

Rosalie, in charge of the entrance to the Towers which was set back a little from Church Road, would see not only pedestrians but those who had arrived by car or coach. The eighteenth-century red brick gatehouse was over a hundred yards away from the Towers and served as a shop as well as its main function. It was a fairly modest building sited not to interfere with the imposing view of the Towers in all its glory while at the same time announcing that the entrant should bend the knee at the honour bestowed on him. Sir Jeffry had thoughtfully provided the odd gargoyle and turret on the gatehouse too, even though his plan was clearly designed not to detract from the outrageousness of his beloved Towers.

'He told me he wanted the background picture,' Alison continued. 'What I thought of Daphne, Mike's role at the Towers, Dan's, Robert's and even all the dancers' roles. Plus he asked if I could remember anything unusual about yesterday – apart from Daphne's death, of course.'

'And could you?' Yesterday had seemed just a normal day to Cara – up to closing time.

No reaction from Max, who had clearly decided to return to his dreams of Lavinia Fontana.

'No,' Alison replied simply. 'But you know how things fly out of your head just when you need them.'

'I do,' Cara agreed fervently.

'He did ask why I went to the orangery at that time.' Alison shuddered.

'What did you tell him?' Fine detective she was, Cara thought. That basic question hadn't even occurred to her.

'I wanted to see Daphne about that book about the Towers that Mike told me she was writing. It was news to me. She was likely to rub some people up the wrong way. Including Max and me.'

'I'd heard about that.' Cara pricked up her ears. There seemed to be several other books being contemplated too, but Daphne's chance of writing the kind that Tanton deserved seemed unlikely to say the least. 'Do you know what she was planning for it?'

'That's what I needed to pin down with her,' Alison said gloomily.

'Did she know you were coming?' The new role of sleuth was battling with Cara's concern for poor Alison, who must be worn out with answering questions like this.

'Oh yes. I said I couldn't see her until after five thirty and the orangery is quite near the room where they change, so I thought that would be handy for her as a meeting place. And it's nice and comfortable with those tables and chairs around. Sometimes she didn't bother with changing anyway.'

'Did the other dancers know she was staying on?'

'They probably did,' Alison said.

The absent-minded professor was suddenly alert. 'Simon Harris knew.'

Alison looked lovingly at him. 'Thank you, Sherlock.'

Cara awarded herself a pat on the back. Something at last to feed DCI Mitchem's appetite.

'Good afternoon, Ms Shelley,' he greeted her.

Cara gritted her teeth. It was confrontation time, but the DCI had caught her inside the kitchen just about to plate up some of Virginia's sandwiches in case the police suddenly descended on her for a late lunch. She'd thought they might have disappeared down to the village pub, the Farran Arms, but now *one* policeman had arrived. To do him justice, DCI Andrew Mitchem had walked over to the café to see her, instead of summoning her for a formal interview in the Towers. Annoyingly, he'd stalked inside to the café's counter.

'Good afternoon,' she returned guardedly. Sammy didn't even bother to look up from his precious new batch of huffkins, for which the dough was currently just at the point when they entered the oven. He had insisted on making them, regardless of the fact that the huffkins had not gone down well with the police judging by only one having been consumed so far. He had insisted on making more, probably seeing it as his duty to keep the tradition alive.

'A few questions please.' The DCI's beady eyes were here, there and everywhere. She had no idea what he was making of his surroundings – but she was wary.

'Go ahead.' Good to show cooperation. Cara moved casually round the counter to wave him to one of the inside tables laid for the less sunny days. At this time of year they were rarely used, but during the winter and rainy days she often had to open up the first floor for customers.

'Thank you.' He chose a table by the window overlooking the grassy slope down to the lawns and accepted a cappuccino from her. Pause. Then: 'Question one. Why call this café the Happy Huffkin?'

Don't be thrown, she told herself. He's just buttering you up. 'I'm glad you asked me that,' she replied gravely. 'Well, as you know, Kent is well known for its hop gardens and cherry orchards, although there are not nearly as many as there were. Londoners used to come down to pick hops for their annual holiday but – ' she injected a virtuous note into her voice – 'I don't have a licence for selling alcohol so all we can do is sell hop tea which is non-alcoholic. And it isn't very popular,' she added honestly.

'Thank you,' he replied, equally gravely. 'And the huffkin element?'

She was well aware that he knew very well what it was by now, but why not deliberately play his game and humour him? 'They were invented here ages ago,' she began solemnly, 'for the cherry pickers to eat during the picking season. Kent was famous for cherries too. King Henry VIII was most impressed and brought a new species of cherry here. The cherry fits well with jam and cream into the dimple in the middle of the huffkin.' She had spoken kindly, as to a child. 'But a sausage does not,' she added innocently.

He ignored the sausage comment. 'Charles Dickens agreed with you about the cherries, though he added a couple of things for which Kent is famous, such as fair women.' He lifted his coffee mug to her in mock homage but before she could manage to retort he continued. 'I did my homework earlier, so I know how the huffkin dimple came about. Fascinating.'

'Only if well cooked – as ours are – they're delicious.' How much longer would they continue this fencing match, she wondered.

'I'll look forward to having another one here, with – or without – sausage. Sammy,' he continued without even a pause, 'tells me he saw nothing amiss at the orangery yesterday, and I gather you didn't either. Were you together all the afternoon, barring toilet visits?'

She thought back to yesterday, admiring the way he slipped from personal to impersonal. Even his face looked impersonal now. 'Yes. I expect you've seen we have two reasonably modern ones tucked away in the bushes behind the folly. Alison thinks they're where the eighteenth-century gentry relieved themselves, especially as they don't ruin the view. And,' she added meaning-fully, watching his reaction, 'there's no way either Sammy or I could secrete ourselves out there and dash over to the orangery and kill poor Daphne all in five minutes or so. I'd have noticed if Sammy was away longer than that and he'd have noticed my absence too.' She hesitated. 'I really don't see any way that any of the few visitors who stayed after five o'clock here could have rushed across to the orangery. You said she was killed about five thirty and they'd all gone by then.'

'Security systems kick in at six thirty, I'm told, after the staff have all left.'

'And,' she said, 'so would any other people who had permission to stay on, like Daphne herself and Simon Harris.' She waited hopefully for his comment but there was none.

'Would you have seen other stragglers from the gardens wandering by as well as your two couples at the café?'

She thought for a moment. 'Yes. I was out there clearing tables after they left, and anyway with the doors to the orangery locked no stragglers could have got in.' She saw him closing his notebook. 'Is that all?'

He nodded. 'For the moment. Thank you, Ms Shelley.'

Was there a note of interrogation in his voice when he reached the 'Ms'? She was about to say 'Cara will do' but quickly changed her mind. 'Not at all,' she murmured politely.

'I may need to talk to you again when the lab results come in,' he added. He made it sound like a penance.

FIVE

'Thanks a lot,' Cara said with relief as Sammy produced a rack of clean plates. A dozen or so complete strangers had suddenly descended on the Happy Huffkin's outside tables, despite the Towers being closed to visitors. It was Friday afternoon. Normally the Towers would be open Wednesday to Sunday, but not now. Who on earth were these people? Police in disguise? Secret Service? Was James Bond going to descend from the skies? Or Doctor Who?

None of these, though almost as amazing. Everything fell into place as she recognized one of them at least, although why they were here was anyone's guess. They must be the Twerps, unrecognizable in modern dress as she usually saw them in full eighteenth-century glory. They always arrived together, left together and took their tea in the changing room before their performance. Dressed in bonnets, puffed-out sleeves, silken gowns, skirted coats, breeches and pantaloons together with powdered wigs, they were familiar figures as they energetically danced to and fro on the lawn.

Today Rosalie and Keeley were here too, although they were sitting at a table by themselves. It was a rare sight as they weren't the best of friends, each of them carefully guarding her own territory so far as work was concerned. With Keeley as housekeeper and Rosalie masterminding the flow of visitors and entrance fees, their roles dovetailed, but Cara knew that all too frequently there were few doves around.

It occurred to her that she knew very little about Keeley and Rosalie's private lives, and there again they were likely to be different. So why were they sitting together? Keeley was Miss Modern, with her high heels, tight jeans and sexy tops. Rosalie was Miss Loyal, who believed in the tried and true, but Keeley remained a mystery. Did that matter? Normally no, Cara thought, but with Wednesday's tragedy it very well might. Why the cosy chat, she wondered, watching them depart. No chorus of farewells followed them, so their being here must be coincidence. It had been noted, however, for she could see a whisper or two going around.

There were well over a dozen Twerps here, mostly women, although there were several men – reluctant husbands? Presumably the police had requested, but not demanded, everyone should attend and some had taken advantage of that. One Cara recognized as the fiddler and another was Simon Harris, sitting at the larger table with five women and two meek-looking men. He was noticeably at the table's head. *I bet he is,* she thought grimly. Without Daphne he could strut about like a pigeon in the mating season, although pigeons would be a lot fatter than skinny Simon. How old was he? Probably late fifties? He looked cock of the roost and enjoying it. His female companions, clad in trousers and summer tops with greying hair in contrast to the flower-bedecked and ornamented hair and costumes of their dancing attire, looked anxious and the men – other than Simon – looked as though they had come here by mistake. 'Nothing to do with me' was their silent message.

'The indignity of it all.' Simon's high-pitched raised voice followed Cara around as she hurried in and out to fulfil orders. 'Would any of us have wished Daphne harm?' he squeaked. 'Of course not. The reputation of our troupe goes back at least thirty years. It's ridiculous even to think any of us might be involved. Why would we want to harm poor, sweet Daphne?' he added virtuously.

Was this the same man whom she had caught screeching profanities at poor, sweet Daphne a week or two ago, Cara wondered. The election for chair of the Tanton Whirlers had been under discussion after their performance, which, as it had been raining, had taken place in the dining room. Daphne, she had been told later, had won the battle with Simon. It was true that he was a close second, but Daphne had then promptly announced to the world in general that the leadership of the troupe's dances, including who should choose them, would of course be her prerogative, not Simon's. That hadn't been tactful but Daphne would have been so hurt if anyone had pointed that out. No one had, not even Simon.

How would Daphne's murder affect the Tanton Whirlers, Cara

wondered as she moved around gathering orders, issuing bills
and removing dirty dishes. Once talk jerkily resumed after
Simon's rhetorical question, it seemed that the general opinion
was still entirely that Daphne had done nothing to deserve it,
although Simon remained ostentatiously quiet, smirking to
himself. The matter of the succession was probably still
outstanding, of course.

Could any of these people be a murderer? What did murderers
look like? Cara shivered, aware that it was all too possible. Stupid
thoughts sped through her mind although she was doing her best
to keep a suitable expression of welcome combined with sympathy
on her face.

Nevertheless, it was interesting to note that they looked so
different here to her usual view of them. Clad in their finery
while dancing, both the men and the women assumed a kind
of anonymity, but here in everyday dress their personalities
began to reveal themselves more clearly. There was a distinctly
waspish lady sitting at the smaller table for four and at the
larger table expressions were beginning to register: inquisitiveness on one or two, reticence in others and, judging by the
murmur of their chattering voices, one or two still greatly
shocked and sympathetic.

Suppose the murderer was amongst them. Would Wednesday's
timetable have fitted in with that? Cara made some quick calculations. Most of the troupe arrived in vans fully clad for the
dancing ahead, some came by different transport and changed
here. The pianist and fiddler were amongst the latter as far as
Cara could remember, but they all seemed to have left together
save for Daphne. Could any of them have evaded notice and
remained in the house? She went over it again in her mind.
Dancing took place at three o'clock on the lawn outside, lasting
about three quarters of an hour or a little longer. At four thirty
the house had closed and Dan Dickson's team of volunteers
would have checked all rooms were clear before they departed
at five o'clock and noted those remaining, staff or otherwise.
Daphne had died about five thirty and anyone wanting access
from outside would have needed keys. Overnight security
wouldn't kick into play until six thirty, so the attack could have
been carefully timed for that reason. Even Sherlock would have

difficulty in working his magic around that situation, Cara thought. On Wednesday, Daphne's presence would have been recorded, so would the staff's and so would Simon's, unless he had disguised himself as a Greek god.

At least she had that clear in her mind, as DCI Mitchem doubtless would as well. It was also a factor to take into account as regards motive. It was common knowledge that Simon was all too eager to take over the running of the Tanton Twerps, and perhaps he was even writing a book, but could those two factors really be sufficient reason for murder? Rule number one, she decided. Don't eliminate anyone just because the motive seems weak.

The occupants of the larger table seemed engrossed in their conversation, as Cara waited on them – slowly, in the hope of gathering gems of information. Luckily they seemed to assume she didn't count; she was invisible – a useful if sometimes annoying attribute of her job.

'Of course she was asking for it,' one of them half whispered.

'Asking for what?' her bold neighbour asked sharply. 'Death?'

'How could I know?' was the annoyed reply. 'She liked secrets.' Her voice grew lower. 'I saw her talking to that manager on Wednesday. He didn't look very pleased.'

That was understandable, Cara thought, taking her time over removing plates. Dan's cheery if patronizing manner with visitors quickly wore off at times.

'Poor Daphne,' a male occupant at the larger table ventured to say. 'She had a lot to put up with.'

'Did she? What?' The conversation returned to Mrs Waspish who had clearly been keeping half an ear open from her own table.

Knowing glances were exchanged. Cara reluctantly fielded the last plate. Then:

'That husband of hers.' Daphne's defender was looking uncertain whether to cringe or defend his sex.

The reply to this came from a prim-looking lady with a suitably hushed voice. Nevertheless, it reached the other table which had caught on to the fact that something interesting was happening. 'He's having an affair.'

An *affair*? Daphne's upright supportive husband, Mike? Cara had to bite back a laugh. This was surely sheer nonsense. She simply didn't believe it and gasps from the audience suggested it wasn't common knowledge or, she corrected herself, rumour.

'Who with?' demanded one. 'He wouldn't dare. Not with Daphne around.'

'Someone *here*. At the Towers.'

This had to be rubbish. Cara was convinced of that. It was someone's idea of a joke, and others seemed to agree with her.

'It was Daphne who was killed, not some casual girlfriend,' someone pointed out feebly.

Mrs Waspish's moment of triumph had come. 'Of course. I always understood that Daphne was very well off. She was *rich*.'

Another shock. No bricks without straw though, Cara forced herself to bear in mind. Even though these far-fetched 'bricks' were clearly lacking straw, she couldn't leave at this high point. She had to hear the full story if she was to dismiss it. 'You mean he might have been scared because if he was having an affair and he and Daphne split up he would lose out big time, financially?' she asked.

Her query went unheard in the hubbub, which seemed to be boiling down essentially to one pertinent question: who was considered the lucky or unlucky lady who had won Mike's attention? Was she here at Tanton Towers, or one of the Twerps, or a villager? This glib statement about Daphne's supposed wealth could well be a misunderstanding, Cara thought. In any case she couldn't see Mike in the role of adulterer or so desperate for money that he would kill for it.

'Another pot of tea,' someone ordered, and to her annoyance she was therefore obliged to leave temporarily. By the time she rushed back with the required teapot, the conversation had progressed significantly.

'I still can't believe it,' Mrs Waspish announced to the assembly with relish. 'Fancy Rosalie Atkins having an affair with Michael Hanson.'

Rosalie? No way. Cara couldn't believe that either. She didn't know much about her outside of working hours, as Rosalie didn't live in Tanton village, but it seemed to her there was a mountain of fiction being blown up out of a molehill of truth. Mike might have found a sympathetic ear in Rosalie, but surely not more than that. These were eager harpies – no, Cara reproved herself – they were merely curious people keen to solve the murder in their midst, as indeed she was herself.

She noted with definite relish the titbits of conversation that followed. Murmurs of disbelief battled with oblique references to the number of times Rosalie and Mike had been seen together, to Daphne's dislike of Rosalie, and to Rosalie being apparently footloose and fancy free while all the time she was harbouring a passion for Mike. One staunch defender maintained it must be someone else who was Mike's lover, but was defeated in the rush to place Rosalie in this privileged position.

Cara sided with the defence. Affairs just didn't fit with Mike. The Twerps saw far less of the Towers' staff than he did, so how could they speak with such certainty? Anyway, Mike was good-looking, but he was fifteen years or so older than Rosalie. Still, who was she to judge the partners that other people chose? She herself hadn't exactly excelled in that respect.

Nevertheless, she reminded herself, here she was trying to be an unbiased detective and she had to admit that if the gossip about Daphne's wealth were true, Mike would be a rich man. Taking on board rumours was all part of her job. She noted that a few heads had nodded at the mention of Rosalie, but she knew Rosalie better than the Tanton Whirlers did. For instance, Rosalie did not wear her heart on her sleeve, she was quietly efficient – and therefore must be a bit of a mystery to loquacious ladies and gentlemen such as these. It didn't mean that Rosalie was having a roll in the hay with anyone, let alone Mike Hanson. Rosalie was no sexy Delilah. Mike was quiet too, methodical, devoted to his job and Tanton's history, plus, she still believed, he had been devoted to Daphne – and not for the sake of her money.

Conclusion: Mike was not devoted to the efficient, self-contained Rosalie, but she should still check this out. Whereas only the police, she reasoned, would have access to Daphne's finances, she might make more progress on the subject of Rosalie's alleged affair. Robert Broome would be a good start as he was friendly with Rosalie. Go steadily, she warned herself. He too had to be on the list of suspects, especially as, if anyone, she would have partnered Rosalie with Robert, who was also dedicated to his work for the Towers.

Robert Broome, unaware that he was being yoked with Rosalie in sexual bliss, was at his desk when Cara arrived at the Archives Room and was apparently staring into nowhere. Odd, she thought, since usually when she accosted him he was full of excitement over some recently discovered document. At present she had no interest in documents and nor, it seemed, had Robert. She was still reeling from the staggering news – or rumours – about Rosalie, but Robert didn't look in a mood to cooperate. She'd have a go anyway.

'I came to see if anything was wrong?' she asked him as tactfully as she could manage. 'Are you still upset about what happened on Wednesday? I'm sure Rosalie must be,' she added with crossed fingers. If there were any truth at all in the rumours about Rosalie having an affair, this might draw him out.

Silence. She thought Robert was going to give her a brush-off but then he blurted out, 'It's that inspector.'

No more about Rosalie then, Cara decided. She'd made a false move, but she was learning. Nevertheless, it seemed clear that Robert's mind was not on Rosalie. It was DCI Andrew Mitchem again. 'He's been grilling you?'

'I must tell him,' he said woefully. 'I saw him yesterday and answered all his questions but I forgot *it*.'

'What's *it*?' Cara asked patiently.

He looked as though he was sorry he had spoken, but he eventually replied, 'I told him that I arrived about three o'clock on Wednesday and I was still in the building to hear all the screaming below and hurried down to see what had happened. He didn't ask any questions that I didn't answer.'

'What's the problem then?' Digging information out of Robert was pure archaeology. Dig deep for a lot of mud around the nuggets.

'It's complicated,' Robert said pathetically.

'About Max?' It often was as both their offices were on this floor. 'Lavinia or those books again?'

Cara had quickly learned the lesson that at Tanton there was no such thing as too many books. However, she knew that books were a touchy subject with Robert. His predecessor had left shelffuls of books about Renaissance art, many of which were stored in what was then a separate storage box room and was now the Archives Room annex. There were rare books and documents there, supervised by several ancestral portraits including the severe-looking lady who, Daphne had assured her, was the famous first wife whose ghost so scared her husband on his wedding day to the second lucky – or unlucky – lady.

Robert was proud that he had been the first archivist to dwell up here after the Great Change three years ago. An archway united the Archives Room with the annex, where Max had insisted that the art books should remain, along with more that had overflowed from the small library he kept at one end of La Galleria. Unfortunately, with the shelves in the Archives Room itself already full, this had led to Robert having to lodge his own precious histories of Kent down in the grand Library on the ground floor.

The Library was huge but it was not what the twenty-first century considered a library – a point Robert had argued vigorously with Dan Dickson time after time. In Sir Jeffry's time the Library was as much a place of entertainment and casual meetings, even dances, as it was a library. As a result, books were there in plenty lining the walls but they were placed in a stately order of how they *looked* rather than because of their contents.

Cara had also marvelled at the fact that the Towers' Library didn't even provide easy access to its shelves, merely long ornamental ladders. Robert had told her once that the books seemed to glare down at him as if commanding him to take them back to Archives. Since then, Max had acquired yet more volumes on Renaissance art but Robert had stood firm about taking even more into his own domain. Max had therefore reluctantly turned a room in the family wing into a library, but the subject was a tender one. Robert was still left with the problem of how to consult his books and always locked up the Archives Room at five o'clock for an hour in the Library before he headed for home.

Today he had more on his mind than books, however, and it was not Lavinia Fontana.

'Not the books or Lavinia,' Robert blurted out in answer to her question.

'So what's really worrying you? Something about Daphne?' Cara asked.

'Yes,' he said miserably. 'I forgot to tell him I met Daphne not long before she died. I was at the foot of the stairs and she was coming down from here. She was very upset.'

Time to play Dr Watson, not Sherlock, Cara instantly thought. This was important. 'When did this happen?' she asked, trying to keep her voice calm.

'On Tuesday, the day before she died. She wasn't here to dance. The Towers wasn't officially open, but I'd come in to do some research. She . . .' He hesitated, and then it came out as he seemed to be reliving that awful moment. 'She threw herself into my arms.'

A picture of a plump, sturdy Daphne, many years older than Robert, throwing herself anywhere – let alone into his arms – flitted across Cara's mind, but she hastily dismissed it.

'The reason I forgot to tell the inspector about it,' Robert continued, clearly eager to get whatever it was off his chest, 'is that I made the most interesting discovery yesterday morning. I found a document little more than a rough note about the delivery of bricks to the cellars in 1784 when the house was being built, and so Daphne went right out of my head. I was so surprised at her action on the stairs because I'm afraid she often tended to annoy me. I had to reprove her recently for not replacing documents in the Archives Office and ask her kindly to replace them tidily. She had promised me she would not fail to do so in future.'

'But that's not what upset her?'

'No. When she had herself under control she said it was to do with the book she was intending to write, so I accepted her apology and we parted though once again I discovered books and documents had not been replaced correctly.'

That book again. Could that be the cause of *murder*? She couldn't rule it out – there could well be others whose territory she was stepping on with this apparently popular project. But murder?

'Do you know anything more about this book of hers?'

Robert hesitated – perhaps he thought she wanted to write one too? Finally, he began. 'I had talked to Daphne about it,' he admitted. 'My opinion was that she would have needed help with it, as there is so much history involved. I suggested she let me help her with that, but she refused. Isn't that strange? The guidebook we already publish had quite enough history for her purposes, she said. You must admit, Cara, that that was an extraordinary statement. What kind of book would she write? Our present small guidebook is splendid, of course,' he added hastily, 'but hardly enough as a basis for a history of the Towers.'

'I'm afraid that's the way things tend to move now,' Cara said sympathetically. 'More pictures and less text.'

'Appalling.' Robert took up this theme eagerly. 'You might find it hard to believe, but my belief is that Daphne was only interested in legends and stories which so often have only the slightest base in history and therefore cannot creep into a true history book. Daphne did not understand the difference and I'm afraid I was rather annoyed. You see, Cara . . .' Robert hesitated. 'As you'll remember, I have plans to write my own history of Tanton Towers, with permission from Max, of course.'

Yes, she did remember. And there were plenty of others too. Simon's for one, as he was often skulking around after hours perhaps with that in mind. Dan had already published two books on antiques and might well be planning another. There would be one heck of an overload of potential books.

'I just can't believe,' Robert said, 'that Alison and Max would encourage Daphne to try her hand at writing a book, even if just about smugglers.'

No, Cara thought, as she walked back to the Happy Huffkin, nor could she. But that showdown – if that's what it would have been – never came about because Daphne had died. Typical Daphne, to barge ahead before checking that the road was clear with the people most concerned. Books were precious things, especially to those who had written them. Could competition have broken out between the various candidates? Had Daphne ruffled feathers beyond someone's endurance? Had it driven someone to murder? It was certainly worth considering, despite her earlier lines of enquiry that Daphne's death might be down to rivalry over the Twerps society leadership, a love affair with Rosalie or the depths of Daphne's pocket.

Take it step by step, Cara, she ordered herself. Given that Mike
was no Dr Crippen, the truth must lie somewhere else whether
involving Rosalie or not. What had upset Daphne so much on
Tuesday? So much that she was killed the next day.

Max had lured Alison to La Galleria with a mission in mind. It
was quite clear that Lavinia was at the heart of this ghastly matter,
if only the police would see that. He also had to convince Alison.
Her visits here were rare because he knew full well that she saw
it as his private domain, just as her study in the family wing was
devoted to Jane Austen. He could never understand the Austen
attraction but nevertheless he supposed her passion for her subject
was just as great as his own.

'I'm busy, Max,' she had told him plaintively. 'Rosalie, Dan
and I are up to our eyes with press and police and goodness
knows what.'

That surprised him. 'But it's five o'clock. Hasn't the hullabaloo
died down now?'

'Hullabaloos aren't affected by time,' she said grimly.

'Call Cara. She'll help.' That was always the quickest solution.
Meanwhile La Galleria was obviously the real target, and he
strode over to his favourite painting. 'I still think Daphne's death
is to do with a gang-planned theft of one of my Fontanas. Just
look once more at this superb portrait, Alison. That's why I kept
it safely downstairs before La Galleria was born. You can't deny
Lavinia has shown us the heart and soul of Queen Elizabeth I.
It displays the essence of the woman. Look at it. She has her
victory over the Spanish Armada stamped all around her like that
famous portrait of her. No one knows who painted that one, but
Lavinia certainly painted this.'

Alison looked and sighed. 'It's no use, Max. You can wheedle
me all you like, but I still don't think that this is her finest work.
You're on the wrong track. The real jewel in this collection is that
self-portrait of her. You can't ignore her use of chiaroscuro.'

Max strode along to inspect the said self-portrait, and reluctantly nodded. 'I agree it's an excellent portrait but compared
with Queen Elizabeth it's flat. No inspiration whereas Elizabeth
is full of life.'

'How and why?' Alison annoyingly demanded for the

umpteenth time. 'Lavinia could never have met Elizabeth. She's not known to have come to England and Elizabeth never took holidays in Bologna.'

He tried not to look smug. 'No, but I stick by my theory.'

Alison groaned, but he stood firm. 'We agree that Lavinia knew the Carracci Academy in Bologna,' he continued.

'Certainly,' Alison replied cautiously.

'To which the Flemish Renaissance artists flocked. And where Lavinia could have met them. She also knew her father's apprentice Denys Calvaert who was Flemish and later ran his own training academy for artists in Bologna in competition with the Carraccis. And we agree that Flemish painters were touring England in the late sixteenth century and could have painted Elizabeth from life. The Spanish Armada time.'

'I know where you're going, but it's tenuous.'

'Keep to the probable, darling. Lavinia saw one of those paintings, liked the idea of an important *woman* subject and decided to paint her own version of it.'

'Problem,' Alison instantly queried. 'If drawn from life, why did a possibly unknown Flemish painter lug his work all the way to Bologna?'

He glared at her. 'All sorts of reasons. Possibly it was his entry pass to be part of one of the academies.'

Alison was taking her time to answer this, he noted. 'Fairy tale, but possible,' she conceded. 'I still prefer that wild young man Lavinia painted.'

Max glanced over to the said painting which was another favourite of his.

'Painted in her Bologna days,' Alison went on. 'Probably at the Carracci Academy. And, good though it is, it doesn't have the life and sparkle of the Elizabeth. He's very dashing though. Almost . . .'

'Almost what?' he asked suspiciously when she paused.

'I can't quite work that out. But it's Lavinia at her best . . .'

The argument had to stop, he told himself. 'We can't go on like this, Alison. There's no escape for us this way from what's happened here.' A pause, then he surrendered. Max sighed. 'Who would Jane Austen pick out as the guilty party if she had been a sleuth?'

Alison thought for a moment. Jane Austen was her own special
field. 'Emma would be a victim. She was just like Daphne: the
cause of her own undoing. Don't stop to think, rush in and pursue
your own track, no matter what.'

'Accepted. Now for Lavinia,' Max replied. 'She planned things,
carefully. She learned from others and gave her own opinion.'

'Unlike Daphne.'

'Yes.' Max braced himself to continue. 'My love, I can't help
feeling that not only La Galleria but Tanton Towers itself is
dangerously exposed now murder has descended on us.'

'Will it change everything?' Alison asked soberly.

'Perhaps. Even Tanton Towers is not immune to invaders from
the outside. We have no boiling oil handy to throw down at them.
The police have come marching in and we, my darling, are as
much under suspicion as anyone else here. We have to play our
part. The real world is here and the skies are darkening.'

SIX

Another frustrating day, Cara thought gloomily. She'd assumed she would be at least catering for police and a few of the staff while Chief Inspector I'm-in-charge Mitchem went about his work. Not so. Here she was with Sammy, both of them standing like lemons waiting for custom. Usually Saturdays were their busiest. This one was not.

It was a desolate scene without visitors dotted everywhere like a Lowry painting. It presented a distinctly gloomy landscape with rain threatening. Against the clouds the turrets and towers stood out forcefully like warriors awaiting battle. Perhaps they were objecting to this intrusion into their deepest secrets. The occasional police officer could be seen drifting past along the terrace, but Chief Inspector Mitchem had not put in an appearance – not to outside viewers anyway.

She had assured Sammy that his presence wasn't essential today but he had turned up all the same, although the tray of freshly baked huffkins remained untouched. She'd had enough, and with Sammy's permission to abandon ship she decided to walk up to the gatehouse, ostensibly to see if the press were still gathering, but she was hoping to find Rosalie there. The Haven, usually alive with people changing shoes, seizing umbrellas, flinging anoraks here, there and everywhere, looked deserted apart from one pair of Wellington boots left outside. Whose? Why? Did she care? Not today, thanks.

She peered in through the Library windows as she passed, but there was no sign of life there either. At least when she reached the gatehouse she found Rosalie installed for action and she could see one or two hopeful media representatives. Even they weren't exactly champing at the bit, but slumping in a couple of canvas picnic chairs.

'Hi, Cara.' Rosalie waved at her as she approached, bearing her basket with coffee and a huffkin stored within.

Cara immediately cheered up. Looking at Rosalie, it was hard to believe that anything was amiss at the Towers, save for a lack of visitors who would normally have been pouring past. And, Cara thought in relief, it was even harder to believe that this efficient, good-natured and decidedly attractive woman was Mike Hanson's secret lover. Surely she could forget that, Cara hoped, but then reluctantly had second thoughts. It was too early to toss *anything* away.

'Coffee time,' Cara called out.

'You're an angel,' Rosalie informed her as Cara unpacked the basket.

Did Rosalie look like someone guarding a secret love affair, Cara asked herself. Nonsense, she thought impatiently. What would that someone look like?

'It can't be much fun out here,' she observed. 'Why on earth do you have to be marooned out here when there are no visitors allowed?'

'Dan thought it preferable to having the door to the Towers guarded by police if Mr and Mrs Public turn up hoping to see the scene of the crime.' Rosalie shrugged. 'Actually, I'd rather be out here than in the Towers. I can pretend that all this isn't happening.'

'It is though,' Cara said soberly. 'Do you know how Mike's faring? Is he on his own?' Another mistake, she realized too late. This was hardly tactful if the rumours about their love affair were true. Nevertheless, she steeled herself to don her mental Sherlock deerstalker, and was much relieved when Rosalie answered quite normally.

'He popped in earlier. He said he couldn't bear being alone.'

'Does he have family around here?' Cara asked.

'Not a close one,' Rosalie answered with no sign of any great interest. 'He has good neighbours, so he won't be alone for company if he wants it. And,' she added, 'he can always come to the Towers.'

Cara was taken aback. Whatever the truth about this rumour, Rosalie seemed to know Mike very well. Cara thought of the Towers staff as a family. They worked together, they liked each other, they disagreed sometimes, but they clung together. Now she was forced to doubt whether that was so. It looked as though they could be sheltering a murderer in their midst. Did she really know anyone here?

By the time Cara passed the Haven on her way back to the Happy Huffkin, she was wondering whether she was getting this out of proportion. The Towers had been here for over two hundred years. In its time it must have suffered many deaths and probably murders and yet today it stood here comfortingly as if to say 'this too will pass'. The only snag was that unless this murder was solved, its scars would remain.

Huh, she thought scornfully. So what do you think you can do, Cara Shelley? Just march in and wave a wand so that all the Towers' troubles will vanish like magic? Well, have I got news for you, lady. This is going to be tough going, but you're going to get there. The widow's mite in the Bible achieved something – so you can fork out your own mite.

Where lay her path? It was all very well for Christie's Poirot, teasing out suspects, working out motives, ruling out possible culprits one by one and then triumphantly declaring the villain. Easier said than done, however determined she was. The turrets and towers of Tanton might be keeping their secrets more efficiently than she could unmask them.

Then she thought of the first tray of huffkins she'd watched Sammy prepare. Solving crime must be a little like baking. It began with an idea, an inspiration, a matter of choice. Had she chosen her recipe? Yes. It was contributing to solving this crime. Assembly and mixing ingredients? She could do that. Then the kneading of the dough. OK. Leave it to prove itself. Hopefully yes. Put her thumb print in it – the traditional sign of the huffkin – and put it in to bake. Then would come the point where she'd take it out of the oven, judge her own work, so that she could present a fully baked huffkin to DCI Andrew Mitchem.

Cara cheered up. It seemed so simple. At present she reasoned that she was still at the mixing of ingredients stage and all these were stacked up on the table before her: Dan, Ewan, Robert, Simon, Rosalie and even Miss Clip-Clop Keeley. She could see two of them conveniently making their way across the lawn to the Happy Huffkin, which cheered her up even more. Dan and Miss Clip-Clop were on their way. It looked an odd combination, especially with Dan so formally clad in suit and tie and Miss Clip-Clop in her usual high heels, tight trousers and tunic. At least the rumour hadn't burdened poor Mike with her instead of

Rosalie, unless of course it had focussed on the wrong victim. Anyway, Mike wasn't having an affair with anyone, she was still sure of that.

'Good to see you, Cara,' Dan greeted her heartily as she settled them at a table. 'This makes everything seem a tad more normal.'

Normal? If only.

'Why close almost the whole house?' Keeley said crossly. 'The police ought to stay in the orangery because that's where poor Daphne was murdered.'

Keeley was difficult to fathom out, Cara thought. So neat, so tidy, so efficient. But where was the heart of her?

'Because, my pet,' Dan answered her indulgently, 'it might have been one of us who murdered her, and in our haste we might have left tracks anywhere like slugs.'

Miss Clip-Clop giggled. 'I'm not your pet and I'm not a slug.'

Cara was in two minds about the latter at least, but then contritely remembered that she had once thought of the Towers' staff as one large happy family.

'Of course not, Keeley dear,' Dan replied. 'You're a treasure. Anyway, the police seem to have the idea that one of us is the guilty party. Nonsense, of course, but apparently all the volunteers have been checked out and none of them was still wandering around past closing time. Nor were the dancers.'

'Just us then,' Cara quickly asked, seeing an opportunity. 'Plus Rosalie and Simon.'

Dan shot a decidedly odd look at her. 'That could well be. I myself was in my office at the time she was murdered, but he's always prowling around for one reason or another. He has some mad idea that Max and Alison are going to give their blessing to some book he wants to write.'

'That's your province, Dan,' Keeley murmured, fluttering eyelashes like crazy.

Dan tried to look modest. 'Indeed. But my next, *The Treasures of Tanton*, has been stalled until the Towers gets back to its usual self.'

The book market was definitely going to be overcrowded, Cara thought. What with Robert's, Daphne's, probably Simon's and now Dan's, it would be well served.

'There will never be a normal again,' Keeley said decidedly.

'It's always going to be known as the place where a murder took place.'

Cara fumed, but she couldn't dispute that now. Dan got in first.

'Not,' he said firmly, 'once the criminal is unmasked.'

'It won't happen,' Keeley announced. 'I was in the toilet, getting ready to go home when the murder took place, but I bet the others here haven't any alibis.'

Not the time to fight her logic, Cara decided, trying to keep a pleasant smile on her face.

'The murderer will have to declare himself before Ewan's open day. He's quite sure that the opening of that tunnel will be salvation of the Towers,' Dan said heavily.

'Will it still go ahead?' Cara asked. August would be here in a few weeks' time and she'd heard nothing. Surely it would be too soon after Daphne's death for it to be the success Ewan wanted? She felt an unexpected rush of warmth for Ewan. Although he made very little attempt to conceal his determination to be top dog here, he was a man with ideas and she was amused by his clear passion to forge ahead. Charm was one of his weapons, or had been until he turned it on her sexually, on which she had speedily put a damper. She was years older than him and he had taken the rebuff with good humour, which was one up to him.

'Not a chance,' Dan said offhandedly. 'Did you know that Daphne was insisting that she should lead the tour parties through it, to Ewan's extreme displeasure? She said she needed the money. She always did. She was always badgering Mike for it.'

Sometimes ripe plums just fall off the tree and Cara gratefully clutched at this one. Daphne was short of money? In that case Mike was clear of accusations that he killed her for financial reasons. Sherlock's deerstalker was working. Yippee!

'What did Ewan think about Daphne taking over his role as tour leader?' she asked.

'He was mad as hell,' Keeley contributed smugly.

'And she was winning too. Of course,' Dan murmured, 'her murder puts an end to that. One does wonder how far dear Ewan would go to fulfil his dream. I couldn't help recalling that he is very frequently in the cellars, so handy for the orangery.'

A step too far, Cara thought indignantly. Dan seemed rather too anxious to divert attention from himself. True, Ewan had, according to Dan, fallen out with Daphne and he would have had quite a job ahead of him if she had inadvertently set her mind on outdoing him over the smugglers' tunnel.

'I rather gather, Cara,' Dan continued airily, 'that you're getting very interested in our few little squabbles here at the Towers.'

Keeley raised an elegant eyebrow. Not a hair out of place. Just a supercilious smile. 'Are you? Do take care, Cara. A lot of care.'

Cara watched them depart wondering just what Keeley was insinuating. Was it a threat, she wondered uneasily. It would be Keeley's idea of fun to drop such a warning and then vanish. Anyway, Ewan himself was striding past, probably on his way back from the smugglers' tunnel and heading for his office on the ground floor of the Towers. He was an interesting man to look at, Cara thought, shorter than most members of staff, and slightly resembling a somewhat slimmer Napoleon in the determination of his jaw and figure. He only needed a cocked hat and he could pass for him any day. However, he could beat Napoleon at charm.

'Here, sit down and have a huffkin,' she called out. 'They're a good remedy for frustration. There's just one left before we close.'

He hesitated, but the huffkin won. With no other customers, she seized the chance to talk. 'What's going to happen about your open day?' she asked as casually as she could.

'Going ahead. Middle of August it is, a special opening on Tuesday the sixteenth,' he said cheerily.

'That's good. Are the police still searching the tunnel?' she asked. She noted that he was getting his way over that after all.

'Officially yes. But I haven't seen anyone there today. Anyway, there's no point looking for clues; the murderer would have needed a key – if that's what's on your mind.'

That key again. Rosalie would have one – all of them did and that included Mike, of course. 'That doesn't mean it's one of us,' she commented. 'Someone might have given a key at some point quite innocently to an outsider.' That didn't ring true, even to her.

'Let's hope so or we're all in trouble,' Ewan retorted. 'Daphne might have irritated us all but not to the extent we'd kill her. Except perhaps Mike,' he added.

'You're joking.' Cara tried to keep her temper. 'Why would he?' she challenged him. 'That would have taken planning and her death was a spur-of-the-moment attack.'

Ewan shrugged. 'We all have skeletons in the closet and the great god rumour floats around. Anyway, I was in my office for part of the time and nipped along to the Snug for a cuppa before I knocked off for the day. Sorry I didn't have time to come here, Cara.'

'Thanks,' she said shortly.

Ewan laughed. 'Well, you'll be pleased to know that for the open day I'm doing a special tour with due respect to the murder.'

Did Alison know that, Cara wondered when he left. The general opinion was that there wasn't a chance the open day would happen. Ewan now maintained it would. He had, she noted, made no mention of Daphne's intention to take over the leadership of the tours.

'It'll work out,' Sammy grunted, appearing at her side as she was taking the half-eaten huffkin back to the folly. He read her expression correctly.

'I doubt it. But at least he isn't writing a book,' Cara remarked. 'Thank goodness for that. Still, Daphne blithely barging in on Ewan's prerogative in leading tours in the tunnel must have been a blow. Just as Simon's eye on leading the Twerps would be to his pride. All a matter of prestige.'

Sammy had his eye on her. 'Them police. Worried about them?'

'Anxious,' she admitted.

'DNA,' Sammy said succinctly. 'That's the answer.'

That sounded so simple as the solution to Daphne's murder. 'But DNA could be present on Daphne for all sorts of reasons.' Cara could see trouble ahead.

'The husband most like.'

'Wrong, Sammy,' she shot back at him.

She was ignored. 'Look who's coming,' he said.

Her heart dropped. She needed time to think over what she'd

learned before girding her loins for battle and now here he was. Andrew Mitchem was ambling towards them as though life were all tea and cakes.

'Tea?' she asked him politely, as Sammy departed chuckling. 'Or is this official?'

'Yes, but coffee please and any biscuits going. We need to talk.' He hadn't sat down, which was odd.

'About what?' she asked guardedly.

'This case. You're involved with the house as well as being an outsider. Mixed loyalties. True?' At last he sat down as she went in to fetch the coffee, giving her time to consider this angle. He could wait for his biscuits *and* an answer.

'Up to a point, yes,' she conceded when she returned bearing a tray with the coffee and three handsome cookies.

'A case of my country right or wrong?'

Whoops! She might be facing a trap here. Too much honey around. 'No,' she replied, 'save for Alison and Max being concerned.'

'Then we'll leave them out of it, if it pleases you. And also your friend Sammy skulking inside. Back to Daphne Hanson. Tell me more about her.'

That astounded her. 'You must know it all by now.'

A somewhat theatrical sigh. '"All" is not a word I work with. It's no matter if I already know some of it. Tell me about her love life, her pets, her silly jokes, her temper, her hobbies, anything. Don't defend her, don't castigate her.' He began to drink his cappuccino during the silence that followed. 'I'll start you off,' he said. 'Happy marriage?'

'It seemed so.' Tread *very* carefully, she advised herself. There was a fly in the ointment. The pleasure of telling him about her demolishing the money motive for Daphne's death would come at the cost of throwing the spotlight on Rosalie. 'Daphne could be irritating to us at times, so I suppose she was to her husband too,' she began. Then she took the plunge.

'Someone said that she was well off, implying she was killed for financial reasons.' She wouldn't bring Mike's name into it if she could avoid it, obvious though the connection was. 'But I have evidence,' she continued, trying not to sound too Sherlockian, 'that Daphne was far from well off. So that can't be a motive for her death. Of course, you'll have access to the will and so you'll know the situation already.'

No reaction. Then: 'Rumours fly fast with very light wings.'

Where now? Plunge, Cara decided. 'There's another one flying around too.'

'There always is,' he said helpfully.

'It's just gossip, of course.'

He waited. The rotter. She was just a fish on a hook to him. 'I heard a crazy story about her husband having an affair with Rosalie Atkins,' she told him. 'Nonsense, of course.'

'Probably not Rosalie,' he replied matter-of-factly. 'I'm told that would be Keeley Martin.'

'*Keeley?*' She had been felled with one blow, but managed to rally. 'Are you sure? If he's having an affair with anyone, which is simply not credible, then it would far more likely to be Rosalie.'

'A busy man,' he commented.

'Mike just isn't the sort to have an affair,' she replied hotly. 'You don't know him well enough. He would never betray Daphne. She was a gentle, loving person, even if she was irritating sometimes.'

Andrew Mitchem had no comment on this. Instead he said, 'Cara – if I may – how would you assess a pyramid? Just from one side?' He was fiddling with the fork and seemed – or so it appeared to Cara – to be thinking of something other than pyramids.

'No,' she said. Calling her Cara? What was this all about? Anyway, why not play his game? 'All sides.'

'Exactly what I do. Once I'm back to the beginning I know where I am. Nothing has been hidden in one today, so I'm grateful for your starting the walk around this pyramid with me.'

This sounded ominous to Cara. 'It's what's buried inside it that counts.'

Silence. Foiled again. She took a deep breath and talked as requested. He didn't interrupt as she went over the same ground: what she knew of Daphne, what had happened that afternoon, that morning, who else she had seen, and so on.

He made no comment until she had finished. 'Coming back to her husband,' he then said. 'What about him?'

Dangerous ground. 'He had left by the time you said she died.'

'How did he leave?'

He must know this already, surely. 'He and Daphne lived at the other end of the village from me. He usually brought Daphne here but not always drove her back because of his working hours. So he left by the gatehouse entrance as usual.'

'There's the old tradesmen's entrance past the family wing, plus the pedestrian entrance in the woods.'

Cara kept a straight face. 'Of course. But he did speak to Rosalie on the way out.'

A silence. Then: 'Thank you,' he said gravely.

More dangerous ground, if Rosalie or Keeley was indeed having an affair with him, Cara thought. Rosalie's evidence would be suspect. But there *was* no affair. Cara asked herself whether she was still sure of that. Answer: yes, yes, *yes*!

'But,' Andrew Mitchem continued, 'suppose he decided to return on foot through the smugglers' tunnel?'

Caught. 'Anyone on the staff would know where the key is. But,' she added speedily, 'Daphne's murderer would know better than to use it for their own purpose, even with a key.'

'Why?'

'Ewan wouldn't be pleased and could well have been in the tunnel himself. He's in and out of it getting it ready for visitors, but otherwise it's locked. It has to be, otherwise casual visitors including children might be strolling along it. He's having a grand open day to launch it.'

Andrew Mitchem did not comment. 'This dancing group, the Tanton Whirlers. How seriously do they take themselves?'

Cara greeted this with relief. He must have Simon in his sights now. 'Extremely. I think there are about twenty of them altogether and they rotate who dances where and when. A lot are early retired, some still working, but they all take the honour and the glory very, very seriously. They often win trophies.'

'I'm told Simon Harris is the new leader. Do you know him well?'

New leader? His dream had come true, she thought meanly. 'No, but we're friendly enough. I suppose that makes sense,' she added doubtfully.

'Perfect sense. Next, do you think Daphne Hanson was killed

for what she represented – an obstacle in someone's way? Or for what she was?'

This was a corker coming out of the blue. She hadn't thought of Daphne's death in those terms. Could the two be separated though? 'Perhaps the second,' she began uncertainly, 'the kind of person she was.'

'You've portrayed her as a gentle, lovable woman with irritating ways. How come she was murdered for who she was then?'

'Hold on.' Cara grappled with this. It wasn't fair but she had to find a reply. 'She was single minded,' she told him. 'She liked her own way. She was inquisitive. But we all liked her,' she added hastily.

'So we're back to her being an obstacle in somebody's way, in your opinion.'

'There could be an element of that,' she agreed. She was falling behind in this race, but it was an interesting one.

'Inquisitiveness about what?' he asked. 'Take Professor Farran Pryde's art collection, for example. Was she interested in that?'

So that's the way the wind blew – naturally enough, Cara conceded. 'She never talked about it to me,' she replied truthfully. 'Anyway, I don't think there's a Picasso tucked away in disguise amongst the Fontanas.'

'Ho hum,' Andrew commented. He grinned. 'Thank you, Cara,' he added, rising to his feet to leave. 'How much do I owe you?'

'It's on the house.'

Did that count as bribery? As well as the 'Cara' and 'thank you', she received a casual hand wave as he strode off. What, she wondered, had that been about? A free coffee and cookies were the only things she seemed to have served him with.

Meanwhile, she had to admit that his dissection of the case gave room for consideration. She went over it again. An obstacle in somebody's way. Could that be as Mike's wife, or as a rival for the Tanton Whirlers' leader, or leader of the smugglers' tunnel trips, or because of rival books? She hadn't mentioned the latter to Andrew Mitchem. Should she? Was it just tittle-tattle or a valid motive?

She battled with herself but she had to tell him. Impulsively she shouted after him but instantly regretted it. No choice now so she marched quickly towards him, kicking herself for not thinking this through earlier.

He was waiting for her to come up to him – typical, she thought crossly. 'I forgot to tell you something,' she said lamely as she reached him.

'Tell me now,' he said.

'It's the book she was writing. And I don't know that it caused trouble. That's only hearsay.'

'I love hearsay.' And, perhaps seeing her hesitation, 'I can forget it whenever necessary.'

'She was writing – or wanted to write – about the legends and smugglers and so on at the Towers.'

'And the problem about that?'

'Jealousy,' she said darkly. 'Other people are writing or want to write books about the Towers.'

'And the problem about that if they're all different?'

'My guess,' Cara said truthfully, as she'd no facts to go on, 'is that honour and glory come into it somewhere.'

'Also the first on the market might sell more,' he suggested. 'Especially if the Towers were backing one and not the other.'

'Alison and Max wouldn't do that,' she said indignantly.

She noticed the way he always cocked his head to the left when he was thinking about something. Would some great pronouncement come out of this?

'Thanks, Cara.' He nodded and continued on his way.

No great pronouncement then. She'd been a fool to come rushing over. No, she hadn't, her second thoughts decided. There could just be something in it. After all, envy was a cardinal sin. Where did this leave her, she wondered as she watched Andrew Mitchem disappearing into the orangery area, still roped off to all outsiders.

And that's what her thoughts on the case were. Roped off – although that didn't mean they were invalid, she argued to herself. Considerably more cheerful, she returned to the café with the dirty mug and plates. No sign of Sammy at the service counter, but he was undoubtedly still around somewhere, probably tucked up in the kitchen. 'Skulking' was the word Andrew Mitchem had used. So what? One can learn a lot from skulking.

Suppose, just suppose, this stupid story about Mike's infidelity were true. How would she then feel about Mike and his possible involvement with Daphne's death? She considered this, staring at the cup of tea in front of her. She knew the answer. She just wouldn't believe it unless Mike himself admitted to having an affair. And even then would it shake her belief in his innocence of murder? She knew the answer to that too. No. It just didn't fit.

Conclusion: she thought of Indiana Jones and his leap of faith across the canyon beneath him: Result: 'Indy, here I come!' she vowed.

Right. Now she needed to work out a way forward independent of DCI Mitchem's approach. For this purpose only, she must not rule out Rosalie's possible relevance to Daphne's murder, nor – far-fetched though it was – the story about Miss Clip-Clop that had reached the great DCI. She had to do her best to prove them wrong, and for that she had to find new avenues, for there, surely, would lie the answer. She would have to adopt Sammy's beady eye for any blemish in his work (or hers) if she was going to help remove the shadows that had fallen on the Towers.

Those towers looked so imposing, so indestructible, held so many secrets. All the turrets, for example, flourished as additions to the building, but they were architectural red herrings. She was aware that she'd have to ignore red herrings of her own, if she was to get anywhere with finding out what happened to Daphne. Moreover, that had to happen quickly if the Towers was to return to its former glory, and the longer the shadows lay over the building and the staff the harder that would be.

As DCI Mitchem had his own way of going about this case, there was all the more reason for her to continue to pursue her own line. She'd therefore leave it to him to follow up the ridiculous rumours about Mike. She wasn't a trained professional detective like Andrew, but . . . She caught herself. Why was she thinking of him as 'Andrew' suddenly? Because of the 'Cara'? Mistake. He was DCI Mitchem. Did he think that her knowledge of Tanton Towers and its staff was a *dis*advantage because she might be prejudiced? If so, she disagreed. Until this crime was solved there, would be a dark cloud over everything. There was a murderer around. And, she realized uneasily, she was caught up in this nightmare.

At that moment Sammy reappeared. 'Done early. No customers much.'

Cara sighed. The café would be busy once visitors were able to come in again, but even so she realized that somehow the Happy Huffkin had been temporarily pushed to the back of her mind.

'Once the gates are open again, the Towers will be back to its normal happy self and so we will be,' she reassured him.

'Dreamland, duckie.'

'No, it's not,' she said obstinately. 'This awful murder has to be solved quickly because until then it's like a malignant worm eating away at it.' Over the top, perhaps, but there was something to it.

Sammy chuckled. 'Keep going.' He doffed his cap and wandered off.

That was Sammy's charm, Cara thought. He looked scruffy and aimless, yet he 'went on cutting bread and butter' like the well-conducted lady in the Thackeray poem when faced with a crisis. Well, thank goodness Sammy did, only with him it was baking.

Where was Andrew Mitchem seeking his prey, she wondered. Was he in the same quandary as she was? The rumours about Mike's secret affair and Daphne's perceived wealth were obvious targets but had produced nothing. He too would see the potential in the rivalry for leadership motive, both for Ewan and for Simon, but the book angle was already beginning to seem weak. How had it affected Daphne? What attracted her to it? The power of writing a book? Of being the first to write one? Or was she fascinated by the stories that would go into it, in other words the history of Tanton Towers?

History. Cara did a double take. She remembered Daphne rejoicing in the story of Sir Jeffry and his first wife's ghost and her own assumption that it was the legend factor that appealed to Daphne. But suppose she was wrong? Suppose it was more the history of that legend and the history of the smugglers' tunnel that appealed to her, rather than their just being romantic stories? That would, Cara realized, account for Daphne's interest in La Galleria, more perhaps as a historical part of the Towers than for the artistic works it contained. Daphne was inquisitive by nature and very determined to follow up anything that captured her attention, especially if there was something she believed needed dealing with. Could that have caused her death? Daphne would not have examined her own motives; she would have pushed straight ahead with what she thought was interesting.

What else could there have been of historical interest in La Galleria that might have hooked Daphne's attention? Anything other than the paintings' subject matter and their journeys from Italy to Tanton? Their valuations, perhaps? But there were far more valuable items in the Towers than those in La Galleria, all of which had to be guarded. There was jewellery, the plate, furniture and so on, and other valuable paintings in the Library and elsewhere. Nevertheless, according to Max it was Lavinia Fontana's work that interested Daphne.

Cara knew that Lavinia's paintings currently fetched a wide range of valuations, from the high hundreds to the occasional high thousands, but if she were an art thief would she pick on elaborate plans to rob La Galleria? And could that somehow have led to Daphne's murder? Hard to see how even fanatics of Lavinia's work would go to such lengths to obtain the painting of their dreams. Non-fanatics certainly wouldn't with rivals such as Reynolds and Gainsboroughs elsewhere at the Towers. Mike was the Towers' accountant and in the past had been involved with art and antiques insurance companies, but that would only be of relevance if there had been thefts in La Galleria in recent memory. There hadn't been, and nowadays security was as tight by day as it was by night. Conclusion: Daphne's interest was firmly on the history of the Towers and especially on that of La Galleria.

Cara looked at her watch. With any luck Max might be in his office, she guessed. But he wasn't. Nor was he in La Galleria. She finally tracked him down in the family wing living room, where he was sitting with Alison and reading the weekend news-papers. They looked warily at her.

'No fresh troubles,' she assured them hastily. 'Just possibilities.'

As usual, she relaxed in the different atmosphere here than in the public rooms. On entering through the not-very-noticeable door, she felt like Alice stepping through the looking glass. Gone was the stately mansion and here was a true home.

Cara accepted the offer of one of their comfortable armchairs but turned down the offer of a drink. She needed a clear head and Max was a great one for aperitifs – especially experimenting with them.

'I've had the honour of a visit from DCI Mitchem,' she explained.

'Ah.' Max looked pensive. 'He's a good fellow.'

Really? Steady, Cara, she advised herself. 'It made me wonder even more why Daphne was interested in La Galleria, whether it was for Lavinia Fontana or whether it was because of Lavinia's role in the Towers' history.'

Max was clearly flummoxed. 'No idea. Have you, Alison?'

Alison shook her head. 'That was just Daphne. Curious about everything.'

'A Christie-type Miss Marple?' Cara asked.

'Good heavens, no.' Alison paused. 'I took her on a brief tour a week or two ago and I remember she asked whether there had been any robberies there in the past.'

Cara clutched at this straw. 'And were there any?'

'Sorry to disappoint you, but there are none recorded in the house archives. Robert says the records aren't complete, but I think there would be a fine old uproar from Max's predecessors if there had been a problem with theft. Why are you asking? Could it have led to her murder? Hard to see how, although Daphne did like her secrets, of course.'

'She didn't share any of them with you, even by hinting?' Cara tried hopefully.

'Not that I remember. The last thing she was rattling on about was the origins of Strip the Willow, the charms of the Sir Roger de Coverley and what should be their *pièce de résistance*. She'd had an argument with Simon Harris about it. He was getting quite vehement because, as a man, he felt the choice should be his, but Daphne wouldn't shift. She did upset people.'

Max cut in firmly. 'That's why I like Lavinia. None of this sexist stuff in Rome. Once Lavinia went to live in Rome in 1604, she became one of the gang with all the famous artists of the day, notably Caravaggio, not that he was exactly covering himself in glory at the time. But everyone was drawn to Rome despite the fame of Bologna's Carracci Academy, where she'd been one of its early stars. Of course, excellent though her Minerva and her portraits from the Rome period are, I still feel her earlier work is superior in many ways. Such as the—'

'Max,' Alison broke in. 'Daphne . . .'

She was ignored. 'Remember that magnificent exhibition in Washington in 1998 devoted to Lavinia and other female artists from that time? Quite remarkable.' Max had that dreamy reminiscent look on his face which Cara had come to know meant he was back in his Fontana comfort zone.

'Yes, I do remember it,' Alison said patiently. 'But one also has to place them in the context of *all* the artists of the time. The sex of the artist should be immaterial. It is the product that . . .'

'Not entirely,' Max interrupted.

Time to break this up, Cara decided. 'Why do you think Daphne asked you about thefts from La Galleria?'

Max and Alison both laughed. 'Sorry, Cara,' Alison said, 'I don't think it was because Daphne had secret plans for running off with Lavinia's masterpieces. She was so eager to write that book she was planning.'

'But had she actually begun it?'

'I don't know. I was gently going to enquire about that, because I knew it would be a minefield and upset people.'

'Not so much they would murder her, though,' Max said firmly. 'Why would a book on smugglers and ghosts and stuff like that whip up scholars like Dan Dickson or Robert Broome into a frenzied murder attack? We couldn't stop her – or Simon Harris – from writing a book about the Towers, but they would only have a lukewarm blessing from us.'

Alison took up the baton. 'The reason we weren't keen on the idea is that Daphne's book in particular might take Tanton Towers into a realm we didn't want. By which, I mean that Daphne in particular was all too likely to make a hash of it even if she didn't mean to. She would chat about the tunnel and Fontana giving the Towers an image that could be picked up by the media as *our* view of what the Towers is all about. We've got our smugglers stories, its legends, its eccentricities in its ownership, but there is much more to the Towers than that. As we see it, they all settle down into a harmonious whole. We have a ghost or two, we have weirdo Horace back in the early days, but they are

just part of an overall story of a family that had both its eccentricities and its service to politics, art and general citizenship.
It's developed its own character and we don't want it
overbalanced.'

'Yes, I see that.' Cara agreed wholeheartedly with this speech.
That was what she loved the Towers for too. She began to realize
just how deep Alison and Max's feelings about it went. They
had to treat the Towers both as an onerous responsibility and as
an everyday job. That was what Cara saw every day, even from
Max. But it was much more than that. Much, much more.

SEVEN

Some days were better than others, Cara thought gloomily. She'd taken the woodland path up to the Towers and, even in the present circumstances, it should have been soothing. Today it failed. Daughter Kate had rung from Cambridge to tell her – with obvious pleasure which made it worse – that she had landed a job in the south of France for the summer and wouldn't be able to make it back to Tanton – except perhaps for a weekend, she had generously offered. No mention of her earlier plan of a trip to Indonesia, so maybe boyfriend Rod was history.

Now even the Towers was letting her down, Cara thought mutinously. Instead of providing a refuge from private problems, it too had its problems. She'd just have to get on with the job, she supposed.

She unlatched the gate, took a deep breath and marched onwards and upwards towards the café. There stood the Towers in front of her, massive, immoveable and calming in its magnificence. Although the house was closed on Mondays and Tuesdays, some of the staff were often present, and usually she would see Mike in his second-floor office. Rent was paid online now, but it had become an established routine to report to him anyway. Today it would surely be Dan standing in for Mike, even if such humble issues as money would be an issue at the moment. These were not normal times, and as Alison had insisted that she should pay for police and staff lunches and teas there were things to discuss. The tea and coffee machine in the Snug was rarely used if the Happy Huffkin was open.

Duty done in the café, and with Sammy's blessing, Cara set off to the Towers, aware that for no reason at all she was growing tense with anticipation. Once in the Great Hall it continued, because there seemed to be an odd feel to the house, as if it were as empty of atmosphere as it apparently was of people. Perhaps the house too was waiting for the resolution of Daphne's murder. Even the grandees staring down from the huge oil portraits all around her seemed to be wondering what this upstart was doing on their premises, and the carved lady at the end of the balustrade of the grand staircase was glaring at her in disapproval. Goodness knows why, Cara thought mutinously. She was doing her best. Dan's office was on this floor so she decided to try that first and was rewarded by seeing the door ajar.

Her tactful knock was perfunctory as silence seemed to be reigning inside, so she went in. 'I've come . . .' she began, then stopped. Dan had a visitor. Mike of all people. She hadn't seen him since his first brave appearance on Thursday. He was sitting in the armchair hidden behind the open door and now clambered to his feet. He looked crumpled, she thought, both in his clothing and his general appearance. To say he was under strain would be an understatement, and with the always immaculate Dan present this was even more apparent.

'Sorry, Cara,' Mike said, as if reading her mind. 'I was tired of my own company.'

'Understandably,' she said warmly, 'and it can't help you seeing all these cordons and police around.' There were no police to be seen this morning but their stamp was everywhere.

'It actually does help in a way,' he replied, clearly struggling to be 'normal'. His mind was somewhere else. Then out of the blue he burst out, 'It was Alison who found Daphne – and then you, Cara, wasn't it? Daphne loved this place.'

Cara struggled to come up with the right words, especially since she felt guilty at delving into his love life behind his back. 'The Towers won't be the same without her,' she managed. It was a platitude, but it was true. Daphne had become part of the show, the exuberant figure in the flying robes as the fiddler threw his all into the music. She remembered the familiar cry of 'Strip the willow!' as Daphne bounced down the line swinging first with the left hand, then the right.

'I still don't understand what she was doing in the orangery,' Mike said. 'And certainly not so long after the others had left.'

'Some may have stayed on.' Cara tried to make this sound casual. 'Did you see any of them, Dan? Simon, for example. He might have stayed on for research for the book he's planning.'

Dan shook his head. 'Perhaps. I wouldn't have seen him. I was closeted here with the day's receipts.'

Mike seemed deep in his own thoughts. 'Daphne usually walked home if I'd already left. I suppose she might have been muddled about when I was leaving and thought I was coming to fetch her. But why go to the orangery if so? If she was waiting for anyone there, it wasn't me,' he said forlornly. 'I had driven up in the morning, and then left around four fifteen. I'd already warned her, so who was she expecting to meet there? Why stay late?'

'Alison,' Cara said immediately. 'She'd agreed to see her sometime after five thirty.'

'I knew about that. There must have been someone else as well.'

'Someone who offered her a lift?' Dan suggested.

'They killed her instead.' Mike was shuddering.

'Look, old chap, don't brood about it,' Dan said soberly. 'That's the police's job to find out.'

'No, it's mine,' Mike said flatly. 'I owe it to Daphne. She was a jewel and I've lost her.'

Seeing Mike now, the rumours about his having an affair seemed more and more unlikely to Cara. The great DCI had only said he'd been *told* about it, not that he believed it. The evidence must surely have been wrong.

'Could it be,' she suggested, 'that whoever else it was whom Daphne had arranged to meet in the orangery was there to discuss the book she was going to write?' Mistake.

Silence, then: 'Looking at me, Cara?' Dan said jokingly. 'I trust I might be excluded,' he added, not so jokingly. 'My work is far different from dear Daphne's field and I was not interested in hers.'

'Cara's right though,' Mike said heavily. 'Writing that book meant a lot to her. Not that I ever saw anything of it. She kept it to herself to surprise me when it was all finished, she told me.'

It was beginning to seem as if nobody had seen this book, Cara realized, and yet she had certainly been keen on writing one. Who else entered the picture besides Dan, Robert and Simon? Ewan, of course, despite his denials. Ewan, who was go-ahead, young enough to see a profitable career ahead of him propped up by his prowess as a leader of the tours, perhaps providing pamphlets of smuggling stories written by himself. Anything to win media publicity. He would see Daphne as a rival. Cara tried to push the thought away. Shadows were falling on the Towers in earnest and the unity she had taken for granted was fast vanishing.

There was a snag in her theory. 'We don't know,' she pointed out, 'that Daphne was set to meet anyone other than Alison there and possibly Mike. The fact that she died in the orangery doesn't mean she'd been there all the time since the house closed.'

This still didn't please Dan. 'Where was she then? Who was this mysterious visitor?'

'I don't know,' Cara had to admit. She was treading on very dangerous ground here. 'After the visitors are chivvied out at four thirty, you make quite sure that no dancers or visitors are left inside, don't you, Dan? So we're back to stage one: her killer has to have been in the house at that time.'

Silence. She had put a foot wrong with Dan, and Mike was in no state to discuss his wife's death rationally.

Might as well play the last card, she thought. 'Even though La Galleria wasn't involved, Max must be worried about his collection's safety, especially as Daphne was interested in it,' she said.

'I see no need for him to be,' Dan said coolly. 'Security's tight there and nothing is missing. There's no possible connection between La Galleria and Daphne's death.'

'Art wasn't her thing,' Mike agreed. 'Poor Daphne. She didn't know a Correggio from a Caravaggio.'

'She liked the idea of women's rights, though,' Dan chuckled, now that they were on safer ground. 'And Max's Lavinia certainly flew the flag for that in her male-dominated society, even if she didn't flaunt it.'

'Nothing changes, does it?' Cara replied brightly.

Neither man commented, but at last Dan said: 'What was it you came for, Cara?'

The subject was closed but she sensed all too clearly that Lavinia was a no-go area.

Ewan was sprawled in one of the gatehouse chairs. He felt on top of the world. 'Didn't know Mike was your lover, Rosalie.

Flying close to the wind, aren't you?' He grinned. Nothing like taking the bull by the horns.

Rosalie looked startled. 'I didn't know either. What on earth are you on about? Is this your idea of a joke? An affair with Mike Hanson? It's quite absurd.'

Ewan tried to look contrite. 'Sorry. The grapevine, at fault. Begins with a small seed and ends up with a juicy story.'

'Small seeds have to be planted,' she retorted grimly. 'Where did it start?'

'I don't recall,' he replied. Press on, he told himself. He could hardly tell her it had begun with him as a safety measure. 'But I'll rack my brains to remember. Can't have the police getting too interested.'

Rosalie was looking aghast and he had a moment's compunction. He liked Rosalie, but it was high time he diverted gossip away from himself. He needed to know what was going on in this murder enquiry.

'Why do these "some" people think he's having an affair at all?' Rosalie said angrily. 'Daphne would soon have put a stop to any frivolity like that. It's all nonsense.'

'Dangerous nonsense though,' Ewan continued. 'Might have nasty results.' Not for him though, he thought. In theory there was no problem about the whole world knowing that he was having it off with Keeley once in a while. Why not? They were both single – well, Keeley was almost single and her divorce would be coming through soon. It had been fun but, in the midst of this witch-hunt by the police, it was better to keep a low profile. That's why, just for a laugh, he'd thrown her name into the rumour mill along with Rosalie's.

Daphne would have been a distinct threat to his career plans. The Towers was a springboard with the next step being his open day on 16th August, and that would have been ruined by her ridiculous ideas about leading the tours, not to mention her unsubtle hints that she knew his credentials weren't exactly as he had claimed when taking up his job here. Granted she was no blackmailer, but what she thought of as jolly comments were threatening to say the least. He'd been working here for over six years now and he had to make a move. Daphne had now gone. Murdered. The more it looked as though the husband had done it, the sooner normal life at the Towers could resume and that couldn't come soon enough for Ewan.

Cara was brooding with a mug of tea over the next step forward. Tea often produced answers, but today it wasn't obliging. She tried again. To sum up: with Mike's rumoured love life unproven, Daphne and her love of history had to be the more probable path to the solution of her murder. Daphne had been faced with an enemy in the orangery. What had she discovered that might have brought that about?

Before this murder, Cara had never questioned the united front of the Towers' staff, and it was proving harder and harder to do so now. Nevertheless, it was now a given that someone on the staff or someone who had access to the Towers after public hours had killed Daphne.

Take Simon Harris again. Could it really have been his life's ambition to be the head of a dancing troupe, fun though that might be? He'd succeeded, even though Simon wasn't a fun person as far as Cara could tell. And, she reasoned, if life had let him down in one respect – perhaps his job, marriage or sex life if any – he might partly be clinging to the dancing troupe as his contribution to the world, in which case he might stop at nothing. OK, psychiatrist, how likely is that, she asked herself. Not very, but just possible, she replied. But add into the mix his history of the Towers being under threat from Daphne's project, and the picture looked much stronger.

Conclusion? History ruled somewhere in Daphne's life, whether her target was the Towers or La Galleria or the smugglers' tunnel or all of them. Cara sighed. Perhaps she should join the race to write her own history of Tanton Towers. It certainly deserved a history, but it wasn't her own forte unless everything she knew about the Towers could be miraculously transferred on to paper or screen to make one readable glorious whole.

She remembered her gasp of enthusiasm when she first arrived and had learned that there had been a house here for centuries before Sir Jeffry had swaggered up the hill and decided to fulfil his dream of towers and turrets. Then Robert had told her that he was sure there'd once been a hill fort here. 'It's not certain,' he had said excitedly, 'but the nineteenth-century dig strongly suggests it.'

Nineteenth-century digs didn't strike Cara as something that Daphne would have been interested in. Sir Jeffry was a different matter as he had commanded the smugglers' tunnel to be built. What was he like as a person? She didn't know much more than Daphne's story about his imminent wedding to number-two bride. Cara sympathized with chosen wife number two, but there didn't seem much scope for that resulting in a twenty-first century murder.

Next had come Sir Jeffry's son Thomas, the elder of twins. Thomas was the good but dull twin who studied art and bought the basis of the Lavinia Fontana collection, and the other twin was the incorrigible Horace, the curse of the village and given to prancing around in the nude and jumping out at people unawares. His ghost was said to have haunted Thomas in fury because he felt hard done by, being born the younger son.

There were other Farran stories, such as that of Sir Jeffry's great-great-grandson Reginald. By that time the Pryde had entered the family name thanks to Sir Jeffry's grandson marrying for financial reasons into a family insistent on his perpetuating the name. Reginald served with the Royal West Kents in Zululand at the time of the Zulu wars and was present at Rorke's Drift in 1879. He was said to have returned to England and, after his death five years later, haunted the state bedroom in case his beloved wife had replaced him – no doubt clashing with the ghost of Great-Grandfather Horace every so often, Cara invented as an add-on.

Those were the only ghosts in the Towers that Cara knew about, although no doubt there were more. None of them could have anything to do with Daphne's death even indirectly if she was planning to include them in this book she was apparently writing. Of the smuggling story Cara knew no more details other than the basics, but it would be a more fruitful line to follow up. It was the smuggling era that had appealed most to Daphne, and therefore might have been the chief feature of any such book. Getting to grips with the smuggling angle, however, meant talking to Ewan again and he might be cagey on the subject given his proprietorial attitude to the tunnel. The answer to that: she'd try

Alison first. Surely there must be something more about Daphne
and that tunnel that might give her a push forward.

No such luck. 'I can't help,' Alison said regretfully, when Cara
had tracked her down to the Snug. 'I thought she just liked the
story of their storing the casks in that old tumbledown building
on the hillside, and then bringing dear old Sir Jeffry's own special
casks to the cellars.'

Nil desperandum. 'What happened to it after that?' Cara
enquired hopefully.

'Pass.'

Mental groan. It was going to have to be Ewan, Cara realized,
dismissing her doubts. She would have to cope with them. She
tried to analyse her hesitation, and it came down – oddly – to
the fact that he smiled too much. Didn't Shakespeare have a
character who could smile and smile and be a villain? Don't be
daft, Cara, she told herself uneasily.

Ewan greeted her as warily as she did him. This time she
found him in his office, which was oddly tucked away by the
side of the smaller staircase linking the first and second floors,
probably to be discreetly away from the grand bedrooms and
bathrooms of the public rooms. Wary or not, though, he was
doing a great job at being his usual bright and breezy self.

'It's about Daphne's book, Ewan,' she began. Was it her imagination or did that bright smile seem even more forced than usual?
'Did you ever see it? Neither Alison nor I did.'

'Never,' Ewan promptly replied. 'She bombarded me with
questions like cannon balls though. She sucked every last word
about that tunnel out of me, but what happened next, if anything,
I've no idea. I reckon she was a would-be writer who was never
going to write.'

For Cara, this was more evidence that it was the history that
appealed to Daphne and the gathering of stories. 'Why did the
smugglers appeal to her so much?'

'No idea.' Long pause. 'She said she would be taking the
parties around on open day,' he said at last.

Something odd here. 'Didn't she need your permission to do
that?' Cara said. At last he was co-operating, but she'd still take
it carefully.

'Apparently not.' Ewan snorted. 'She just swept in and

announced it. She didn't know her history, only the fancy stuff with no facts. All she wanted was to tell the stories about Sir Jeffry being fond of his booze and how the smugglers either stored the stuff down in the woods or lugged it along the tunnel to the cellars.'

Cara fastened on to this. 'Why would Sir Jeffry have a tunnel secret from the household but then display the goods in a cellar where in theory anyone could have seen them?'

He shrugged. 'Sir Jeffry's wife and kiddies wouldn't go down there. Only the butler and footmen maybe.'

Was Ewan being a little too dismissive? Cara wrestled with the now-familiar tug of loyalties between her friends and the knowledge that it was probable that one of them knew far more about Daphne's death than he or she pretended. Plough on, she ordered herself. He's getting uneasy.

'The Revenue could easily check there,' she pointed out. 'Do you think Daphne was following this line up?'

Another shrug from Ewan. A dead end. 'What do you want to know all this for, anyway? It's clear enough why she was bumped off. Good old Mike was having it off with Rosalie and she found out.'

Good. He was getting annoyed. 'I've heard that,' she said earnestly. 'But there are two conflicting stories going around as to who his lover is, which is important, and the DCI will surely be hauling them in for questioning because they might be parties to the murder.'

She sensed a sudden stillness in him. And then he spoke: 'I can tell you who it isn't. It's not Keeley. We don't broadcast it, but we're a couple.' He glared at her. 'Satisfied? You can tell your chum the DCI that.'

And that, as Christopher Robin said, was that, Cara thought as she left. It wasn't proof positive, of course, as Keeley could theoretically have a whole bunch of lovers. But it was another titbit of information that she'd have great satisfaction in sharing with Andrew Mitchem.

In this she was thwarted. There was no sign of him at the Towers and a phone call to his office resulted in DCI Mitchem's polite response that he would take note of her call. Very well, Cara thought rebelliously, so she was free to follow her own path to solving this awful crime. Her first step would be to talk to Alison again, she decided. Surely between them they could take her theory further if only to dismiss it. There was no proof that it had anything to do with Daphne's death, but how could she tell? She still had a hunch she was on to something, and so she'd run it through her mind again before tackling Alison.

First step: Sir Jeffry, who in 1784 had decided to build himself a mansion and castle combined, so planned a home that would obey no rules of conformity but make use of the best architects of the day to fulfil his dream. He liked the pleasures of life and, in those days of high taxes, the pleasures of life were not only expensive but annoying if they weren't immediately at hand. He had therefore set out at some point to ensure not only that he had plenty of the good side of life – including brandy and gin – at hand without flaunting it before the Revenue. He had built his tunnel to enjoy these amenities.

Did he hold gin, brandy and port parties in the cellars to keep them hidden? What was the etiquette? Did the ladies retire from the dining table to leave the gentlemen to pop off into the cellar for their foul liquor? Or did they wait till the butler struggled in with it? In Victoria's time Cara knew that chamber pots were kept for the gentlemen in the dining room discreetly to save them the bother of rushing to urinals, so presumably the ladies had left at that point while the gentlemen drank their booze, but did that apply to Sir Jeffry's time too?

Was the story of the smugglers' tunnel the only kind of history that interested Daphne? Surely not. Daphne had struck Cara as a person who would demand every detail of whatever interested her at the moment. She would want to know therefore what happened to the stuff once delivered to the cellars. Did the butlers (did they have butlers in those days?) rush out to fill glasses? They could hardly drag the casks inside. Perhaps they kept some in the kitchens. No, Sir Jeffry wouldn't risk that.

With a sigh of relief, she felt she'd arrived at the end of her own tunnel towards the truth. Well, if not the end, at least a stopping place. At last she managed to track Alison down. This time it was in the Library.

'Sir Jeffry must have had his own methods of concealing

the casks once they reached the cellars,' Cara pointed out eagerly. Alison had been contemplating a sad-looking vase of roses that were due for retirement. Typical Alison, Cara thought fondly. She always wanted to give flowers their full moments of glory.

'Sir Jeffry must have had his own methods of keeping it away from prying eyes,' she continued once she had brought Alison up to speed on her thinking. 'The Revenue gents might demand to look around if they became suspicious. So surely he wouldn't have left his supplies in the cellar? Those casks would be a real giveaway.'

'A cask would look somewhat odd in the drawing room, don't you think? Or even in the dining room.'

Cara giggled. 'Agreed, but he can't have popped out of the dining room or down from his study to the cellar every time he fancied a swig.'

'There are jugs and things,' Alison countered vaguely. 'Anyway, he'd send the butler to the cellars to collect what he wanted.'

'How would he know the butler wasn't being paid off by the Revenue? Extreme perhaps, but quite possible.'

'Then he'd . . .' Alison stopped and Cara could see she had her full attention at last. 'He'd have taken some to a more convenient place than the cellar. Maybe bottled. Robert told me that the bottles were probably ceramic in the eighteenth century as glass was taxed heavily.'

'That sounds unlikely for good old Jeffry because they'd be clumsy to present at elegant soirées. Doesn't wash, Alison.'

'Then you do some washing,' Alison replied amiably.

'OK,' Cara replied with dignity. 'Wash I will. Consider that I am Sir Jeffry forced to obtain his brandy or other delights from the continent, owing to the hideous taxes which our wicked government had imposed on such necessities.'

'Objection!' Alison held up her hand in protest. 'Sir Jeffry had no fear of hideous taxes. He was rich enough to build this place in 1784.'

'Sir Jeffry,' Cara whipped back, 'would nevertheless refuse to pay good guineas over to a government that had wrenched the money from him for their own unstated purposes. Objection overruled.'

'I will regain my seat,' Alison said with dignity, 'and hear your case to the full.'

'Consider that Sir Jeffry has dined well with his family or friends and wishes to indulge in a glass of brandy. The family might of course be withdrawing to the withdrawing room, but—'

'Objection!' Alison's hand shot up again. 'Ladies stayed right where they were in the eighteenth century.'

'Even if they did,' Cara said grandly, 'they were unlikely to enjoy the sight of their beloved Sir Jeffry lugging a cask in, with or without his butler's assistance.'

'Accepted,' Alison said grudgingly. 'So what does this old codger ancestor of Max's do?'

'He has a place to hide it in the dining or drawing rooms, where a manservant or Sir Jeffry himself could discreetly reach it.' Cara had played what seemed to her a trump card that had conveniently tumbled into her hand.

It fell flat. 'So what?' Alison asked.

'There must be lots of places.' Weak reply and Cara knew it. She thought desperately of all she knew about country houses and the Towers in particular. Right. Attack, she ordered herself.

'We know the Towers was built by a man who loved eccentricities. Who loved Gothic mysteries,' she said, thinking as she went. Then inspiration struck her. Attack Alison on her own home ground. 'Think of Jane Austen.'

That did it. Alison was hooked. '*Northanger Abbey.* A house full of secrets. What secrets did Sir Jeffry build in to this place right from the beginning?'

'Got it!' Cara was triumphant as she scrambled to think of other country houses she had read about. 'A hidey-hole.'

No instant applause for this either. 'A what?' Alison said blankly. 'Oh, come off it, Cara. This house wasn't built until 1784 and the era of priest holes and whatnots died out with the Roundheads over a century earlier.'

Cara wasn't going to give up that easily. 'But Sir Jeffry liked history. Suppose he just wanted his own hidey-hole to hide smuggled goods just for the fun of it.'

Silence. Then: 'Proof?' Alison asked meekly.

'In the pudding,' Cara shot back at her.

'Where's the pudding?'

'Not yet cooked,' she admitted.

'Then let's look. Just one thing . . .' Alison paused. 'Why are we spending all this time on Sir Jeffry, Cara, when we've Daphne's murder on our hands?' she asked quietly.

Hit for six. Cara thought quickly. 'Her murderer might have hidden there,' she tried. A weak response but she didn't need Alison's silence to tell her that. She scrabbled back in her mind, trying to track her thought processes.

She was rewarded. 'Daphne seems to have been obsessed with the Towers' history and therefore with the smugglers' goods as well as the tunnel. Suppose she was on to the same idea – a hidey-hole?' she cried in triumph.

'Why would someone want to kill her for it?' Alison asked reasonably.

'I don't know,' Cara admitted. 'But I'm going to find out. Just as soon as DCI Mitchem lifts that cordon.'

For once, Andrew Mitchem seemed to be on their side. When Cara arrived on Tuesday morning the cordon was still firmly in place, with its unspoken message of 'this is our territory'. Half an hour later, after she had sorted the day out with Sammy, she was amazed to notice that it had vanished. Once again she could look across the grass to the Towers without that constant reminder of Daphne's death. With the search for her killer becoming more and more urgent, it was never out of her mind for long. Nor, it seemed, Alison's as she came across to the Happy Huffkin to give her the news.

'We're opening again very soon now,' Alison told her gleefully, 'now the cordon's down. Want to play hidey-holes this afternoon? There are only one or two case specialists around and no police.'

'You bet,' Cara said fervently.

Oh, the freedom of being able to wander into the Towers without that cordon, Cara rejoiced as she went to meet Alison in the early afternoon. The dining and drawing rooms had a slight unloved feel to them but there were few other signs of the police occupancy. The dining room was a large and pleasant room. It wavered between being an attractive but very formal room, from which family portraits gazed down with pleasure or disgust at their descendants, and having a warmth about it with its dark panelling, discreet red-flowered-on-white wallpaper and a magnificent Angelica Kauffman ceiling. Even the Reynolds portrait of Sir Jeffry himself seemed to smile with approval of that. Or was he smiling about something else – such as his smuggled brandy, Cara wondered as she and Alison entered.

This was a room that shouted history at you and Cara's excitement grew, at least for a moment. Then silence fell as she and Alison looked at the room from the point of view of their mission. Here lay the answer to Sir Jeffry's brandy habits. Cara was sure of that. But where?

'The problem with hidey-holes,' she remarked at last, 'is that they're hidden.'

Alison began to laugh, then stopped. 'I shouldn't do that,' she said. 'Daphne was here so recently, but we have to go on. Where do we start?'

'It has to be handy,' Cara replied, 'because if Sir Jeffry was in urgent need of brandy, he wouldn't want to clamber up on ladders to look behind portraits and so on. Nowhere high up.'

'Agreed. What about the serving area? That would make sense, because if a hidey-hole had a reasonable size cask in it or several ceramic bottles, the butler or whoever had easy access to it. And that's the end nearest to the cellars underneath.'

'But what if this butler were in the Revenue's pay?' Cara reminded her.

'True. What about behind those cupboards? They're original?'

'Sir Jeffry couldn't shift those to grab his ceramic bottle, much less a glass one.'

'Perhaps they were installed after his time.'

'Let's leave them till last then.' Cara pondered. 'Is the posh panelling original?' When Alison nodded, Cara asked, 'Is there any of it that would move if we struck the right one? Let's look.'

Feeling somewhat foolish, she ran her hands up and down the edges of the carved panels, taking the anti-clockwise route round the room, with Alison going clockwise. Her hopes of striking lucky did not materialize though, and they gravely shook hands as they met at the end of their journeys.

'Nothing my way,' Cara said ruefully.

'Nor mine,' Alison replied. 'What does that mean?'

'That we haven't searched thoroughly enough. What about the window seats?' In the bay window recesses the seating stretched straight across the far window and along the adjoining windows as far as the dining room itself. The padded cushions had velvety covers, and beneath them were wooden panels matching those in the rest of the room.

'These aren't nearly the size of the wall panels, so how could they open?' Alison asked doubtfully.

'Same way, I suppose, and they're large enough to take large bottles or even small casks. If we start pressing bits of it as we'd just been doing round the walls, we might feel something give.'

Alison sighed. 'I don't want to be discouraging, but it's going to be a very clever little hidey-hole to have eluded discovery all these years.'

'You never know. It might have been used as a Victorian cupboard for pornographic literature.'

'Very funny,' Alison retorted. 'It's more likely just to have hidden the urinals for Victorian gentlemen who got caught short once they'd pushed us women out of the way.'

Cara's turn to snort with laughter. 'I'm relying on Sir Jeffry to reveal his secrets. Here goes. You start with this window and I'll take the next one.'

'Max is never going to believe this,' Alison muttered, as she obediently went down on her knees.

Cara promptly went over to the next window to follow suit. Deep in their so-far unrewarded work, neither heard the new arrival.

'What *are* you doing?' An astonished Max was striding towards them.

'Trying to find a hidey-hole,' Cara yelled at him.

'Really?' Max squatted down next to her at the end of the panelling running along under the velvet seating on one side of the bay, and began to inspect her work. 'You need more light on the situation,' he announced.

He put a hand up to the sill to steady himself as he tried to get to his feet, the hand slipped, he leaned his weight against the wall to steady himself again – and there came a large groan. Not human. Wood. *Something was happening.* Cara held her breath. Then as she moved nearer to track it down, Max completely lost balance, knocking her to the ground with him. Alison rushed to their aid, but even as they rolled over and scrambled to their feet Cara realized that Alison was distracted.

That was what Alison had been staring at. Now Cara could see a black hole in the middle of the panel where the carving of a portly Greek god had disappeared. A hole through which Cara discovered she could put her hand. She pressed the lever that poked out to greet it. All three feet of the panel obligingly slid back to reveal a large cavernous space.

Save for an old china bottle lying on its side, it was empty.

EIGHT

Someone had to break the silence. Max had extracted himself from Cara's involuntary embrace and, painfully, they had clambered to their feet. It was Alison who spoke first after clearing her throat meaningfully.

'You've made your point, Cara,' she said. 'But what has this to do with Daphne? Did she find it? Remove anything from it?'

'I don't know,' Cara was forced to reply meekly. 'If so, she would have been excited over its discovery, but why would anyone care enough about that to murder her? And she certainly wouldn't have taken anything from it without spreading the news, at the very least to Robert. She'd have insisted on trying to find out its history.'

'Perhaps,' Max murmured straight-faced, after his obviously painful tumble into the Towers' history, 'her murderer hid away here to beat the security checks.'

'Very funny,' Cara retorted. 'Daphne was connected to the smugglers' tunnel, and *that* links to this hidey-hole.'

Max wasn't convinced. 'I don't see smugglers staggering into this room with casks of brandy. A little too noticeable.'

'Darling,' Alison said patiently, 'Cara and I have already talked this through. We think it was a hidey-hole for Sir Jeffry to have drink available in here while the casks remained in the cellar.'

Max was frowning. 'Why bother to build something as elaborate as this hole instead of stuffing the cask or jug or whatever behind a table? Why build it at all?'

Cara took this one on. 'Perhaps Sir Jeffry yearned for a priest hole and he wouldn't want to keep rushing to the cellars. Nor would the butler. He would want a quantity at hand and as an eighteenth-century gentleman who was building a "small residence" for himself and family, Sir Jeffry would have had carte blanche to stick in any little oddities that took his fancy.'

Still silence from Max and Alison. 'It's possible,' Max agreed at last. 'Where does that leave us?'

'With a fascinating piece of history for your tours,' Cara replied. She took a deep breath. 'I still believe it could be a stepping stone to finding out what happened to Daphne.'

'*If,*' Alison said, 'Daphne found it at all. As you say, if she had done so, she would have come rushing to tell us. We've lived here for umpteen years in blissful ignorance.'

'She might have been scared,' Cara said, thrown into doubt at the basic assumption she had made. 'Perhaps she found something in there and removed it?'

'There are a lot of "perhaps",' Max observed. 'No proof.'

'No proof *yet,*' Cara added hopefully.

Sammy was definitely not pleased. Words were seldom his method of conveying dissatisfaction, however, and when she returned from the dining room he chose a patient head-down approach as he trudged past her with a trayful of coffee and his special cookies for the one occupied table. A quartet of two women and two men were seated there, probably specialists called in by the police. Her absence had been in the interests of the Towers, Cara assured Sammy hastily, then could have kicked herself. It sounded like an excuse but it had been true.

Once in the kitchen, hands washed and apron donned, she did her best to play her part. Not that there was much of a part to play now, with more customers unlikely to arrive. A trayful of huffkins stared at her hopefully but probably in vain.

'News.' Sammy finally spoke. 'Mr Hanson.'

'What news?' Cara was instantly alarmed. The extra-long wait before he spoke again was her punishment for her late arrival.

'This morning. Hauled in for questioning.'

'*What?*' Coming out of the blue, this was appalling. Was it just for a chat, she wondered, or was he arrested? It was ominous either way. Sammy must be exaggerating because Alison and Max had said nothing, so maybe this was simply an extension of Sammy's earlier dictum that 'the husband had done it'. 'It can't be serious,' she added, 'because he has an alibi. He left the Towers long before Daphne was killed.'

'Reckon they think he sneaked back.'

Relief. That old chestnut. 'Surely they can't think he whizzed back through the smugglers' tunnel. They'd have more than that to go on if they've arrested him. Anyway, planning a trip through that tunnel is hardly in line with a spur-of-the-moment murder like Daphne's,' she reasoned.

'Maybe,' Sammy commented darkly, putting the tray down heavily with a clatter of crockery to signify his disagreement. 'Heard the other news, have you?'

Cara sighed. She really was in trouble with Sammy. 'Probably not. What news?'

'Towers opening up tomorrow. Manage that, can we?'

Tomorrow! This was good news indeed. Wednesday would herald normality. 'Yes,' she said fervently. 'Does Virginia know?' This was vital if they were to arrange the cakes and sandwiches so quickly. Somehow Virginia always managed it, so fingers crossed it would work for tomorrow.

Sammy gave a cursory nod. Of course he would have told her. 'Two coaches,' he growled. 'Two o'clock and half past.'

'Only half an hour gap? Are you sure?' she asked. Why book that in? They'd be overwhelmed. It was busy enough at the Happy Huffkin with an hour's gap between parties, but only half an hour between them would result in chaos.

Sammy grinned. 'Best be here when they come then, eh?'

His revenge was complete.

Hardly surprisingly, there was no sign of Mike when, two hours later, Cara had fulfilled her tasks to Sammy's satisfaction and returned to the Towers to find out whether he had returned. The police questioning was obviously going to take longer than she'd hoped. The Towers seemed deserted until she met Alison descending from the second floor and was swept off to the Den, the small room just inside the family wing and as welcoming as their living room. This room too was a mixture of styles. The Den mingled Victorian comfort with modern experimentation, including a coffee machine. The message the room exuded was: 'Any decisions to be made? Step right inside.'

'Any news of Mike?' Cara asked anxiously. 'Do you think this inquisition is still connected to rumours about his love life?'

Alison ruminated. 'Could be, but it's a big jump to a murder charge.'

'Whether it's Rosalie or Keeley involved – or both.' Cara

caught Alison's eye. Laughter is a fine tonic, as the saying goes, and it certainly helped at the moment.

'Busy man then,' Alison commented, straight-faced. She sobered up. 'If you're right about history and Daphne's book somehow being the motive of her death, that wouldn't bring Mike into the picture.'

'Agreed. And the history line fits in with Daphne's character,' Cara maintained. 'She did so like poking her nose into the past. It could have caught up with her.'

'You'll have the DCI to contend with if you poke too far.'

Cara bristled. 'He can't stop me talking to you or the Towers' team.'

'Depends what it's about,' Alison warned her. Then she saw Cara's expression and groaned. 'Don't tell me. Lavinia Fontana!'

Cara laughed. 'Don't despair. Robert said Daphne was interested in the Archives too so perhaps she found something there to grip her imagination. But she did favour stories from the Towers' history, like the famous Sir Jeffry, of course.'

'And presumably Max's other ancestors too, including Horace's larks. There was his twin Thomas who married the beautiful Fiorella in Rome during his Grand Tour. I blame her for being a descendant of the great Lavinia, because that's how we ended up with Thomas's collection of works by the great lady. How on earth did she cope with those eleven children? An early working mother, even though she did have an obliging husband to help out.'

'How did Thomas stagger home from Bologna with stage-coaches full of portraits?' Cara asked. 'They must have had a lot of minions to help out. Why did Max become so interested in it? Just because of his ancestors?'

'We went to Italy on our honeymoon,' Alison recalled gloomily. 'A wonderful honeymoon except for Lavinia. We visited Bologna and suddenly there were three of us in this marriage. Previously he'd ignored the family collection here, and then, lo and behold, Lavinia was tops. Not only did he fall in love with all the paintings already here, but added several more. Nearly all of them are acknowledged Lavinia Fontanas with one or two "school of" or "attributed to". And there are the drawings as well. I've become an expert in recognizing enigmatic faces. Oh, and you might have noticed there are a couple by Lavinia's father, Prospero, and one by her husband Giovanni Paolo Zappi – just so that they aren't left out of the fun.'

'Was Daphne interested in how the paintings were executed or what they were about?' Cara asked.

Alison thought about this. 'I don't think she knew anything about fine art,' was her eventual conclusion. 'So the answer's no.'

'Except that Daphne was interested in Lavinia. Have there been any thefts or fakes that would fit in with the smuggling angle?'

'None recorded in the Archives. Some paintings have been added since Thomas's time, as well as Max's three or four. There's nothing to suggest any doubts about their authenticity save for the one or two "school of" or "attributed to". I don't see how there could be any fakes, because this is the same collection that Max inherited plus a few more of his own and according to the Archives it hasn't otherwise grown significantly for a hundred years or so. I think Max's father added a few drawings, but unless a genuine painting was replaced by a fake I don't see any fodder for Daphne there. Fakes would have been a step too far for smugglers. In any case,' she added, 'until La Galleria was established three years ago, some of Max's treasures in the collection were down on the first floor next to his office.'

This was a humdinger, Cara thought. *Nil desperandum.* Press on. There had to be more to this. 'Did Daphne question you about all the other treasures in the Towers – the furniture, the porcelain, the other paintings and so on? And the Library – did the rare books interest her?'

'Interesting point,' Alison conceded. 'I remember her clambering up to look at a book or two in the Library, but I don't recall any questions about any of the paintings in the Towers as a whole. She never asked about the Reynolds, for example. Or the probable Van Gogh. What does that imply?'

'Nothing yet,' Cara conceded, 'but it might if Daphne's only interest was in Lavinia. But,' it occurred to her, 'that might be because she was trying to please Max.'

'No,' Alison immediately replied. 'Daphne didn't think that

way in my experience. It's easy to butter up Max by admiring the portrait of Good Queen Bess, but I doubt if Daphne even noticed he is besotted with it. The only time I remember her looking at it was to admire the necklace round her neck.'

'She didn't get excited about the jewel room?'

That was where, under heavy security, the family jewels of the Farran Prydes were displayed. Some of them were indeed spectacular, Cara thought, including a magnificent ruby in a diadem worn by Max's ancestors at the coronations of Queen Victoria and Edward VII.

'No. DCI Mitchem asked me that, but Daphne seemed interested only in Lavinia,' Alison replied.

'That's interesting.' So, Cara deduced, Andrew Mitchem was following the Lavinia Fontana line too. Not unreasonably, she conceded.

'Shall we have another look, Sherlock?' Alison suggested. 'Something might come to mind. I took Daphne on a quick tour of La Galleria a month or two ago.'

Cara pricked up her ears. 'Yes please. Now?' Even if the delay did upset Sammy, it was worth it. She'd sort that out tomorrow. Despite her previous visits to La Galleria, each picture might take on a new meaning and perhaps give her a clue as to what Daphne's interest was. Probably it was merely a story about an ancestor's purchase of a particular painting, but perhaps it was more. If nothing else it might jog Alison's memory as to what had inspired Daphne into her sudden enthusiasm for Lavinia. 'Did she ask you for a tour?' Cara added.

'Yes to both questions. And the police asked me about that too. She bearded me in the Den one day, asking if she could stay on after the dancing ended. She did that on several occasions after that, presumably for her book. Simon Harris stayed on sometimes too. I gather they were punctilious over telling Dan when they were doing so.'

'What did Robert think about Daphne's book?' Cara asked as they left the Den. 'As archivist it can't have been much fun for him with rivals about to steal his thunder.'

Alison laughed. 'Robert was well placed. He, like Dan, has carte blanche to wander around any time he likes. Plus of course he's the one in charge of documentary evidence and even though

Daphne had what I'd call a more populist approach to history, she would have needed his help.'

'He's not a Lavinia enthusiast though,' Cara commented, 'or perhaps only in so far as she affects the Towers.'

'Correct. He glories in the history of how the collection was put together, so his favourite picture is the same as Max's.'

At the very least, Cara thought, this tour might give her a clue as to what Daphne's main interest might have been. The most likely was that her nose for interesting stories had detected possibilities in La Galleria. Today with the all but empty building and the afternoon sunshine penetrating its windows to light their way it seemed even grander, particularly marching up the grand staircase with Alison. She imagined herself swishing the full petticoats of the eighteenth century. Where would she be heading? On the first floor she could swish by the stately bedrooms and even bustle into a rare original bathroom. Then she could graciously pop up the still rather grand staircase to the second floor as lady of the manor inspecting her territory. There would be no Lavinia to greet her then, so the second floor would have been very different to today's La Galleria, Archives Room and Max's office.

Meanwhile in today's jeans and tee-shirt and with no petticoats to flounce, Cara could fully appreciate that La Galleria was a splendid sight, with its long gallery lined with impressive paintings, many of them portraits of dignitaries of long ago staring down benevolently. Sir Thomas had done his best with the collection he had lugged back from what was now Italy, and adorned the gold painted ceiling with original Fontana drawings or oils at intervals. It was almost as though Michelangelo had popped down to approve its grandeur.

'Let's look at Max's pride and joy first,' Alison said, leading the way.

'You don't like his pride and joy?'

'I'm not convinced by it. Too many ifs. Here she is.'

Cara gazed at the painting which of course was the Queen Elizabeth I portrait, with Her Majesty staring challengingly out at her. That was a lady who wouldn't like being crossed. Cara had once had a schoolteacher like that – terrifying. She had tried standing up to her once and won. Mistake. Revenge was duly

taken. This lady before her now looked not only in command
but as though she had won the lottery.

'It's genuine though?' Cara asked.

'Oh yes,' Alison replied. 'Lavinia painted it all right, but there
still remains the question of how did Good Queen Bess of England
meet Lavinia Fontana in order to sit for her portrait? Theories
are all very well, but I'd be happier with proof. Very few portraits
of Elizabeth I were painted from life and this isn't one of them.
She's really gloating in this portrait, isn't she? Max maintains it
doesn't matter that it's not directly from life, provided the portrait
itself has life. This one, he says, has. I disagree.'

'There's no doubt that it's her and not some other sixteenth-
century queen?'

'No doubt at all,' Alison answered immediately. 'There's a well-
known portrait of her at Tilbury welcoming the returning heroes
and another of her displaying regal glory as the victorious monarch.
Like this one,' she added, 'it's laden with jewels. Look at that
enormous ruby she's wearing. It's possibly the missing Regale of
France, the huge ruby given by their king in homage to the murdered
Archbishop Thomas à Becket, which so mysteriously disappeared
when Henry the Eighth's men got their claws on it. It was last
seen around the neck of his daughter Queen Mary so it's entirely
possible that Elizabeth then snatched it for herself.'

That was a story that would have interested Daphne, Cara
thought. Even so, would it have any relevance to her death? The
gossip about Mike's purported affair still seemed to be masking
the urgency to follow up other motives for her death that might
lead to her killer. 'Could this be a fake?' she asked, still staring
at Her Majesty Elizabeth I. The queen stared haughtily back at
her as if challenging her to get on with the job.

'I doubt it,' Alison replied, 'for the good reason that it's never
been listed as a recognized Fontana, although that's not surprising
as it's been here since Sir Thomas snapped it up and he bought
it from Lavinia's descendants. Max's theory is that its existence
stems back to a Flemish artist who came to Bologna, possibly
one who worked with her father and ran some kind of training
academy for artists. Flemish artists were all the rage then in
England as well as on the continent and Bologna was a centre
for art too. Max believes that she saw either a drawing or painting

of Elizabeth which had been drawn from life by one of the Flemings. The subject must have appealed to her. Strong women. Women's rights and all that. Our Lavinia was the first widely recognized female artist and, while obeying all the rules of current society herself, she had a subtle programme for indicating that our time was coming.'

'Was it the women's rights angle that interested Daphne?' Cara asked.

'I've no idea. I don't recall her being particularly interested in this one – or any of the paintings come to that. She was busy looking everywhere so I can't be sure. She was intent on peering out of windows and even at the floor.'

'Maybe she was hunting for trapdoors in the floorboards,' Cara said hopefully, 'as another entry point.'

'Or a hidey-hole or two?' Alison said ironically. 'Perhaps thieves crept into them while they were waiting till sundown to creep out and do their dirty work.'

Cara laughed. 'That's a blow beneath the belt.'

'Good. Victory to me. Now, look at this self-portrait by Lavinia. She painted quite a few but this one is different from the others.'

It was a painting that Cara liked too, the one with a woman gazing out at them, a secretive lady with a composed expression and slight smile on her lips. A calm woman, a woman of strength.

'I agree. She does look as though she's bursting to tell the world that she is as accomplished as any man.'

'Look at her use of light and dark to emphasize her message,' Alison said.

Cara couldn't judge that, but that was a woman she'd like to have known. And here was another favourite of hers, she thought, as they reached the portrait of the young man glaring out at them from his oil-painted image. She liked this ruffian. His fierce eyes challenged the observer, his neatly trimmed beard almost quivering with anger at the world he lived in.

'Who do you think he could be?' she asked. 'Francis Drake after bashing the Spanish Armada to bits?'

Alison laughed. 'No idea, but he's a tearaway, I agree.' A pause. 'Cara, where are we going with this?'

Honesty made Cara reply. 'I don't see a clear way forward yet.'

'Perhaps there isn't one here.' Alison looked round the gallery. 'Maybe we're barking up the wrong tree.'

Was she right? At least Alison used the word 'we' not 'you', so Cara comforted herself that she may still be on the right track. She'd continue along it. No more false avenues of love affairs for her. She had been expecting too much from one piece of the jigsaw. Alison's beloved Jane Austen heroine, Emma, rushed headlong into trouble. Just like Daphne. And that, Cara decided, was a trap she would avoid. If, of course, she saw it coming.

NINE

It was well after closing time and she still had to sort out tomorrow's needs with Sammy, Cara realized wearily. Once again, here she was, putting her new mission before work, and that wasn't fair on him. Tomorrow would be a different matter. She summoned up courage and put a smile on her face.

However, as she rounded the corner of the Towers her heart sank. There was still a customer sitting outside the Happy Huffkin. Then to her relief she realized it was Mike. He was back safely. Thank goodness for that, but why on earth had Andrew Mitchem hauled him in for questioning? Guilt at her absence from the café made her fulsome in her greetings as she sat down to join Mike. No need to tell Sammy she was back as he would have noted her arrival. He had a sixth sense of her comings and goings.

'I'm taking advantage of a few hours' rest,' Mike said ruefully. 'It might be in the press that I'm being questioned and I don't fancy being prime attraction for visitors, so I might not reappear tomorrow if it's OK with Alison and Max.'

'I don't blame you.' Cara saw his point. 'Are the police still heckling you?'

'They haven't said so. Where were you? I thought maybe you'd been carted off too.'

'No, but Alison and I have been in La Galleria.'

That took Mike by surprise. 'Why's that? Was it about that book Daphne was apparently writing? I thought she was concentrating on smugglers.'

'She seems to have had wider interests than that,' Cara said diplomatically. 'The Fontana collection is part of the Towers' history so I imagine that's what fascinated her.'

'You think she was killed for her knowledge of that? Daphne was hardly into big-time heists,' Mike said drily. 'Anyway, there's nothing in La Galleria worth the risk of big-time heists or even petty thefts. I should know. I've been valuing stuff like that since my student days and anyway Dan and I keep our eyes open for threats to the Towers' assets. The ones to worry about are tucked all over the rest of the house, not in La Galleria. Look elsewhere, Cara.'

Elsewhere? Was this help or setback, she pondered as he took his leave. As well as false affair rumours, it now seemed La Galleria as a motive had gone to join them. It was clear that Daphne had not been artistically minded. All the staff at the Towers had worked in the arts world before coming here and were well clued up in it, so the idea that Daphne had deduced something that they hadn't was a non-starter.

No missing works of art, no fakes.

'Cakes?'

She must have spoken aloud because Sammy appeared at her the doorway. 'Ordered,' he told her. 'Virginia. Cakes one o'clock sharp.'

'Sorry, Sammy. I was muttering *fakes.*'

Sammy trudged over to the table and took a seat with folded arms, a sure sign that he was brooding. 'What fakes? Up there.' His head jerked in the direction of the Towers' second floor.

He continued brooding and Cara knew better than to interrupt this important process. 'It's who you know,' he said eventually.

'What is?' Cara asked blankly. Accustomed though she was to Sammy's grasshopper mind, this leap she could not follow. She did her best. 'You mean Max knows about fakes?' That didn't make sense.

More consideration. 'Maybe.'

'Who?'

'This Lavinia lady.'

Caution needed. 'I'm not sure I'm with you, Sammy.'

He glared at her. 'All those nobs.'

Light began to dawn. 'The portraits she painted?'

Sammy nodded. 'Knew all the nobs, Lavinia did. Why fake them? No kids' kids to want them? No aunties, no uncles.'

A long speech for Sammy, but he was right. Descendants would have bought them at first, but otherwise Lavinia's reputation would have to be sky high in order for all her work to be worth a small fortune and thus worthy of being faked. Lavinia – Cara sent up a silent apology to Max – might not be quite in that class.

Nevertheless: 'What about her religious paintings?' she asked. 'There are several in La Galleria.'

'Who'd buy them?' Sammy asked.

'Religious institutions.'

'Buy, yes. Ten Commandments. No stealing. Faking's stealing.'

It was David meeting Goliath in this argument, Cara realized, but she was doing a poor job as David. 'Lavinia would have had hundreds of descendants, all of whom would multiply over the years.'

'Wouldn't buy fakes,' Sammy said obstinately. Then he added, 'That Daphne. Lovely lady.'

Cara gazed at him dumbfounded. Memories of Daphne flooded back to her, dancing graceful cotillions, Sir Roger de Coverley and her flying figure as she stripped the willow on the lawns. All that dancing full of joy only for her to meet that awful death. Sammy was right. Daphne deserved her help as much as Alison and Max did.

So far, however, she seemed to have achieved precious little that seemed relevant. The rumoured unfaithfulness of her husband, a Twerp jealous of Daphne's dominance, and her love of history, about which she might or might not have begun to write. Out of that territory, all Cara had to show was a false move with an old hidey-hole that kept Sir Jeffry happily supplied with booze. Big deal.

Sammy was watching her. 'Pecker up,' he advised. 'The DCI chap not doing much either.'

That cheered her up. She remembered what she'd thought after she had first met that gentleman. Tomorrow is another day. And now tomorrow had come. Good.

Today was the day. It was Wednesday at last and she rejoiced. Tanton Towers would reopen its doors at two o'clock and be itself again. Even the thought of coach parties didn't disturb Cara too much. Life would be returning to normality. Meanwhile, in the interests of presenting a unified front to the world, the Happy Huffkin was open for staff earlier than usual. And here came Dan Dickson strolling up. He plonked himself at one of the outside tables and grinned as he saw her coming over to him.

'Alison told me that you and she had a pow-wow in La Galleria and decided I must be Daphne's murderer.' He roared with laughter. 'Joke,' he added.

Cara tried her best to laugh in return but failed. 'Most amusing,' she said sourly.

To do him justice, Dan got the message quickly. 'She told me there had been talk of fakes. Did you mean paintings bought in good faith but were fakes,' he asked seriously, 'or those that were switched at a later date? Or do you mean copies rather than fakes?'

He didn't wait for an answer, but grandly swept on: 'It depends on when such fakes or copies were put there. If they were always there in modern times, it doesn't affect us now except to disappoint Max. If they were switched with originals, if that were recent, then the thieves would have to work out how to get to La Galleria unobserved by modern security. Plus the fact that the frames too would prove a problem, both to fake them and because they'd affect the ease with which the paintings could be stolen. Photos might be easily taken to enable the subjects to be faked, but to remove the originals together with their frames would physically be a real challenge.'

Cara decided to play at being a meek learner (which she supposed she was). 'Could there be old fakes here amongst the originals?' She drew up a chair to sit with him, mentally crossing fingers that Sammy would get the message and not object to yet another dereliction of duty.

'Sure there could,' Dan replied. 'There could even have been a fake, or at least a copy, amongst the booty that dear old Sir Thomas brought back in triumph.'

'Would Lavinia have been famous enough to be worth faking at that time?'

'Could be. Lavinia Fontana had a high reputation during her lifetime in Bologna as well as in Rome and it would only have increased as the years passed. Thomas could well have dropped into Bologna for a quick pint and found plenty of people eager to sell him so-called original Fontanas.' Another guffaw from the complacent Dan.

He had his patronizing voice on now and Cara was fully aware of it. Life, Cara realized, was already changing at the Towers. They used to be a united group of which she was an honorary member, but a momentous event can start tiny cracks appearing and even the Towers might not be immune to this. Here was she, still regarding Dan as a suspect, not the friend she had grown accustomed to. She was also aware that the theory that La Galleria had something to do with Daphne's death was rapidly joining the affair rumour in being relegated to the background, if not the trash bin. Still, she had to carry on.

Oblivious to her reaction, Dan was still holding the floor.

'The Victorians,' he announced grandly, 'were great fakers, only they didn't see it that way. They saw their work as copies in the style of the old masters.'

She couldn't resist the opportunity. 'Or mistresses,' she murmured firmly. 'Plenty of women painters around even in Lavinia's time.'

This was a mistake because it brought forth yet another guffaw and announcement.

'Old mistresses? Not our spotless Lavinia, who did everything by the book,' Dan laughed. 'From virgin, to respectably married, then a nice bunch of children – and inside was her raging desire to conquer the artistic world.'

Keep on target, she told herself. 'Are the prices her work carries high at present?' she asked meekly.

'Not bad.' He looked at her curiously. 'What's brought this about? It's a murder case we've been dumped into, not art theft.'

'I know it's probably irrelevant,' she replied quickly, 'but as Daphne seemed to be interested in collecting all the historical material she could, I am too.'

He shrugged. 'It's true she used to bore me with questions about Sir Thomas and the grand tour, but she wasn't much interested in art itself, despite Mike trying to explain to her what it's all about. Believe me, ghosts and smugglers were her thing, together with juicy stories about the Farran Pryde family history, including the old chestnuts about Sir Alfred losing the knighthood and Horace wandering about in the nude scaring the locals.

'Tact,' he continued after Cara's polite laugh, 'wasn't our Daphne's forte though.'

'Did Daphne consult you about her book?' she asked.

'No. I'm fairly sure it doesn't exist.'

End of that, then. Cara pressed on. 'Could she have been killed because she found out about a planned theft from the collection or anywhere else in the Towers?' Dan was in charge of them so it was a fair question.

Evidently he didn't think so, as his reply to that was also dismissive. 'I'd back our security system against any master thief idiot who tried his luck anywhere in the Towers.'

'And before that kicks into action?' She knew that most of the valuable items were indeed alarmed, and eagle eyes were guarding them during the tours. The smirk on Dan's face annoyed her though, but she couldn't retaliate as company was arriving. Robert Broome and Ewan were strolling up towards them and Dan leapt straight into controlling the situation, ignoring her question.

'Glad to see you both,' he boomed. 'I'm in need of rescue.' Hearty laugh. 'Cara seems to have the idea that there are fakes within the collection, so I hope she's already solved the murder for us.'

Let him think he's winning, she decided. 'Theoretically,' she said, trying to present a sweet smile.

'So *theoretically*, chaps,' Dan said cheerily, 'one of us probably murdered the poor woman.'

Two could play at this game. 'Not my job to decide which,' Cara replied equally cheerily.

Robert must have been thinking on other lines, because he abruptly switched the subject. 'There are valuable original documents in the Archives. Old ones, dating back long before the house was built.'

'Old Sir Jeffry was a bit of a hoarder,' Dan laughed. 'I thought he just sat up in his study to rule the roost.'

Robert flushed at the dismissive tone in Dan's voice and Cara was about to intervene when Robert replied firmly, 'Sir Jeffry was a most interesting scholar in his own way. There are also most fascinating documents concerning the delivery of bricks and stones to the cellars for shoring up the foundations of the house. He was very much concerned with the practical side of the buildings as well as exercising his powers of design with the turrets and towers, and there is no doubt therefore that he was personally involved in every aspect of the building and—'

'Bravo, Robert,' Dan interrupted him in hearty tones. 'Proving the originals are genuine is vital. For paintings,' he continued firmly, 'provenance is often recorded on the rear of the frames and is a vital element in detecting the fake from the original. Anyway, I'd like to make it clear that there *are* no fakes in La Galleria.'

Why were they trying to outdo each other, Cara wondered. Were they anxious to hide something or was she seeing bogies everywhere? Time to step in, she decided, or rather backwards as they were plunging back into fakes again. 'Presumably, Dan, that would apply to all the paintings in the Towers, not just Max's collection, but Daphne doesn't seem to have been interested in them, only in La Galleria. So, Ewan,' she said, turning to him, 'how do you see the chances of fakes or thefts from the collection? Could your tourists be involved? On the tours they could perhaps take photos easily, one flash of a phone—'

'No way,' Ewan interrupted. 'No bags allowed on the tours, no photos to be taken, and each group is covered by three volunteers in all, with one of them checking from the rear. There's only been three incidents this year, none resulting in photos that escaped our notice.'

'That's an oxymoron in its way,' Dan murmured. He turned to Cara. 'So there we are – not guilty. I'm damned if I see where all this is leading though. Have you joined the police force?' Smug glance at Robert and Ewan.

'In all but name,' Cara shot back. 'Haven't we all done that? Don't we all want to find out who murdered Daphne?'

A moment's silence, then: 'Yes,' Robert agreed earnestly.

'You're doing a great job, Cara,' Ewan joined in eagerly. 'And thanks for that hidey-hole you discovered with Alison. Brilliant. I gather you think it was used for Sir Jeffry's illicit brandy. Great. I can work with that. Trace the life of a brandy cask, perhaps.' He sat back, looking rather pleased with himself, Cara noted.

Dan must have decided to join the majority, for he joked, 'What's next, Cara? Are you going to dress up like one of those female pirates and creep along the smugglers' tunnel for Ewan's tours? Or did Daphne come up with that idea too?'

He'd made a mistake, for Ewan immediately leapt in again. 'Remember the open day, Dan? I'm planning a big show for that. I'll be leading the troops along but we're still in the middle of painting and decorating. It's fully passed its safety tests now and the security is fixed.' He looked at his watch – and his arm ostentatiously shot up to view it. 'Let's get going. The hordes will be descending on us shortly.'

Cara watched them in frustration as they departed. That pushed the idea of fakes in La Galleria into the background again. Back to Simon Harris then. Simon, who had carte blanche to roam around the building after the dancing sessions. Simon, who was longing to be top dog in the Tanton Whirlers. Simon, who wanted to write a book about the Towers. As of course was Robert, who was in the building but should have been in the library at the time of the murder if he followed his routine. Robert, who also wanted to write a book.

There were far too many books at stake, Cara thought crossly. It sounded such an innocent wish to write a book, not one that could lead to murder, surely. Not unless one had a very big ego indeed. Andrew Mitchem wouldn't think much of that for a motive.

Her heart sank. It must be bad luck even to think about him. Crossing the lawn towards the Happy Huffkin was his tall and now familiar figure. He wasn't hurrying, merely strolling across like a gentleman of leisure. Why did that annoy her so much? Stupid of her.

'We're not officially open for another ten minutes or so,' she declared as he reached her. 'Luckily,' she added, belatedly conscious of how childish she was being, 'we're open unofficially.'

'I'm officially here,' DCI Mitchem assured her blandly, 'but I can make it unofficial if you prefer – on one condition.'

'Which is?' she asked cautiously.

'That you or your colleague Sammy can rustle me up a huffkin.'

Cara looked at him suspiciously but he seemed to be serious. 'We've only sandwiches and scones at present,' she told him truthfully. 'But we can rustle you up a huffkin if you can wait half an hour or so.'

'You're too kind. A cheese sandwich will do splendidly. Unofficial then.'

Fulfilling his order gave her breathing space to pull her wits together as she hurried inside to sort some kind of sustenance for him. Should she tell him her not-so-bright ideas about fakes and Daphne's love of history or let him take the initiative? She would need some cards left in her hand, she thought, as she arranged some banana bread in addition to the sandwich on the tray, although ten to one he wouldn't even ask her for her views.

The decision was taken out of her hands. Once his lunch was before him, he speedily took the initiative. 'Great,' he said approvingly, looking at the banana bread. 'Now you can tell me as much or as little as you wish about what's going on.'

'OK, but the gates are about to open, so I might get diverted if any of them make a dash for a cup of tea.'

'You'll be sold out, thanks to the media coverage.'

'Won't the tours get in the way of your work?'

He shrugged. 'We won't be stomping around with flat feet and helmets. Can I ask you a few questions?'

'Still unofficially?' she asked guardedly.

'Very much so. I take it that the staff – including yourself – usually all get on well. Has that changed?'

She considered this. 'It's rocky,' she admitted. 'I get the impression we're looking at each other and wondering . . .'

'Whether you're looking at a murderer,' he finished for her. 'Don't worry, I don't suspect you.'

This caught her off guard. 'Thank you,' she said demurely. Be careful, she warned herself.

'You couldn't have whipped over to the conservatory, killed someone and be back again without your Sammy noticing.'

'Thank you for that too.' She meant it. 'But I want to find out who killed Daphne just as soon as possible. For different reasons than yours, of course.'

'Not necessarily. I can't stop you, Cara, but I can give you good advice. *Stop*. And if you ignore that, then take care every single step of the way.'

She gulped. He was serious about this. 'Is that official?' she asked.

'Not yet.'

Silence. Another impasse. 'Are you any further along?' she managed to ask at last.

'Unofficially yes. How are you weathering this?' he asked.

This personal note came out of the blue and she wasn't prepared for it.

'I'm still trying to get used to the idea that Daphne won't be dancing away like crazy on that lawn any more,' she said frankly.

'Are you going to continue exercising your detective skills?'

There was no point in denying it. 'Will you have secret agents watching me?'

'No. I'll be watching you,' he replied simply. 'I gather information wherever I can and put two and two together, just as I imagine you are trying to do. I noticed victims retiring crushed just before I came along here.'

That made her laugh. 'Are you going to lock me up for impersonating a police officer's role?' she asked politely.

'No. You'd make a rotten one.'

'Why?' she asked indignantly.

'You're too transparent.'

That didn't sound too awful, if distinctly worrying. 'So you came here just to order me to mind my Ps and Qs and stick to my own trade.'

'Are you going to ignore me?'

'Not necessarily,' she whipped back at him.

'One good reason for listening to common sense. As you're so transparent, you might be to a murderer. On the other hand,' he said thoughtfully, 'you might find out something useful.'

She glared at him. 'That was the general idea.'

'I'll give you more advice.'

This was getting steamy, Cara thought uneasily. He was staring at her as though she were an arch criminal. Play it cool, she told herself. 'Whether or not I want it, you can give it to me.'

'Listen, watch, think. LWT – got it? *Don't ask* and take care.'

She considered this. 'But theory is one thing, practice another.'

'Then for heaven's sake remember LWT.'

'While you play Big Bad Cop?' She blurted this out and then regretted it.

He sighed. 'Officially, then. It's dangerous, Cara.'

'How do you know?' she asked. The 'Cara' seemed to be a fixture now.

He took his time in replying. 'Policing is like huffkins,' he said at last.

She stiffened. This was a blow below the belt.

'The case,' he continued, 'is the bun, slit so we can butter and devour it.'

Sneaky, very sneaky of him. Well, he asked for it so here came her reply. 'And the hole in its middle?' she asked through gritted teeth. 'Would that be the motive for Daphne's death?'

'Yes, and I can't yet fill it for certain. There are options. We've got firm evidence on timing, prints, even motives, but the hole's still empty. *That's* where the danger lies.'

Just what was bothering her. That empty hole was motive. It was time to talk, she realized. 'I know you can't tell me officially what you think or what might be relevant. But,' she continued sweetly, 'there's nothing to stop me telling you what I think.'

'Nothing,' he agreed. 'So tell me.'

Amazing that this was happening. 'Here goes,' she said. 'It could be that Daphne discovered something in her enthusiasm for the Towers' history and, whether or not it went into a book eventually, it cut across other people's plans. Or it could be something to do with Max's Lavinia Fontana collection. Or it could be the theft of one or more of the other valuable antiques in the Towers. Or . . .' She hesitated. 'It could be to do with her husband's falsely rumoured love life or Daphne's supposed wealth. But that simply can't be true,' she then burst out. 'I suppose you have to consider all these awful possibilities however ridiculous until facts rule them out. What a beastly job you must have at times,' she concluded fiercely.

'Agreed.' He said no more, just sat there looking at her. Then he picked up the remaining piece of banana bread.

'And I feel dreadful,' Cara added fiercely, 'for having put the huffkins into your oven, so to speak, to be baked by you.'

That made him smile. 'I do bake quite efficiently.'

She glanced at him, aware that some kind of Rubicon had been crossed. No, she couldn't handle that now. Instead she glanced at her watch and rose to her feet.

'It's gone two o'clock. The Towers is open again.'

TEN

Where did the great DCI's comments leave her? Cara was well aware that curiosity can kill more than cats and that could have been Daphne's undoing. And if she wasn't careful, Cara realized, it could be hers too. That was his message which she was trying to take on board. Her message to him would be that she had to push ahead – albeit with caution. How, she reasoned, could she do that when she didn't know from what direction danger might be coming? Whether it was Daphne's inquisitiveness, her barging about regardless of its results or Mike's private life, it raised a threat to more than cats. The threat was to her, Cara Shelley.

At least a relatively normal afternoon lay ahead, despite there being two coach parties to cope with instead of the usual one. There were no threats in that, only tension. As yet there was no sign of any customers as the first coach party was on the house tour and any individual visitors would either be tagging along with that or wandering round the grounds, not yet ready to indulge themselves with tea and cakes. She hadn't spotted any yet but they might be in the woodland or the Grotto out of her sight.

The Twerps too would be arriving shortly for what Simon Harris had apparently decreed would be a memorial performance for Daphne. Anyway, she and Sammy were – she hoped – ready for the invasion, with napkins, tablecloths and china set for action. Just these outside tables needed adjusting and their parasols opening.

Then she spotted Rosalie hurrying towards the Haven, clearly intent on some important mission. She would not have left her volunteer deputies in charge of the gatehouse, otherwise, least of all now. Nevertheless, Cara decided she couldn't miss this opportunity.

'Hi, Rosalie. Have you got a minute?' she called out, running over to her. She'd seize this chance to clear the slate over this alleged affair once and for all. She was in luck.

Rosalie stopped. 'Yes. I wanted to warn you anyway.'

'Tell me the worst,' Cara said resignedly. Get this problem over first, whatever it was.

'There's another coach party coming. Three thirty.'

'*What?*' Visions of as-yet-unbaked huffkins, sandwiches and cakes rushed through Cara's mind. How would she and Sammy cope? 'The poor things will have to run through the house, not stroll,' she said grimly.

Rosalie managed a grin. 'Alison's agreed with Dan that the house can stay open for another half hour and the Twerps have been adapting to that. Simon's dreaming up an ongoing performance outside with stately pavanes and what not instead of country dances.'

Daphne's probably self-appointed successor was clearly in control. Cara rebuked herself for cattiness. 'Good idea,' she said firmly. As it was, she supposed.

'There's singing in the dining room too.'

'The Twerps are singing?' she asked blankly.

'No. Keeley offered.'

'*Keeley?*' What on earth had she got to do with it, Cara wondered. Her head was spinning.

'Amazingly she's a trained opera singer, but had to give it up for some reason.'

Cara was sobered. She had known nothing about Keeley's background although she had been working as housekeeper at the Towers for at least two years. That was a lesson to be learned. The staff at the Towers were no longer a united whole, as Cara had thought. It seemed every one of her colleagues probably had secrets, including, she acknowledged, herself. She had never chatted to them about her daughter's father.

'Isn't the dining room too close to the orangery?' she asked, perturbed. 'Everyone will have their minds on the murder.'

'No way,' Rosalie replied. 'Dan said the police are OK with the orangery being open now, but Alison and Max are keeping it closed out of consideration for Mike.' She hesitated. 'Could I run something by you, Cara?' she asked diffidently. 'Just a quickie.'

'Go ahead,' Cara urged her. Her hopes shot up. This could be leading somewhere because it was rare for Rosalie to be bothered about anything. She usually just fixed it.

'I told the police everything I could think of about Daphne,' Rosalie began, 'but I've still been thinking about it. I was concentrating on what happened to her in the orangery and not that I'd passed her earlier that afternoon. It would have been well before five o'clock because the gatehouse wasn't yet closed. Daphne was very quiet and that wasn't usual.'

No, it wasn't. Cara held her breath. This was vital information. 'Did you get any idea of why? Was it the sort of quiet that suggested she'd had a row with someone or just a general brooding?'

'I've no idea,' Rosalie said helplessly. 'It was only a fleeting impression, and she was more murmuring than talking to me. I gathered she was expecting to speak to Mike, but when I told her he'd left she said she'd wait for Alison. I suppose I've been holding back from telling the police because of some stupid rumour they've got hold of that I'm having an affair with Mike. As if.' She hesitated, then said firmly, 'Doesn't anybody realize I'm gay? I live with my partner and my mother.'

'*Gay?*' Cara repeated stupidly. So much for the rumour of Mike having an affair with Rosalie. Well and truly off the cards. First, though, this story about Daphne, which could be of vital importance. 'Tell the police what happened that afternoon,' she urged her. 'Right away.'

She watched as Rosalie hurried on her way, and turned to return to the Happy Huffkin. What was the great DCI going to make of her story about Daphne? Or, she realized with pleasure, of a suspect exiting from the list of those possibly connected with her death.

Why had it never occurred to her that Rosalie was gay? That, Cara comforted herself, was the strength of the Towers' united front. Until that united front was faced with murder, their lives outside working hours were their own. She doubted whether anyone other than Sammy knew about her daughter Kate.

She permitted herself a twirl round one of the folly's temple pillars. She'd managed to dispose of the rumours surrounding Mike. The path was now clear to follow the other avenues to the truth about Daphne's murder without trailing that gossip with her. Take care, Andrew Mitchem had told her. And she would. All the same, she could speculate on this 'murmuring' that Rosalie had heard. That wasn't usually Daphne's style. Had she had a put down from someone about her book? Was she worried that Alison might put the stoppers on that project because of the rival claims? Simon Harris at least would be only too eager to trumpet the importance of his own cause, especially since he was obviously leading the Twerps now.

There was, Cara decided, a lot going on. Was there danger here or in the Towers? How could she tell? She had to press on. This afternoon it was going to be busy at the Happy Huffkin, but she had a problem. As if by magic, Sammy appeared to give her a hand with putting up the parasols and she summoned up her courage. Sound casual about it, she decided.

'Sammy,' she began cautiously, 'I may need to go over to the Towers during the afternoon. Could you check—'

'Virginia,' he cut across her grumpily. 'On her way.'

'Thank you, Sammy,' she said humbly.

At last. Now that he was back at the Towers ready for the performance of his life, Simon Harris began to relax. He knew he'd been right all along. The Tanton Whirlers dance troupe would rise to the occasion under his leadership and would be proving it today.

A pity that that woman Keeley had insisted on singing some kind of dirge, but the dancing on the lawn would still be the main attraction. Their colourful expert display would remain in the visitors' minds, not the squeaky voice of a novice. He had ordered a special dress rehearsal yesterday and they had practised the quadrille endlessly. He had even organized publicity for the Tanton Whirlers after demanding a meeting with the editor of the *Tanton News* for a full-length feature and, better, had wooed a journalist on the *Kent History News* for an article praising the troupe, thus making sure that his name was in as the new leader.

Daphne would never have tolerated the press swarming around. Pity about her death, but at least it had opened the path to a brighter future – despite Cara whatever-her-name rushing around asking questions, so Simon had heard. But there had been the police interviews, of course, all because of some trifle he had not told them earlier. Nothing much, and it was easy to forget something like that – as he had told them. He had stayed on after the Tanton Whirlers left that day. He had had no choice. Daphne had been crowing that Alison was going to discuss her book with her on account of her claiming to be the best historian.

He couldn't have that. He had hoped to have a word with Alison and Max before that. It hadn't been possible, and now Cara was snooping around.

A busy afternoon, but Ewan was geared up for it. The second group was already about to march through La Galleria. He had no wish to run into Cara Shelley though. He was definitely uneasy. He'd gathered from Dan that she was somehow involved with this Daphne business and from what he could tell she was on good terms with the police, or at least with the DCI, so it would be good policy to work with her – provided she didn't step over the boundary line on to his patch. She had come perilously near it with that hidey-hole discovery – she was also too close to Alison and Max for his liking. She needed watching – especially at present.

The Towers would have yet another coachload arriving shortly, and he'd already had to rope in more volunteers to take parties round the house. He had told them it didn't matter too much what they said, as most of the groups would be agog to get near the orangery, the scene of the crime, thanks to all the publicity there had been. Dan and Alison had agreed how to treat the subject – basically give the groups such information on the murder as they could but hold back opinions or word-of-mouth stories. He'd done well so far, he reckoned, but now they were on hallowed ground, the Lavinia Fontana collection. So here goes, he thought, smiling at his captive audience. Two thirds of it were women, mostly clubs but some independent tourists. Easy.

'Lavinia Fontana,' he began brightly, 'is a model for today's women. The first professional female artist and still one of the greats. She had her life planned, did Lavinia. She decided she'd get nowhere in a world dominated by men unless she played by the rules. The daughter of a well-known artist of Bologna at the time, Prospero Fontana, she continued to live with him, even when she married and had eleven children.' Smile at audience.

'Bologna was heaving with brilliant artists during her lifetime,' he continued, 'but she carved out a career as a portrait painter as well as getting commissions for her religious works. Think of it. All those children and building a time-consuming career too. Her poor old husband was left to do the baby rearing – nice one, Lavinia.'

Cue for laughter. Ewan kept the smile on his face with some difficulty as inwardly he was churning with suspicion. He'd just spotted Cara, who had suddenly turned up and joined the tourist group. What was she after? Obviously she was hell-bent on some mission to do with Daphne's murder, but why her sudden interest in the Fontana collection? Fakes? He'd heard rumours about that angle, but she'd never shown much interest in art before, not even in the Reynolds portrait of good old Sir Jeffry.

Did that mean she was linking this fake issue with Daphne Hanson's death? Not good. It was bad enough to have had Daphne snooping around his territory without having Cara as well. Trust her to be the one who had badgered Alison and Max into revealing that hidey-hole. Infuriating that she was grabbing the limelight, even though he could make use of it in his tour. He and Dan saw eye to eye, luckily, so although he was in theory answerable to Dan there was usually no problem. But Ewan didn't like spies, and there she was at every turn. Almost worse than Daphne. Well, the problem of Daphne had been solved – and now that Cara had raised her head over the parapet perhaps that problem too would be addressed.

'Is this where the lady was murdered?' someone piped up, ignoring the fact that he was in the midst of glorifying the achievements of Lavinia Fontana.

'No,' he replied with all the charm he could muster, 'but the case is still ongoing. Soon, however, the late Daphne Hanson's co-dancers will soon be greeting us in the adjoining room to the orangery where the murder took place and where we have now made the most amazing discovery thanks to Daphne.'

That should put Madam Cara in her place, he thought with satisfaction. A tribute to Daphne and a put-down for her. Nevertheless, she was a Grade One nuisance and he'd have to do something about that . . .

No wonder Daphne had met obstacles in her path if everybody was guarding his patch as vigorously as Ewan seemed to be,

Cara thought. The presence of Virginia, together with the lovely Lucy, had enabled her to slip away as planned, irrespective of Sammy's reproachful eye.

She'd wanted another look at one or two of those paintings to see what might have attracted Daphne, but she had stupidly run into Ewan's tour to his obvious annoyance. The glances he kept giving her were proof that she was ruffling his feathers – though she couldn't see how.

As Ewan swept the group past, Cara had another peek at Max's beloved painting of Queen Elizabeth I. See what a woman can do, she seemed to be saying as she stared back at Cara in scorn. Trying to do my best, she muttered in self-defence. As the tour crawled on, she had another squint at the self-portrait she liked. Lavinia had been fond of them, but this one certainly seemed different. There she was, the determined artist inside her studio with palette and easel, and outside was the tree in full bloom. Was there something lacking in the painting though? Passion, perhaps? Come off it, Cara, she told herself. Who are you to judge?

She had another look at the painting with the unknown ruffian sitter. There he was, elegantly clad, looking out at unconquered lands ahead, as if determined to leap on his horse and rush off to conquer them. What had Daphne made of it all? Perhaps nothing. Alison had said that all the staff at the Towers had had prior experience of art and antiques, so perhaps Daphne had simply wanted to keep up with the rest of them.

Ewan was getting into his stride now. He really was a crowd-pleaser, Cara thought, although there was no problem about that – in theory at least.

'Her final coup for capturing her market was to move to Rome in 1604,' Ewan explained enthusiastically, 'the main centre for the greats of the day. Rubens popped along there, Caravaggio, and many more. Lavinia must have loved it – probably joined in the fun and painted her fellow artists, as well as all the dignitaries of church and noblemen. They all painted each other. We'll never know the answers to all the fascinating questions these paintings raise.'

He paused, bestowed another beaming smile on his flock, and announced, 'And now we shall return to the ground floor. Our tour will conclude on the lawn outside where the famous Tanton Whirlers dance troupe will be ready to entertain us but first Miss Keeley Martin will be singing in honour of the late Mrs Daphne Hanson in the dining room.'

'Aren't we going to where she was murdered?' came the inevitable demand.

Ewan was ready for this. 'No, but we shall be able to view our latest addition in Tanton's history, a recent exciting discovery by the late Mrs Daphne Hanson.'

Neat one, Cara thought. A tribute to Daphne, possibly unwarranted, combined with a put-down for herself.

Ewan didn't seem to be the only one with a bone to pick with her. Just as she lingered while Ewan guided the procession towards the stairs to the ground floor, Robert Broome emerged from the Archives Office, saw her and immediately and for some as yet unknown reason looked daggers at her.

'Are you leaving?' Cara asked him uncertainly.

'No, I merely came out in case,' he announced loudly to the whole group on the point of disappearing down the stairs, 'anyone has questions about the history of the house. All records are housed here and you are welcome to browse through them – under supervision, of course.'

Nervousness and Ewan's obvious annoyance combined to fasten the tourists' movement towards the staircase down to the first floor. Cara tried not to giggle. Poor Robert. 'All the visitors are interested in today is Daphne's murder,' she tried to comfort him as he turned crossly back into his office. 'Perhaps you should pretend there are jewels or guns hidden in your records,' she added, following in his wake.

'That hidey-hole is all they're interested in too, thanks to you,' he said crossly.

Cara was taken aback. 'But all I did was help uncover it. I don't know the history, as you all do.' That was a good line, she thought, but it didn't work.

Another glare. 'It's a *hidey-hole*. It won't be in the official plans by its very nature.'

'There must be hints or clues somewhere,' she urged him, but he was silent.

Impasse. This wasn't like Robert. She tried again. 'But it will

attract visitors to find out the history and why it was built and
so on. Like the smugglers' tunnel. That's not recorded in your
documents, is it?'

'Only one or two oblique references.' He looked mollified at
least. 'But even Max's own library gets more visitors than I do.
Daphne used to come, and Simon Harris and the occasional scholar
sent here by the National Trust or English Heritage. That's all.'

Max's tiny library, from which the spillover was in the Archives
Room, was at the far end of La Galleria. This was the entrance
door for groups and therefore all too easily bypassed by eager
visitors. Nevertheless, Cara could see why it received more attention than the official Archives Room. Tucked away at the corner
of the house, overlooking the gardens on the front side and the
yard between the servants' wing and the orangery, the Archives
Room was easy to bypass. Max's office was up here too, but
thanks to the distance it was from La Galleria it, like the Archives
Room, was a peaceful working place.

Cara liked the Archives Room and she could understand why
Sir Jeffry had selected it for his study. Its sheer shape was unusual,
with the annex making it a backward L shape. The most unusual
thing about his study was at its far end on the left-hand corner;
it was the base of the large turret that adorned the roof above.
It swelled out from the study itself, with a semi-circular space
around it, and boasted two facing brass frontages, one featuring
an old poem.

Sir Jeffry, she decided, must have been an even more weird
gentleman than she had realized. Every day she admired the view
from the lawn of the admirable tangle of tiled roofs adorned by
the turrets and towers. It was a testament to a time when architectural inconsistency in houses such as Tanton Towers was (or
could be) admired. Hats off to Sir Jeffry.

'What actually happened to his first wife?' she asked Robert
with interest, remembering the story handed down the genera-
tions. 'I know she became a ghost, but had he bumped her off,
or did she die in childbirth?'

A prompt answer. Robert's eyes lit up, for this was home
territory. 'Isabel died after giving birth to a daughter, which is
believed to have been stillborn. The second wife, also an Isabel,
gave birth to the twins, Thomas and Horace.' A giggle. 'I fear

some contemporaries believed the first wife's death to be a case of Henry the Eighth.'

'What's he got to do with it?' Asking questions was the way to win Robert's approval, she decided. As he was already cheering up, she added, 'You mean his nasty way of getting rid of wives who didn't produce the right sex to be his heir?'

'That has been suggested,' Robert said diffidently, rising to his feet, seizing the file on his desk and hurrying past her into the annex.

'So Isabel Number One was a very indignant ghost and Isabel Number Two got the plaudits. In the marriage stakes, she didn't have much to boast about, compared with Lavinia Fontana,' Cara continued cheerfully, following him into the annex. Clearly Robert was anxious to get rid of her, although not, she hoped, in Henry VIII's style.

Joking, however, was clearly banned in a room dedicated to serious history or so Robert's severe expression had conveyed. She tried to make amends. 'Does the first wife still haunt the house?'

'I'm afraid I don't know,' he replied stiffly. 'Certainly not here anyway.'

She seized the moment. 'What would Sir Jeffry do for his brandy up here?' she asked – seriously.

'I really can't say.'

'He can't have lugged a cask up from the dining room hidey-hole,' she mused. 'He must have filled a flask or the butler – did they have butlers then? – would bring one up.'

'Certainly they had butlers then, at least in charge of·liquor. The butler held the key to the wine cellars.'

Could it be Robert was getting interested, she wondered. He did seem to be more involved.

'So he must have known about the hidey-hole in the dining room,' Cara added, 'although it still seems a long way from the wine cellars. Did Daphne ever comment on that with her love of history?'

Mistake. 'History? Daphne did not know what the word means.' Robert was clearly annoyed. 'And anyway, that hidey-hole in the dining room might have other purposes.' He cleared his throat in embarrassment.

She tactfully ignored that. 'Did Daphne ask you about hidey-holes?'

'She rarely asked me anything. I believe I mentioned that she had the audacity not to bother to replace documents or books in my absence,' Robert said grimly. 'Not even the precious letter from Sir Jeffry to the architect about the importance of every single detail. Every i had to be dotted, every o observed. I fear Daphne was too interested in the smugglers' tunnel to care about that hidey-hole, if she even knew about it.'

'Why though? It was presumably legal to drink spirits in the eighteenth century, wasn't it? It was just how one got hold of them that was the problem.'

'Basically yes,' he agreed. 'Too much of a display might cause comment, however.'

She was no further forward. She thought about this as she made her way downstairs, guiltily aware that even though Virginia and her sister were helping out at the Happy Huffkin, the coach parties might be overwhelming it.

Even as she walked though there was still a nagging question in her mind about those casks in the cellar. The cellars were open to all at Tanton Towers – including visits from the Revenue. Surely the smugglers didn't just bring the casks up the tunnel and dump them there? She was still musing on this as she reached the café. The Twerps were in the midst of their performance, watched by a huge crowd – and by everyone packing the tables at the Happy Huffkin.

Virginia had everything under control to Cara's guilty relief.

'Greetings,' Virginia said, whisking by with a trayful of teacups. 'We're low on chocolate cake.'

'I'll place an order tomorrow morning,' Cara said thankfully. Back to reality. Fascinating though the subject of hidey-holes and brandy flasks was, she still didn't know how Daphne fitted into this. Had she discovered the hole in the dining room? A chilling thought recurred. If so, did the same threat lie over her, Cara? She was well aware that she had been broadcasting her interest in the subject without thinking about that.

'Someone wants you, Cara!' Virginia shouted over to her.

She swung round to see – of all people – Keeley Martin running, almost stumbling over the grass to reach the café. No, she realized. It was to reach *her.* Keeley was shouting out her name and was clearly upset.

What had happened? Cara found herself running towards her. 'What's wrong?' she asked, really alarmed now.

'I thought you ought to know. You've been going around asking questions about Daphne and Mike. They've just arrested him for murder.'

ELEVEN

S ometimes bad dreams come true. Finding somewhere quiet to talk was her first priority, Cara realized. Keeley might have got this wrong. She steered her through the crowded outside tables round to one of the pillared terraces overlooking the river, where few customers found their way. It was Sammy's favourite on the rare occasions they both took a break to admire the view.

Take stock of the situation first, Cara decided. Looking at her now, gone was the Miss Clip-Clop she had thought she knew, before she turned out to be an opera singer in her spare time. Certainly it was obvious that there was no truth in her being Mike's lover, for she would have been far more distraught. If there was any substance at all in the gossip, it might be someone else on the staff or in the village.

Cara took a deep breath. 'Are you sure he's been arrested? It's not just another interrogation?'

'Yes. I heard them. He was just marched off.' Keeley had brightened up, now that her news had been broken. 'It was that awful policeman. I saw it happen after I'd finished singing in the dining room.'

'DCI Mitchem?'

'Yes. He's gone and arrested him this time.'

'It won't be for long.' Cara's head was spinning. 'How could Mike be guilty? He left the Towers long before Daphne was murdered. Or are they thinking he nipped back and used the tunnel? That can't be so either because although he'd have a key, Ewan might have been there. Have they charged him yet?'

'I don't know.'

Cara still couldn't believe it. Perhaps Keeley had made a mistake – it was just questioning again. Or had the police made the mistake? Far more likely. Mike killing Daphne because of a love affair or because of her apparent wealth? No, neither was possible, Cara reasoned. She'd proved the wealth issue was nonexistent and the affair rumour was heading the same way. 'Did the police interview anyone else? Did they talk to you, for instance?' she asked cautiously.

Keeley's head, with its so smart haircut, shook vigorously. 'I told them he didn't do it,' she said smugly.

'Good,' Cara said, wondering how this 'evidence' had gone down with Andrew Mitchem. 'When did the arrest take place?'

'Only just now. Mike was downstairs talking to Dan when they came for him.'

She'd missed that, Cara calculated. Perhaps that was as well or she might have thrown herself into another fray with Andrew Mitchem. 'They'll let him go when they realize it's a mistake,' she said firmly. 'Is this general knowledge?'

'I don't know.' Keeley stood up and patted her on the shoulder as she prepared to leave. 'Cheer up,' she said. 'He might not be guilty.'

Cara managed to refrain herself from comment and instead offered a weak smile of thanks. Right, she thought, once Miss Clip-Clop had clip-clopped her way back across the lawn. Time for action! Back into the folly. With a full house, she ought to be in command here, although thankfully Virginia seemed to have everything under control, and Sammy too. He took one look at her.

'Nabbed Mr Hanson. Chap outside said. That why young Keeley's showing off?'

'Does everyone know already?' Cara asked. 'Lots of sage nodding of heads?'

'Word spreads.'

'But he can't be guilty,' she said desperately.

'Could be.'

'He's not the type,' she protested again.

'Met that type, have you?'

Cara reluctantly grinned. 'Mike's not a violent spur-of-the-moment man. Nor could he plan something so extraordinary as attacking Daphne in a public place.'

'Could happen,' Sammy decreed, giving great attention to a mug to inspect its cleanliness.

'Not at Tanton Towers.' Cara stopped. 'I really don't think he could have murdered her,' she added earnestly.

'Reason being?'

'He wouldn't kill her at Tanton. He's far too clever.' Perhaps that wasn't doing her side of the argument any favours, she thought uneasily.

Next task: a must. She needed to talk to Alison and Max. Terrible though Daphne's death had been, it couldn't have its roots in anything to do with the Towers itself and it could affect its well-deserved image. For over two hundred years it had survived all that could be thrown at it, including two world wars, a threatened invasion from Napoleon and other disasters. Literally and figuratively, it towered over the world beneath it, a refuge and an example. She worked here and she had a duty to help keep that image safe. Faced with a challenge like this, her grandmother would have informed her that of course she could do it, chorusing the magic words of an old song about flying elephants. Well, her elephant was definitely going to fly. The DCI had played his hand and now it was her turn.

She was almost thrown at the first hurdle. Passing the Snug, she ran straight into Simon Harris. She groaned to herself. She would be duty bound to ask how the Twerps' performance had gone, but the last thing she wanted was to discuss the awful news about Mike with him or with anyone save Alison or Max until she'd had a chance to really take it in herself. Her best course was to concentrate on Simon himself.

'That was a splendid tribute to Daphne,' she told him warmly. She meant that. After all, even though she'd seen almost nothing of it, the idea had been good.

Simon swelled with pride – visibly. Just as she had expected. She noted the shoulders going back and the head held just that little bit higher. He was not a tall man, save in his own opinion perhaps, but he looked after his own gravitas splendidly. Not gay, she guessed, but perhaps one of those men who remained single until they met someone worthy of the honour of being his wife. He might wait a long time, in Cara's opinion, but given that the female Twerps outnumbered the male, perhaps he'd get lucky – even if the chosen lady didn't.

'Will you continue with all your dancing commitments?' she asked – to please him.

'Of course,' came the grave reply. 'Daphne would not have wished otherwise. Poor woman.'

'It requires such dedication.' Keep it going, Cara told herself. He basked in her words of wisdom. 'I shall be honoured to take the troupe forward. Built on Daphne's foundation, of course.'

'And in writing a book about the Towers perhaps?' she continued desperately as he was blocking her way forward.

That caught him off-guard, judging by the pause that followed, but he recovered quickly. 'Yes indeed. It seems Daphne had been impressed by my example and decided to write one of her own. Mine will be a very minor effort.' Self-congratulatory cough from Simon. 'Our subjects overlapped a little. Daphne chose the exciting theme of the smugglers, but my humble efforts are somewhat broader in subject matter. Concentrating on the eighteenth century, I trace the family itself through to the modern day, especially with regard to its musical tradition.'

Musical tradition? This was a new one on her, Cara thought. Change of subject back to Daphne. 'Did Daphne talk to you about her book?' she asked. Someone must know more about this.

'No,' he snapped. 'She was somewhat secretive over her work. One might say zealous in what she regarded as her territory. Not that I minded,' he added grandly.

'No, of course not. In any case yours would be the more erudite.' Cara mentally congratulated herself for this gem. 'The Tanton Whirlers must be so grateful that such a skilful organizer as yourself is taking over.'

Now walk firmly away, she instructed herself, reproaching herself for intolerance. She glanced back at him. He was still staring after her. Simon was definitely somebody she would not want to meet alone on a dark night.

It took her some time to reach the family wing as she skirted the tourist groups, and when she finally reached Alison and Max's living room door she heard Simon's voice booming on the house phone speaker to her amusement. He had found a new audience. She could even hear the words clearly. 'Quite terrible. That poor woman. I always suspected that husband of hers . . .'

Alison was alone and her face brightened as Cara came in. She motioned to her to sit down, made an excuse to Simon and ended the call with obvious relief.

'Before him it was the *Kent Post*,' she said. 'Wanted to know what we thought about Mike. News spreads.'

'What *do* we think?' Cara said gloomily.

'Confusion worse confounded,' Alison said briefly. 'John Milton. Paradise really has been lost.'

'It's obviously a mistake. It must be. Do you know if they've charged him?'

Alison looked even gloomier than Cara felt. 'No. The press will probably know the outcome before we do.'

'Did the DCI say *anything* to you that could suggest why he's been arrested?' Cara asked desperately. 'It's crazy. Rosalie told me that when she came over to the house sometime before closing at five o'clock she ran into Daphne. She said something about wanting to consult Mike, but of course he'd already left. Perhaps the DCI got the wrong end of the stick over that. Rosalie quite definitely had seen Mike leave at four fifteen, which would have been well before the time she saw Daphne very much alive.' Cara hesitated, but pushed on. 'Keeley is friendly with him – was it she who confirmed the time he left?'

Alison saw her point. 'No, it was Rosalie. She was in the gatehouse at the time. She saw his car leave then – and, before you ask, he was driving it and she had a word with him too.'

Up against a brick wall then. Cara sighed. 'Mike's a friend but we have to put that to one side if we're to find out what really happened. He's been married to Daphne for donkeys' years and, even if it was a planned murder, it would be a very odd choice for him to pick your orangery at that time of day. And if she was killed on the spur of the moment, it's still a very odd place.'

Alison looked at her gravely. 'That's what Max and I have been chewing over. We're no further forward as to who if anyone she was expecting to meet, apart from me and possibly Mike. Max and I talked to one or two of the Twerps, but Daphne hadn't said anything to any of them about meeting anyone. Although one of them did say she hadn't been as chatty as usual.'

'So the police must see this case differently.'

'How?'

'That the only person other than you to meet her there seems to be her husband. Which we know it wasn't,' Cara added firmly.

'It's unofficial,' he said, apologetically.

Cara stared at him in disbelief. This was proving to be one

hell of a day. First the opening day rush at work, then the news about Mike and all the ensuing dramas that had caused. Now she was faced with another one out of the blue. What the blazes was DCI Mitchem doing on her doorstep on a late June evening, apologetic or not? Admittedly he seemed uncertain of his welcome – as well he might. He obviously had some mission in mind, but at the moment she wasn't interested in missions.

'Shall I go?' he added politely when nothing was forthcoming from her.

What to do? Cara's mind went blank. The overhead outside lamp was lighting him up against the darkness of her front garden and its tall hedge and outside the road leading to the village was silent in the dusk. The only traffic usually was mostly to and from the Farran Arms, the village pub. Before Sir Jeffry had the bright idea of building the Towers, it had been the King's Arms, but Sir Jeffry had speedily put an end to that. Robert had once reluctantly shown her the correspondence on the matter, although that was due to his old-fashioned idea that the language would shock her.

She pulled herself together, tempted to say 'Yes' to the invasive DCI. Curiosity (she supposed) held her back. 'No need,' she replied guardedly.

This was grasping the nettle with a vengeance, and she wondered what her daughter would make of it. Kate would undoubtedly think she was making too big a mountain out of a molehill, and would laugh her head off if she did still honour her mother with a visit, which now seemed highly unlikely.

'Come in,' she added, hoping it sounded nonchalant but not ungracious.

Where to take him though? Conservatory? He followed her through the living room, bending under the door beams – but not quite far enough.

'Sorry, people didn't grow as tall in medieval times,' she said after the impact.

Now that really was ungracious, she realized, finding a comfortable chair for him in the conservatory. What was wrong with her?

'You must have English Heritage's eyes on you all the time,' he said.

'Would you like a coffee?' she asked, mollified. 'Or hot choco-late? Wine?'

He smiled at that. 'None, thanks. Have I interrupted supper?'

'No.' Supper had been two of the sandwiches left over from today.

'Then we can stop the formalities. I take it you've heard the news about Mr Hanson?'

She wouldn't beat about the bush. 'Yes, and you're wrong.'

'Time – or rather evidence – will tell.'

'He wouldn't . . .' she burst out, instantly regretting it.

'I can't discuss that, Cara. You know that.'

'Then why come?' she retorted.

No reply. He was looking at the low bookshelves lining two sides of her conservatory. They held cookery books from the past, mostly ranging from Mrs Rundell and Alexis Soyer up to more modern times, all kept near at hand (in the hope she might blossom into being a brilliant cook one day). Then at last Andrew Mitchem did reply.

'I came because of what we've already discussed,' he said amicably. 'Information falling into your hands that might or might not have relevance to what's happened here, plus your own permitted impressions of who, what, when and why.'

Fair enough. She'd give a straight reply. 'A tall order, Chief Inspector. My view is still that her death was because Daphne was bung full of insatiable curiosity.'

'You're convinced that's why she was killed?'

Where would this lead, she wondered. To an official order to stop? 'Yes. What's your problem with that?' She tried not to sound too truculent.

'I'll come to that. Meanwhile, give me an example of what you've learned.'

Go cautiously here, she thought. 'Simon Harris is intent on writing a book about the Towers. Daphne trespassed on his ground, as he saw it, and also with her no longer alive he has taken over the leadership of the dance troupe – for which he'd been hankering.'

'I'm listening. What else?'

Cara hesitated. What was this to do with Mike? Why come here at this time of night, she wondered. Was it that he wanted every little gem of information in the hope he could lock Mike up and throw away the key? She'd have to put an end to that. 'Apart from Simon Harris, these are all my friends you're interrogating,' she pointed out, 'and I don't want to guess at what they felt about Daphne or Mike.'

He nodded. 'Accepted. Now tell me anyway.'

'There are too many books around,' she began, then laughed as his eyes immediately went down to the cookery books on the shelves.

'No, potential ones,' she amended. 'All about Tanton Towers. Chiefly there was Daphne's own book about smugglers and all the romantic stuff about the Towers, but no one seems to know whether she had actually started writing it. Including her husband. Dan is writing or plans to write a book on the historical treasures of the house, and Robert Broome wants to write the true history of Tanton Towers. And Simon Harris is at least planning one.'

'And why did Mrs Hanson's book clash with all these?'

'As I said before, everyone would want to be the first and grab the limelight,' Cara said.

'Is that so important that murder could be a weapon?'

'It's possible,' she said firmly, 'to some people. The limelight might fall on the first to be published, which would attract TV and press interviews.'

'Thank you. What else other than books?'

'The obvious one. I don't see where it fits in but there's La Galleria and the Lavinia Fontana collection. Also, very possibly, the other treasures in the house of course, the Reynolds and jewellery and so on. But Daphne seemed hooked by the Lavinia Fontana works although she wasn't an art historian herself.'

'That rules it out?'

'No. All the senior staff at the Towers have some kind of background in art. But you must know all this,' she said, puzzled.

'Different perspectives,' he said vaguely.

She wasn't going to let him get away with that. 'Have you charged Mike?' she asked firmly.

'There's the CPS to consider.' Another pointless reply. Even she knew the Crown Prosecution Service would have the final say. Then she couldn't hold back any longer.

'Strangulation,' she burst out. 'It's just so out of character.'

A long pause. Then: 'Someone mentioned you had a daughter. Is she as spiky as you?'

She bit back an instant retort, trying to adjust to this new Andrew Mitchem. 'She keeps me in order with her gentle nature,' she said sweetly. Kate would be highly surprised to hear she was being accorded this accolade.

Cara waited for him to ask about her daughter's father, but he said nothing – disappointingly, as she was fully ready for it. But instead he said:

'I enjoy sitting at the Happy Huffkin. One gets a balanced view of Tanton Towers. An outsider's view but a close one.'

'I agree.' She was surprised that he'd nailed it so well.

'Do you like the work involved?'

She considered this. 'Yes. I like people. I like the recipes and cooking. I'm not much good at it yet but I'm interested in the cooks who wrote them. I like the history.'

'Of all the Grand Houses?'

'Wrong. All houses. I've a handwritten recipe book from the 1850s, and even Queen Victoria's cook Francatelli wrote a recipe book for poor working families.'

'Why do you run this café though? Why not explore the world by reaching out?'

'I can reach out from here. The world comes to me. I don't need to travel with my feet anymore.' She stopped, annoyed with herself for going so far.

'I guess exploring is much the same in my work. The history behind the crime, how the crime came about, and putting all the ingredients together and stirring gently.'

He'd been trying to catch her off guard, Cara instantly thought. Very well. 'You're just trying to reach a verdict that way,' she said crossly. How gentle was he being with Mike, she wondered.

He actually smiled again. 'Sometimes. Tell me this. From your café, you can see outsiders before they enter the building, even those you know well. You can see all those people moving about as in a board game or dolls' house. But when you enter the Towers, you might see everything differently. You're part of it yourself. Your perspective changes. Do your opinions change too?'

'No, I'm the same person with the same thoughts.' Where was this going, she wondered uneasily.

'Are you sure? You can still see your friends objectively and be considerate although you're in there with them?'

'I suppose,' she said doubtfully, 'I might feel I was betraying them at present if I talked and listened to them at the moment. Not,' she added firmly, 'about facts that might help you.'

'If you recognized those,' he said.

'I would.'

'Let's try. Even though you believe we've got the wrong man for Mrs Hanson's murder, you are faced with the fact that the right one has to be amongst your companions.'

'That's true, but I still can't chatter to you or anyone else frankly about my friends.'

'Then describe them in just a few words as though you were standing outside them. Not their faults, but just as you see them as an outsider. Robert Broome for example.'

Thank goodness, she thought with relief. She could handle this. 'Quiet scholar dedicated to the Towers.'

'In what way?'

'Through its history.'

'OK. Dan Dickson.'

'Scholar with a mission to rule and inform.'

He chuckled. 'Ewan Chapman?'

'Entrepreneur committed only to his current job.'

'Rosalie Atkins and Keeley Martin?'

'Conscientious, capable manager, and Keeley . . .' She paused. 'I'm holding back on this one.'

'Accepted. Alison and Max Farran Evans?'

'Too close to me.'

'Because they own the Towers and you presumably rent from them?'

'No. Because they're . . .' she struggled. 'Part of me.'

'Thank you, Cara.'

Cara? That seemed to be a fixture. And yet he didn't seem an Andrew to her yet. Just as she was about to offer him a drink again, he rose to his feet. He was leaving. She felt vaguely cheated after she had shown him out and closed the door behind him. Cheated, she supposed, because he had taken her help without disclosing a thing in return. He had just been picking her brains. He hadn't even asked her about the hidey-hole. Why not? He must surely have heard of it as news of it had spread around the Towers, not to mention its being on Ewan's route now. Had he dismissed it as not contributing to his case?

Once again she mused on Sir Jeffry stuck up there in his study longing for a drink and the hidey-hole way down on the ground floor in the dining room. Or would he have walked upstairs clasping a jugful of brandy? If he was going to drink it at meals, however, why bother to hide it in the hidey-hole as though that was going to be frowned upon by his ladyfolk? Was the reason that it might have protected him if there was a raid by the Revenue? Answer: nothing she had heard about Sir Jeffry suggested he was the nervous type.

How would that hidey-hole work? In the middle of or after dinner would he order the butler to open up the hidey-hole and pour him a brandy? And would the same happen if he wanted a drink in his study up on the second floor? What did he do up there anyway? Read books while swigging his gin or brandy? No, there was a library downstairs if he was tired of his wife's company. Write letters and need a good drink by his side? Maybe. Treat it as a getaway room where he could be free of children and wives? Yes, drink in secret. Pornography? Possible, in which case a nice brandy would help things along. Estate affairs? Hardly. He had a steward for that. Or perhaps he kept a small supply of spirits in the study, tucked away out of sight? That might mean he had a hidey-hole of his own there. That turret area would be just the place for it. It looked so innocent. Yes . . .

Hang on, Cara, she told herself with a jolt. You're dreaming, aren't you?

Perhaps not. Could the hidey-hole in the dining room be a blind, to please wives and fool the Revenue?

And if so, why and where was the store kept?

Moreover – she caught her breath in hope – had Daphne found it and for some reason had it led to her death?

TWELVE

She had slept on it. Her decision next morning? It was a theory worth looking into and that was putting it mildly. Nevertheless, Alison was looking unconvinced. Sammy had been placated and the day's necessities at the Happy Huffkin taken care of, and Cara had braced herself to corner Alison. So far it was not going well.

'Why would anyone want to kill Daphne just for finding out how Sir Jeffry got his daily brandy?' Cara was bent on sorting out whether this was a red herring or whether she might have hit a bull's-eye.

'And are we next in line now that we might have discovered it?' Alison asked drily.

She'd blundered. 'Sorry, I'm jumping ahead of myself and falling flat on my face,' Cara apologized.

That made Alison laugh. 'We have it on the best authority that even Homer nods.'

'I doubt if Andrew Mitchem would see it that way,' Cara said ruefully.

'You underrate him. He sees everything as a stepping stone, right or wrong.'

Cara considered this. 'But a stepping stone to what? He wouldn't be interested in how Sir Jeffry fulfilled his brandy desires. I am though. Sir Jeffry would want his brandy actually in his study. He was an eccentric and probably had great fun enjoying a tasty sip or two.'

'We don't *know* he was eccentric,' Alison objected. 'He just has that reputation. His letters and the other documents seem mostly straightforward.'

Trust Alison to take the scholarly approach. She was right, of course, but in Cara's view guesswork could sometimes be helpful.

'If he had eccentricity enough to build Tanton Towers,' she replied, 'he would have been eccentric enough to dream up some scheme to suit his alcoholic desires better than that hidey-hole we found. He doesn't seem the kind of man to restrict his habits to the odd polite drink in the dining room even if the ladies had retired.'

'Probably not. They'd be knocking it back with him.' Alison laughed.

'Suppose,' Cara said, trying to hold back her excitement and be measured and reasonable, 'he had another hidey-hole serving his needs much nearer. In his study.'

A groan from Alison now. 'Don't get carried away. If there's another hidey-hole, why wasn't that discovered long ago? One overlooked is admissible, two are definitely not. The one in the dining room might have escaped much attention, but surely Robert would have discovered a hidey-hole in a room in which he was working?'

Cara searched frantically for an answer. 'It wasn't discovered because Sir Jeffry liked mysteries. He wouldn't reveal his architectural secrets to anyone, especially to his wife. And that – ' her excitement grew – 'could be how the legends about her sprang up.'

Alison sighed in resignation. 'Very well. So how do we start looking for Sir Jeffry's supply chain? Do we need someone else in on this? Dan? Robert?'

Cara ran through the possibilities. 'No, let's keep the hunt to ourselves at first, then call in the big battalions if we can see that ties in with Daphne's murder.'

Alison leapt on this immediately. 'Back to square one. How would another hole link in with that?'

'Because she was murdered for a reason,' Cara whipped back, 'which might stem back to the smugglers' era. I agree it's a remote possibility, but I still can't see Mike in the role of such a passionate lover that he would kill his wife and in such a public place.'

'I agree.' Alison looked weary. 'The Mike situation is ghastly. His DNA could be anywhere on Daphne's clothes or skin quite innocently.' She paused. 'So let's go ahead with the hidey-hole hunt – just on the barest chance that there is one hidden in that old study and that it might help Mike in some way.'

'Shall we call in Dan instead of Max?' Cara suggested, sensing Alison was still reluctant.

'No, I'll do my best to persuade Max,' Alison told her. 'Dan tends not to like new discoveries unless he initiates them, and anyway we are in dangerous waters if I start bringing staff into this hunt. Max could be surprisingly accommodating if we promise not to tip him into a supposed hidey-hole again. He'll be back from the lecture he's giving at the college this afternoon, and Robert's not in today so we will have a free hand to call in Max without involving too many curious eyes. And we won't start till after closing time.'

'A preliminary survey then, to see if I'm barking up the wrong tree,' Cara said eagerly.

Alison giggled. 'You, Cara? Never.'

'Lead on!' Max said grandly.

To Cara's surprise – and Alison's too – Max had been all for it. 'Why brandy though?' he had asked when their summons had brought him to their side. 'Hidey-holes cover a multitude of sins. Let's call it the Adventure of the Scarlet Lady,' he'd chuckled, having advanced his theory that Sir Jeffry kept the hidey-hole to thrust lovers into in the event of an unwelcome intrusion. 'Where is it?' he asked, looking round the Archives Room hopefully. 'Here or in the annex under the archway. If it were here he'd have it closer to hand, but the annex – which was all part of his study – would attract less notice.'

'We don't know,' Cara had to confess, conscious that Alison was deliberately leaving this to her – justifiably, of course. She was clearly enjoying the situation. 'And it's only if there was one at all.'

Max looked perplexed. 'Have you made mathematical calculations as to the likelihood of this mysterious hole?'

'No, but . . .'

'An adventure indeed then.' Max frowned.

Alison obligingly stepped in. 'The odds were the same when Stanley set out to Africa to track down Dr Livingstone.'

'Not the same comparison, my darling,' her husband declared. 'Nor would Shackleton or Scott on their Antarctic explorations provide a competitive experience. Their goals had evidence on their side. From what little you have told me, there seems none in this case. This case seems more in the sphere of *Alice Through the Looking Glass* or the discovery of Narnia.'

'Perhaps, but . . .' Cara began again.

'Nevertheless,' Max beamed, 'whether or not there is a scarlet lady at the end of the trail, let us proceed. Where do we begin? Annex or here? And is Robert joining us?' Max asked.

'No, darling,' Alison began, 'it's his . . .' But Max was already marching across the room.

'We'll start here. Let us study the situation.' He held up his hand to encourage the troops. That was Max's strength. Once engaged on a subject, he gave it his full attention, Cara thought admiringly. 'First, how would the casks or other containers reach this room?'

'That,' Cara admitted, 'is the weak spot. Presumably the staff would lug it up.'

'In which case,' Max pounced with glee, 'why does he need a hidey-hole?'

Cara struggled and came up only with a weak retort. 'It was done at night.'

'The same question,' Max said complacently. 'Why another hidey-hole?' To her relief he then added, 'Nevertheless, let us proceed. I dislike trailing question marks.'

Her doubts deepened as he took command, studied, pushed, pulled every nook and cranny without any sign of magical mysterious openings into secret places. Only the portrait of Sir Jeffry on the wall facing Robert's desk overlooking the lawns gave her any hope. It seemed to be winking at her with one eye, or, as it was described in the tour guide printed for visitors, he had a roguish look. Might that mean something, she wondered.

Max was intent on the turret area bulging out at the rear corner of the office. It was stacked with files, but all these were swept aside by Max in one grand swoop to reveal the base of the turret with its huge eye-catching brass panels, guarding either side. On the left one was etched a large grinning cat, and on the right was the poem that Cara had seen before.

'For I will consider my Cat Jeoffry,

'For he is the servant of the Living God, duly and daily serving him.'

Alison broke the silence that followed. 'From Christopher Smart's *Jubilate Agno*. So what now?'

Cara read the lines again. When she had first come to the

Towers she had asked Max why the poet's cat apparently liked the 'o' in Jeffry the cat whereas Sir Jeffry did not. He had explained that there was no fixed spelling of names in the eighteenth century. Sir Jeffry simply chose not to use the 'o'. Cara had been intrigued enough to look up the whole poem. She remembered it was long and it was fun. Why was it here though?

'Our Sir Jeffry must have met Smart at some stage of his life,' Alison added. 'Smart was born in Kent not that far away from here but that was in 1722, long before Sir Jeffry appeared on this earth. Then he moved first to university then London, where he wrote the whole *Jubilate Agno* including this poem in a lunatic asylum, poor fellow, with his cat as an only companion. It wasn't published until the last century though so Sir Jeffry must have had a prior peek at it.'

'I suppose they might have met,' Max agreed grudgingly, idly pushing at bits of the wall without success. 'Does that advance our mission, however? Nothing so far suggests there is a hidden hole anywhere in this room.'

'No trapdoor in the floor?' Cara asked hopefully.

Max cast a glance at her. There was fitted carpeting over the turret floor showing no sign of anything underneath, but he did not hesitate. 'Rip it up,' he said and proceeded to follow his own order. Cara peered over his shoulder at the underlay on the floor beneath as he stretched out to pull the carpet back, promptly toppling over in his eagerness just as he had in the earlier hidey-hole search. No laughs, Cara promptly decided, while Alison merely stretched out a hand to the fallen hero.

Max graciously grabbed it, supporting himself with the other hand on the nearest panel and began to get to his feet. And lost his balance again, toppling backwards this time.

'What . . .' he began. Then stopped.

They were all staring. The panel with the poem on it was gradually disappearing downwards, not noiselessly but with a quiet rumble coming to a stop with its top a few inches above the floor level. Cara and Alison promptly seized hold of Max, rolling him out of the turret area to sprawl in an ungainly huddle on the floor.

'And there, my friends,' Max declared with great pleasure as he scrambled to his feet, 'is your hidey-hole. So what now? A bit of an anti-climax, wouldn't you say?'

Cara was inclined to agree, as she and Alison peered in. It was just another empty hole, like the one in the dining room. Nevertheless, she thought, it was large enough to take a cask or even two, as the floor looked covered with thick webbing, presumably to save damage to the cask and help prevent noise.

'At least we've found it, and I haven't hurt myself too badly this time,' Max said cheerfully.

'How did you set it going?' Cara demanded.

'I've no idea. My hand was pushing against the panel. At the top. The bit that's showing now.'

'Where did you press it though?'

'About there by the "My Cat Jeoffry" title. I'll try and haul it up to show you.' He peered into the black space and tentatively began to feel around. 'There's some kind of apparatus here,' he called back, 'so it wasn't just an accident that it fell. If I'm right, it means there's some kind of counterweight that will control it once you've heaved it up or down. Shall I have a go?'

'Don't you dare crawl inside,' Alison shouted anxiously.

Max was oblivious now. 'I'll need to know exactly what I pressed.' He withdrew his head and beamed. 'I was holding my fist like this.' He demonstrated, pressed hard in several places and at last: 'Look,' he crowed.

They didn't need to look. They could see and hear the rumble as the rest of the panel slowly reappeared.

'Good Lord, look at that.' Max looked flabbergasted. 'I must have pressed it by chance. I think it was on the "o" of the Jeoffry.'

He'd hit on it – in all senses, Cara thought jubilantly. No wonder Sir Jeffry the joker had been so keen on it.

Alison was on the same track. 'Maybe it was chosen on purpose because he didn't use the "o" in his name.'

'A theory worth pursuing, my love,' Max agreed.

'Just one thing, Cara,' Alison said. 'How does this affect Daphne's death?'

That brought her down to earth with a thud. 'Not yet known,' she replied grimly. 'But we have to find out. If it doesn't, then we could be missing something vital. There is one thing that seems odd to me,' she added. 'The mechanism must be simple

enough but what about air? Whatever was stored there might
need a little at least. Did the atmosphere hit you when you put
your head in, Max?'

'Yes, but no more than in a very old wardrobe.'

'Narnia, Max?' Alison laughed. 'Any good-hearted lions
hanging around in there?'

'It's worth looking for them,' Cara said hopefully. 'Shall we
have one more shot? Let's go down and look at the turret from
the outside. There might be some visible sign of an outlet.'

This might be an anti-climax, Cara feared, as they made their
way downstairs, despite her niggle that something was odd about
that hidey-hole. Would it just prove a red herring on her part
with Alison and Max merely being polite in pandering to her
delusions? Would Andrew Mitchem pursue such red herrings as
part of the job?

She felt reassured as they stood on the lawn peering up at the
roofs plus the numerous turrets, gables and towers. She was, she
reminded herself, looking up at an extravaganza designed by an
eccentric knight nearly two hundred and fifty years ago. Anything
was therefore possible, especially in that mass of architectural
shapes up there. From where she was standing, she could glimpse
over the top of the orangery the tall bushes in the yard that
divided it from the servants' wing which jutted out behind it.
The bushes, she suspected, were a Victorian effort to hide the
hoi polloi from the delicate sensitivities of guests in the orangery.
The solid red brick wall of the Towers, surmounted by its guardian
towers and turrets soaring up to the skies, gave on to roofs that
must have been a nightmare for chimney sweeps trying to attack
their targets from above.

'That must be where our turret is,' Cara said uncertainly.

'Granted. But there's something odd about it, isn't there?' Max
frowned.

Odd? So Max felt it too. Cara studied it carefully, but nothing
that she could see was odd – or was there? Finally she nailed it.
They had been right. Over the top of the orangery shouldn't she
be able to see the base of the turret jutting out from the Towers'
side wall brickwork? Yes, but what she was looking at was the
side wall going upwards with only the merest hint of the turret
bulge before the turret itself rose up in all its glory. When they

were in the Archives Room she had seen a small window in the turret, but looking up from here there seemed to be two windows, one lower than the other. Robert's office windows overlooked the lawns, so neither could be his. She grappled with this, wanting to be quite sure she wasn't dreaming.

'That,' she then declared in excitement, having pointed this out to Max and Alison, 'is the something odd. The Towers' side brickwork from the turret downwards seems to have spread outwards, further out than it should be. That doesn't make sense, so what would My Cat Jeoffry make of that?'

'For tenthly,' a highly pleased Max quoted from the poem, 'he goes in quest of food. If there's some hocus-pocus attached to that turret then My Cat would know all about it. It's merely that we don't.'

'For the electrical fire is the spiritual substance which God sends from heaven to sustain the bodies both of man and beast,' Alison picked up the quotation. She too was excited now. 'Dear old Sir Jeffry's sustenance was brandy.'

'For though he cannot fly he is an excellent clamberer,' Max chortled.

Used as Cara was to this toing and froing between Max and Alison, this time she was joining in, big time. 'Clamberer,' she repeated, trying to sound rational in her eagerness. She failed. '*Clamberer?* Upwards. Look upwards!'

Their gaze too fixed on the brick wall. Clamber up that? A brick wall that stretched from the ground up to the base of the turret. Then there was a joint cry from Alison and Max: '*Jubilate Agno!*'

'That's the clue,' Max crowed.

'Somehow,' Cara said, scarcely daring to hope, 'we've discovered how that brandy and gin reached Sir Jeffry's study. Perhaps it wasn't carted through the house at all.'

'Calm down, folks,' Alison said. 'We can't be sure that the oddity we can see is linked to the turret hidey-hole. All we can see from this point is a solid wall that looks slightly out of kilter running down to the level of the orangery roof. And because the orangery has a brick wall running along its length on that side, we can't be sure of where the Towers' side wall meets it.'

'And that's not helped by the hedges in the yard behind the

orangery,' Cara added in frustration. There must be a way through this. *There must.*

'Cellars. Tried them?' A familiar voice behind them made them all jump. Sammy had joined them. 'Old. Back to Willie the Conqueror. What goes up starts low down. Best get back.' And with that he ambled back to the café, leaving them even more stunned by this remarkable speech.

Alison had been studying the brick wall again. 'The cellars, Max,' she exclaimed. 'He might be right.'

Cara leapt at this. 'Do let's give it a go.'

'One moment. Aren't we getting a touch of Alice in Wonderland here?' Max wore his grave professor face. 'The cellars are stone-built not brick, and they are a long way from the turret.'

'A ladder, perhaps. To be a *clamberer*,' Cara said impatiently, 'you climb up things.'

'Clamberer is but one word in a very long poem,' scholar Max pointed out. 'Before we start tearing stone walls apart, perhaps we should inspect the turret area again. There was no sign of anything going any further.'

'We didn't look carefully,' Cara pointed out in anguish. There had to be something else, there *had* to be. 'If there's a connection down to the cellars, it has to be tucked in under that turret. It would have to run up to Sir Jeffry's study and nowhere else.'

'My Cat Jeoffry leaps up to catch the musk,' Max quoted. 'Very well. You win. Onwards. Or more correctly, downwards.' Even he was getting excited, Cara detected with pleasure.

Downwards it was. Nothing like a cellar to dampen enthusiasm, Cara thought, as they went down the steps into the brick cellars. Thankfully there were two sets of steps, as she couldn't have faced walking down the steps near to where Daphne had been found. Another set led down from the end of the dining room serving area, and – Cara calculated – would be much nearer where any connection with the Archives Room might be found.

'Here,' Max pointed to the inside corner which must be, Cara estimated, where the dining room above met the conservatory. At that point the stonework looked its thickest bulging out slightly into the cellar. 'This is the most likely point.'

All guesswork, but Cara agreed. Nevertheless, although the

stonework reached up to the ceiling, there was nothing to indicate any possible stairways.

'Back to the study,' Alison decided. 'Let's tackle this job from the top first till we know what, if anything, we're dealing with.'

That was sensible but it seemed to Cara as they turned to leave that the bulging stonework was almost winking at them. I've won, it seemed to be crowing. But Alison was right and they made their way up to the Archives Room again, her hopes beginning to rise once more.

'Right,' Max said briskly, as they surveyed the turret area again. 'A thorough search this time. First move?'

'Ripping the webbing off the floor first,' Cara said.

'Agreed.' Max bent to set the panel in motion. 'I heave, you applaud.'

'We'll be too busy hoicking you up to your feet again,' Alison muttered.

'Panel down ahoy!' Max pressed the magic button and the panel slid slightly less reluctantly this time down to the same position as before. 'Would you like to pull up the webbing, Cara?'

'You bet I would.' Cara eagerly changed places with Max and began to tug at the webbing, with Max and Alison hovering by her. She couldn't budge it.

'Is it fixed? Try all the way round,' Alison said anxiously, leaning over her. Still no luck. Then she felt something hard under her hand. A stone? No, too long and narrow. 'There could be something here,' she crowed, on her knees now, leaning inside the hidey-hole to tug harder. And up it came and the whole of the webbing and the wood it protected with it.

Cara could hardly believe what she was looking at. It *was* a trapdoor. Just as she'd hoped. A large one, which lifted backwards fairly easily. And beneath it . . . Max and Alison were on their knees at her side, shining a torch. Beneath it was a huge square hole, perhaps three feet across, and at two corners a few inches down Cara could see two beautifully carved bronze cats on guard.

Max cleared his throat and spoke first. 'They look as proud as though this were a Pharaoh's tomb.'

Alison, peering over Cara's shoulder, yelled, 'Steps!' just as Max bawled out: 'A baluster.'

At first that was all Cara could see, save that the steps and the baluster must surely continue downwards. This, she knew, was *it*.

'What are you doing?' came an anguished cry from behind them. Robert Broome had unexpectedly joined them and was gazing with horror at the sight before him. So much for his not being here today. 'What's that hole?' he cried in dismay.

'Come and see,' Alison invited him shakily, making room for him as he advanced cautiously towards them.

'A stairway. Probably going down to the cellars,' Max said briskly. 'Had you no idea it was here?'

Robert shook his head, still looking mesmerized as he peered down for a quick glance. 'Those cats look like Ptolemaic bronzes.'

Max pulled him back as Robert tried to get closer and Cara retreated. 'A few security checks to be made, methinks, before we let anyone near it. Including us.'

Belatedly, Cara knew what she had to ask now. 'Could Daphne have used this if it is a stairway down to the ground floor?'

Silence. 'No,' Alison eventually said. 'Not her style at all.'

The idea of Daphne clambering up a narrow stairway not knowing whither she was going was remote to say the least, Cara thought. And yet . . . A light shone at the end of this tunnel, metaphorically speaking. 'She might have known it was here though,' she suggested, a picture beginning to build in her mind.

Robert was ashen-faced. 'She was in here once or twice when I wasn't here. But I never heard a hint about this hole. She did like the Smart poem though – she kept questioning me about it and must have decided to do her own research in the annex. That's where she fiddled with my files and books when I wasn't here. But it's possible she did find this.'

'I could go down a little way,' Cara said hopefully, moving towards the open turret door again. Max neatly stepped in front of it.

'Health and safety, Cara. Neither you nor anyone else is going down those steps till we've had the experts in.'

'Do we tell the police?'

'Of course. They – and Lavinia – should be very grateful to us, especially you, Cara.' A pause. 'What, I wonder, would Lavinia have made of this conundrum?'

Alison groaned. 'I knew it. She was bound to have a say in it.'

Max looked at her reproachfully. 'Of course. She was a wise woman. Studying her portraits both of herself and of others, I can spot secrets that Lavinia had in her deep understanding of life but kept to herself. But in my portrait of Queen Elizabeth I understand the importance of strength and confidence in her mastery of life's problems. That is what we need today. You've given us that, Cara, no matter whether this hidey-hole is a step forward or not.'

Cara gaped at him in amazement, as Alison and (rather reluctantly) Robert applauded. 'Me?' she asked.

Max was still in full flow, however. 'There's one more thing I think I should mention.' Now he did pause, beaming at his audience. 'This stairway has been used in the not too distant past.'

'How do you know that, Sherlock?' Alison asked, while Cara was still struggling for words.

Max preened himself. 'There was a biro caught up in the webbing.'

Hidey-holes? Secrets? Unsolved murder? Dizzy with question marks, Cara stumbled her way back to the Happy Huffkin. All that, coupled with Max's amazingly kind words – it was a lot to take in. But where did it leave her in the quest to prove Mike's innocence? Those question marks reared their heads like writhing intertwining snakes. Was the new hidey-hole a step towards finding Daphne's true killer, which Mike most certainly wasn't? Or was it completely irrelevant?

There was more to think about too. That bulging stone wall in the cellars – was it really the end of the steps that they had seen? Somehow it didn't seem in keeping with the elegant cats they'd seen in the turret.

After Max's declaration they had agreed that tomorrow they would look further at what presumably was the end of the stairway. But it was a big assumption to make. Cara had promptly volunteered to go down to the cellar to inspect its inside corner and one more discovery had been the result – or rather a deduction still to be proven. This was if the stairway did extend to the cellar then its entrance would extend to roughly three feet further in from the cellar corner. That didn't fit with the bulging stonewall they had seen and still needed investigation. Poor Robert, Cara thought. He had been happily installed in his Archives Room, never dreaming of the history surrounding him. Or, it occurred to her uneasily, was he all too well aware of what that stairway might reveal? Daphne's murder had ripped through the bond that kept the staff together.

Were they following in Daphne's footsteps with this discovery? It was hard to believe given the sheer importance of the find. She could have been the innocent victim of someone else's plans, given that the stairway had had recent use. The Archives Room was not far away from La Galleria. Could Max be right and Lavinia Fontana played a part in this story after all? There was nothing else of any monetary value on the same floor. It was possible that the stairway had an exit on the first floor too, but Sir Jeffry would not have wanted a door in any other part of the house than his study, given its primary purpose. Too risky, Cara decided. However, if Lavinia was now back in the picture – so to speak – how, when and why had the stairway been active in recent times? It wasn't certain that it had been used, of course, and maybe only the top of it had been disturbed. More information was definitely needed *quickly*. How long would those safety checks take, she wondered impatiently.

Max would tell Andrew Mitchem about the find. No question about that, of course, if only because a possible additional entrance to the cellar and orangery might help clear Mike of suspicion.

The Happy Huffkin seemed a welcoming refuge when Cara called in there before returning home. Exciting though the discovery of the stairway had been, it opened up more than a dark secret. Whether it took Daphne's murder case any further or not, it was a step into the unknown, into darkness, metaphorically as well as literally. And where darkness dwelt, danger could be lurking – and she'd get another lecture from his lordship the DCI.

Already there were lots of questions needing answers, she thought. For instance, could Robert really have been ignorant about its presence after three years working so close to it? Yes, she decided. After all, even Max and Alison knew nothing of it. Sir Jeffry must have chuckled, she thought, when he presided over the plans for the house. And Dan: had he never suspected its presence? Or Ewan, who was constantly on the prowl for enlivening his tours (and career prospects)? Or Keeley in her housekeeping role? Or Rosalie?

Cara shivered, guiltily relieved that she worked here at the café – just a little distanced from the Towers, both physically and mentally. Tomorrow, however, was another day. New doors might then open. But what lurked beyond them?

THIRTEEN

There's nothing like the smell of baking to make you feel that all's right with the world, especially now. The moment Cara stepped over the threshold of the folly on Friday morning, it wafted over her and the world seemed a happier place. Sammy must have come in early today and, since there was plenty of time to prepare for the afternoon, that meant she would have the time to explore the hidden stairway. Her qualms disappeared.

There was an immediate hitch to her plan. Sammy appeared from the kitchen as soon as she called out to him, which wasn't his normal habit. Her heart sank. Grey clouds seemed to be looming.

'Message,' he announced.

Definitely not normal. 'Who from?' she asked, bracing herself for trouble.

'Mr Max. Ten o'clock. Library. Everyone.'

Not only not normal, but formal. What now, she thought feverishly. Would Max have arranged this just to announce the discovery of another hidey-hole? Unlikely. Nor was it normal for him to call a meeting at all. That was Alison's province. Was it to do with Mike? Unlikely to have a meeting to break that kind of news. Had the hidey-hole anything to do with this? Too soon, so again unlikely. Was the meeting just to keep morale high?

Stop speculating, she told herself. Even so, staff meetings like this were comparatively rare, especially at short notice. It wouldn't have happened in Sir Jeffry's time nor in the nineteenth century. No way would the servants from 'downstairs' have been informed of what was going on 'upstairs'. That made her think of the lord who had once murdered his valet and was rewarded by being hanged with a silken noose because of his rank. Fortunately she was lucky enough to be working side by side with Max and Alison.

Good. Keep on thinking about something else. There must

have been murders at Tanton Towers over the past centuries, Cara supposed. She vaguely remembered hearing about Sir Thomas's crazy brother Horace having met a suspicious death when he tried to dispute his twin brother's succession. And the same fate had awaited the sister of Sir Jonathan Farran when he married Lady Jane Pryde and insisted on moving to the Towers with them. His sister had unfortunately turned out to be a practising witch with the nastiest of habits and apparently had to be dealt with. Just stories – but back went Cara's mind to the horror of Daphne's death, which was all too real and recent.

Was it significant that Max was holding this meeting in the library? Would it affect the future of the Towers? Would the murder leave a legacy of horror?

'Wants me there,' Sammy grunted. 'Dough proving.'

The huffkins would have to be sacrificed if the dough didn't meet Sammy's standards. After all, Cara told herself, the meeting might be about yesterday's find. Keeley had arranged chairs in huge semi-circles around Max and Alison's, so that it looked fairly convivial – helped by the appearance of the coffee machine on the trolley. It wasn't going to be enough to serve all these people, for there were more than Cara had expected. She recognized the garden and car park staff as well as the Towers' staff and volunteers.

Max and Alison were already seated facing the semi-circles and their worried expressions brought back her fears. It hardly needed Max's rise to his feet followed by his grim statement to confirm them.

'Last night the police contacted us to tell us that they've applied for permission to keep Mike Hanson under arrest for another two days.'

So there it was. Cara's hopes plummeted. Mike was seriously in trouble. How could this have come about? She had been so sure that the DCI was on the wrong track – not only because had Mike an alibi, but because physically attacking his wife would be out of character. Sudden spurts of anger were alien to him, and if by any wild chance he had planned Daphne's murder, it wouldn't have happened where it did. She was still convinced that somewhere something had gone very wrong.

'The present media publicity is going to continue,' Max was

saying. 'It will worsen not only for him but for us all if he's charged and the case goes ahead. The spotlight is going to be on Tanton Towers and it's probable that some of us will be called to give evidence. That will affect us all not only during the trial itself but in the months leading up to it.' *And not for the better* was the unspoken message.

Give evidence. Cara would almost certainly be one such witness, she realized with dismay. How much of what she had told Andrew Mitchem would she have to repeat on the witness stand? Moreover, it was highly possible that Daphne's true murderer was in this room and would be rejoicing at this awful news about Mike. She looked around at the assembled company. Even Simon Harris was here with one or two faces she recognized from the Twerps. She could see Ewan leaning forward, listening intently. Had he heard about the stairway? Was he already planning tours to run up and down it? Perhaps he was *pleased* about Mike's predicament. Dan looked his usual relaxed self, with his elder statesman expression, which usually meant he was thinking of how to use this situation to his advantage. Cara reproved herself. It was she who had thought the staff so united, her friends – and yet here she was mentally tearing them to pieces.

Keeley was looking utterly distraught, although Alison would surely have warned her of the news in advance. Rosalie, however, looked as composed as usual. Robert, who had been so shaken yesterday (or seemed to be) about the hidey-hole stairway, looked almost as upset now.

Max hadn't finished. To Cara's slight surprise, as they hadn't yet finished the search, he did go on to describe the discovery of the hidey-hole stairway by her, Alison and himself. That naturally brought a lightening of the atmosphere and stirs of excitement.

'Can we use it?' someone immediately asked.

'Not yet. Health and Safety,' Alison replied for Max.

'How does this affect Daphne's murder?' a querulous and familiar voice asked. Cara craned her neck to see who was speaking. Sure enough, it was Simon Harris.

Max's reply was simple. 'We don't know.'

That stairway had been yet another secret for Tanton Towers, Cara reflected as she left the meeting. How many more were there?

Were there more surprises to be found in the Towers, either physical or sinister secrets held close to human hearts? And if so, whose?

Secrets. Despite the welcome news that Michael Hanson was still suspect number one, Simon Harris seethed with rage. He had suspected that stairway must exist and had been keeping it secret to make a grand announcement at its discovery, at a time of *his* choosing. After all, Max treated him as the true historian he was. That had given him carte blanche to study the Towers, but his plans were now ruined. Once again it had been Daphne's fault. She had completely ignored his status, treating him as an amateur. She even dared to tell him she could help his career by sharing authorship with him on his book about Tanton Towers. Then she had gone too far. 'I'm on the track of a great big adventure,' she had cried with such excitement that you'd think she'd walked on the moon. But she wouldn't tell him what it was, so it could have been the hidey-hole in the dining room or this stairway. Daphne was dead now, but here was Cara committing the same crime. She was becoming too inquisitive about Tanton Towers . . .

Secrets. Everyone had secrets. Ewan congratulated himself that, despite that, his career was going nicely now with a clear path ahead of him. Daphne was gone and Mike was likely to be charged with her murder. The rumour he'd spread about him having an affair with Keeley had gone down nicely. Unfortunately, there was now Cara. He had had a lot of time for her, but she was definitely stepping on his toes. Her finding that hidey-hole in the dining room had caught him on the wrong foot. He should be seen to be making these discoveries, otherwise his leadership over the guided tours and associated benefits would be shaken. And now she could claim to have discovered this other more important hidey-hole with probably a huge stairway leading down. That must have been what Daphne was boasting about.

Old Sir Jeffry must have had fun with that stairway, Ewan reckoned. There he was sitting in his study swigging illegal brandy. That was his masterpiece of a secret. One now blown because of Cara and Daphne. There was Daphne, smug as a bug – 'I think I know what happened to the smugglers' brandy.' He should have been the one at the forefront of the discovery. That woman deserved all she got. She'd no idea of the importance of sharing knowledge. He'd decided to have another shot at getting her to divulge the secret, but she wouldn't talk about it. It could have been either the one in the dining room or this new stairway. She'd been as white as a sheet when she saw him the day she died. Frightened of him, maybe. Well, poor old thing, she got her come-uppance. He wouldn't have wished that end on her, but she was all too good at stirring things up and getting in people's way. And, unfortunately, Cara was of the same ilk.

Secrets. Dan thought about his position carefully. Every stately home had its secrets, and sometimes they were secret to the current owners. As in this case. There was nothing to worry about, he decided. Why was there a fuss at all about hidey-holes, especially this new one? It wasn't as if they were true priest holes, because they were eighteenth century in origin. The Towers was full of oddities anyway. That was its allure, so why was Max even bothering to pretend that this was something special? Dan had never been able to understand Max. Was he really the absent-minded professor he liked to appear? It was only relevant as one day there might be a very nasty shock over that Lavinia Fontana collection, which might, he realized, possibly rebound on his own head, even though he hadn't been sure about those paintings. No one would pick up on them now. In his very private opinion, Max's beloved Lavinia Fontana was vastly overrated. Her praises were only sung because she was a woman. There were plenty of women artists around at that time, but Lavinia was her own best self-publicist.

Dan comforted himself that his secret could lie fallow for as long as he liked. After all, it didn't really matter because the collection was never going up for sale. He'd only praised the collection to Max to be tactful. He liked Tanton Towers and luckily the job suited him. It gave him the status he deserved, and Max had been admiring his Lavinia Fontanas so long that he didn't really *see* them anymore. Anyway, on the plus side he'd encouraged Max to buy that Elizabeth portrait. It was a pity that Daphne Hanson had begun fussing around though.

Secrets. After he left Max's meeting, Robert had only one wish: to rush back to his archives where he felt safe. Documents were history; they could not be changed unlike this modern life where there was nothing to be relied on. Everything – and everyone – changed. 'My Cat Jeoffry' had been displayed on the turret base ever since he came to work here. It was a fixture. He could not be blamed. There had been no mention of it when he came to work here although it was true that his predecessor had shown some concern about possible illegal access to the house. He couldn't have meant this dreadful stairway though or he would have specified how and why it had been installed. Robert felt some guilt that he had never mentioned that possibility to Max and Alison. He comforted himself that there had been no need, as there were no available facts pertaining to this.

For five years now, the Archives had become his own private refuge. He had felt secure, a king of his own tiny kingdom. That was until he moved up to this floor and Daphne Hanson had begun her intrusions, tiptoeing around his files with her fingers to her lips. 'I'll be very quiet. I'll just tiptoe around. You won't even notice me, I promise.' She had been pleasant enough, he supposed, but she had definitely been smug, especially recently – he'd suspected that she was holding something back for that foolish book she was writing. He'd even shown her on the Sunday before she died the precious diary of Sir Reginald Farran Pryde which included his service in the Zulu War in 1879 and the birth of Alfred, so well-known for his service in the First World War.

Daphne was obsessed with the smuggler era, however. Her problem was that she didn't realize that history required the careful analysis of every scrap of evidence available. Judgement could only be made after seeing the whole of a subject, not just the part that applauded one's argument. That took time, as his own planned history would testify.

Robert sighed. If only life could be normal again. Life was safer that way. It was all very well for Max to talk about secrets, but what constituted a secret in Tanton Towers? Was it simply the recipe for Tanton Tart, for instance, which Cara had tried to make based on an old recipe she had found, or had Daphne discovered these hidey-holes? She hadn't shared it with him anyway. She had been vague on what her purpose was when she arrived at his office early on the day before that fateful Wednesday, showing no great excitement. Then he had been called away from the office and had returned to a terrible sight.

Not only were Alfred's account books, together with the valuations from his local auction house, Messrs Blink & Marlowe, strewn over the top of the dresser in the annex, but also the diary of Sir Gerald written in 1870 covering his preoccupation with the Fontana paintings. Sir Gerald had guarded them by keeping one loaded shotgun by his bed and another poised for action at a strategic point wherever they were displayed or stored, convinced that they were all under threat from robbers.

And there was the diary before his horrified eyes, Robert recalled with horror. It was open and face-down, thus straining the delicate binding. Even his predecessor had not been impeccable in his handling of ancient documents, but Daphne did not even understand the importance of taking care of them. She was bent on her search for smugglers' stories.

And Daphne herself was simply standing by those valuable books and scattered documents, staring out at nothing, clearly bored with Sir Gerald and only thinking of her smugglers. He had of course reproved her not for the first time on her carelessness. She had briefly apologized but clearly thought nothing of her transgression. It had been that very same day when an hour or two later she had thrown herself into his arms just as he was returning from a speedy lunch up the staircase to his desk. He would not have wished her terrible death upon her, but sometimes fate dictates the unthinkable.

'What did you make of Max's news, Robert?'

Robert stiffened. As usual, Dan was marching in as though he were the major-general of Tanton, which in a way, Robert admitted, he was. Dan lost no opportunity to remind him of that, he recalled bitterly. He would dearly have loved to do some major-generaling himself in his own field, but he never felt justified in throwing his credentials at anyone especially at 'the world'. The 'world' so far as he was concerned was full of social media, where nothing could be checked and everything, however wrong, could apparently be announced as 'truth'. Thankfully he could be sure that his own contribution to the world was valid; the truth about Tanton Towers, with *all* its secrets, was under his control. He was the Keeper of the Records.

'Must have been a bit of a shock to you, finding that hidey-hole stairway in here.' Dan went over to peer at the turret alcove where Max had barred the way to the 'My Cat Jeoffry' panel for safety with a large No Entry sign. 'Or did you know it was there?' he added offhandedly.

'I did not,' Robert said firmly. 'Otherwise Max would have been informed.' Yes, that was the way to put it.

'So our Cara was behind it all.' Dan was still staring at the panel. 'Seems to me she's behind quite a few things.'

On balance Robert decided it would be good policy to agree. 'Yes.'

'Seems odd you had no idea.'

Careful now. Where was this leading? 'No one had,' Robert said offhandedly. Laugh it off, that would be a good policy. 'There's not even a whisper of it in the records. I'd have picked that up immediately.'

'Good old Sir Jeffry again, eh? Keeping the brandy for himself, eh? Or did he use that stairway to lure his mistresses up here unobserved?'

Trust Dan to come up with that idea. Robert was appalled. This was a haven, a study where Sir Jeffry and his successors could devote themselves to the glories of history, not to idle pleasure.

'There is no evidence for that at all,' he retorted sharply.

'Steady on,' Dan replied mildly. 'No need to get fired up. We need to stick together, Bob. We don't know where this Daphne affair is leading.'

Robert hated being called Bob. 'Her murderer might or might not have been caught, but do they really think they have solved the murder?' Dan went very still, he noticed.

'What do you mean by that?' Dan demanded.

'Even if he's charged, they still have to prove it in court. Suppose they can't.'

'Do you mean suppose they have to look elsewhere?' Dan was ashen-faced.

Robert was fired up now. For once he had the upper hand. 'Could be,' he said airily. That would give Dan something to think about and, if Mike wasn't proven guilty after all, Robert didn't want to feel those DCI eyes turn on him.

Secrets. Keeley Martin was sitting in her office which had once seemed a paradise, the centre for the best job she had ever had. Now it seemed a prison. There was a rumour going around that she was having an affair with *Mike.* As if! It had always been Ewan. What would happen now? The police said she might be called as a witness. That was a laugh. On whose side? Mike's? Or the police's? How could her evidence help? Just because she'd seen Daphne crying in the ladies' loo the day before she was killed, and when out of the kindness of her heart she'd asked Daphne what was wrong, she just replied that probably nothing was.

Now even the police seemed to think she and Mike were a couple. She felt like a pawn in a game of chess that she hadn't wanted to play. Ewan wasn't being much help. She wasn't sure she was in love with him but they'd had a good time. It had saved her at a bad point in her life when her partner had just walked out after five years together. Ewan hadn't asked her questions, they just hit it off. She was friendly enough with Mike, but he didn't talk much about Daphne and she had had the sense not to ask. Nevertheless, she'd picked up a thing or two about antiques and all that stuff from him, always her weak point. Her statement to the police had been as honest as she could make it because she couldn't see Mike as a murderer. But who would the police settle on next?

At last Cara was able to survey the scene. The cellar looked full of nothing very much, unlike in the glorious (or otherwise) smugglers' days of old. There was a collection of old bags, disused machinery, empty wine crates and a few old chairs and tables. Fixed to the walls were a cupboard or two and old bookshelves. For all she knew there might be priceless antiques amongst the apparent rubbish, but she wouldn't bet on it.

At the Happy Huffkin she had finished her share of the preparations for the afternoon influx of visitors. *Another* three coach parties were due, so the public interest in Tanton Towers had obviously not diminished and the press announcement that Mike was being questioned for another two days would intensify it.

This might be good news for the café with increased takings and indeed for the Towers itself, but it wasn't for her nor, she imagined, for some of her Tanton Towers' friends. She looked at her watch. Good. Twelve thirty. She had been given the OK by Alison – rather reluctantly but with the pressure of so many visitors she'd given way.

'I thought I'd find you here.'

The familiar voice behind her made her jump. Andrew Mitchem seemed bent on hounding her. What could he be doing here otherwise? 'Why?' she demanded.

He looked contrite. 'When I saw you set off from the café I guessed where you were going. I needed to check out your hidey-hole from both ends.'

'Couldn't one of your officers do that?'

'They could,' he agreed, 'but I'm a mere human being. I can stare at all the evidence before me, agree with it and still feel the need to experience its reality. Walk the ground myself.'

She looked at him suspiciously. He was straight-faced and so she'd take that lofty diagnosis as genuine.

'Does that mean you have doubts about Mike?' she asked hopefully.

'No, Cara. It's still an ongoing investigation.' He obviously saw her indignation, but he continued: 'I assume you're here for much the same reason. You found the hidey-hole yesterday with Alison and Max, didn't you?'

'Yes, but not this end,' she admitted ungraciously. 'It's more complicated than we thought.'

'Let's find that dratted stairway's end. It can't be that difficult.'

'Done.' She grinned, oddly pleased about this practical step forward. 'Though there's nothing much to see so far. It's at that end.' She pointed. 'The cellar goes another three feet further than the orangery wall.'

'I can't wait. Or rather, yes I can. I'll start at the smugglers' tunnel exit to double check whether it could have been used in connection with the case and work my way round this cellar. The tunnel has a security system of its own, of course.'

She glanced at him in surprise. He had done his own homework, not just left it to his minions.

'Yes, but timed as the main house,' she explained, 'so if you're thinking that anyone could use the tunnel to reach the stairway to get access to the house before the security system kicks in, it wouldn't work and especially not now because the tunnel is firmly locked against intruders at both ends except when Ewan or workmen are there.'

'Do you have a key?'

'No,' she said, 'but the staff would have access to it.'

'Quite.' Andrew Mitchem had strolled back to the tunnel entrance – which had a very twenty-first century lock on it. He was staring at the entrance, which looked, Cara always thought, more like a saintly church door than one built for criminal purposes. 'Your Sir Jeffry had an eye for the absurd,' he observed. 'Not only building his own tunnel but a complicated way of delivering the goods.

'Right,' he continued briskly, 'I know that one flight of steps takes you up to the orangery. I'm interested in finding out if that stairway you've discovered in the Archives Room might have influenced my case, so whereabouts are we in relation to that and the famous turret?'

She'd be glad to stop imagining all too vividly Daphne's killer here with Daphne standing unsuspectingly in the orangery above. 'We think the hide-away stairway starts along here marked with a substantial stone base around it.'

'Let's make a start.' Andrew Mitchem strolled along inspecting every inch of the walls until Cara was hopping up and down with impatience. No need for that, surely. At least the cellars boasted modern lighting. To be stuck here in the dark would not be pleasant.

'Here's the point where we think the stairway may be,' she said, stopping at the cellar's inner end. He regarded the stonework thoughtfully.

'Possibly,' he agreed.

'But on the other hand, the stairway must extend about three feet from the cellar end.'

'Let's consider. Does that affect anything?' he asked.

'Yes, because the only possible place the entrance can be is here, but there's no sign of it in the stonework. It's not big enough,' Cara pointed out. 'There's nothing else apart from this old broom cupboard.'

About to turn away, Cara stared at it for a moment. It didn't look much or big enough to miraculously hold a stairway inside it. And then she saw it. 'Nothing but *that*.' With rising hope, she pointed to an old painting on the cupboard door so faded that the subject was no longer visible. This rickety old cupboard had surely stood here for yonks and looked as if it hadn't been in use for decades. True it wasn't big enough, but it was worth looking at.

She pulled the door open with some difficulty, aware of Andrew Mitchem breathing heavily behind her. All she could see were several garden brooms stacked upside down and looking as though they had been there for ever.

'Those brooms look pretty old.' She stepped aside for him to see them.

Pretty old? The moment she had said that, the adrenalin rushed in. How stupid of her. That's what they were looking for, wasn't it? Signs of an ancient hand at work?

Andrew Mitchem peered into the dark interior, grabbed the brooms and pulled them out. Or rather tried to. The first two came out, the second two did not. They seemed stuck to the rear of the cupboard for some reason and were supporting old bottles, one on each broom. That was weird, Cara thought, hardly daring to hope.

'Let's give it a try,' he said matter-of-factly.

Try what? Then Cara saw his point as he tugged at them.

'It's a door,' he breathed. '*Of course*. In fact – ' he gave a final pull at the bottles – 'these are the door handles.'

Two separate doors opened stiffly and slowly towards them. And inside – glory be – she saw the foot of what must surely be the spiral stairway. What's more, there were *bricks* not stonework here. Hadn't Robert been boasting about a document about bricks being delivered in Sir Jeffry's time? She'd assumed they were for the house, but it was far more likely that this was a special order for this stairway. A *very* special stairway. She caught her breath as she looked at it in wonder. On the wrought-iron handrails above the last step sat a magnificent brass cat supercili- ously staring out at them as if to say he was well aware of his heritage, thank you.

On the walls surrounding the stairway were the faded remains of what had once been a huge painted parade of more cats. Stepping cautiously inside with Andrew pressed up behind her, Cara could see on the inner side of each door the familiar panel of 'My Cat Jeoffry', each with several lines of the poem engraved on it. And in front of them were the stone steps of the spiral stairway undoubtedly leading up to Sir Jeffry's study.

'That's it,' Cara crowed in delight. 'We've found it.' 'We'? That seemed a natural word in the circumstances.

'I agree with you,' Andrew Mitchem commented, looking almost excited, 'that from the lawn the extra width of the stairway would be unnoticeable. Sir Jeffry was a clever chap.'

'Good,' she managed to say, her head beginning to whirl as she tried to cope with all the possibilities that this new development opened up.

'We know that according to Professor Farran Pryde it's been used recently,' he continued, 'but it seems odd that over all this time the family hasn't investigated and found it.'

Cara tried to think this through. 'Why should they? We wouldn't have found it if we hadn't been looking for it, even though someone must have used it recently. There's the small window which is visible but that could just have been taken for a window in the house. Air and light could be managed without alerting the house. Anyway, someone in the past must have used it. The baluster is wooden. That would have rotted if it didn't have attention over the years, and the iron too.' She paused, trying to second-guess him.

'Max and Alison knew nothing of it,' she added awkwardly.

'Quite.'

FOURTEEN

The only thing that had been normal about today, Cara decided, had been unstacking the dishwasher ready for tomorrow and the lingering smell of baking scones. Despite the progress they had made over the stairway, she felt flat, as though they were circling round the problem of Daphne's death. Usually she enjoyed this clearing-up process because it was a preparation for the next day in which new faces would present themselves, making her feel part of the Towers' life. Today, it was just a tiring job after all that had happened.

Everything looked the same but nothing was. It was almost – she hesitated, then let the thought emerge – as if Tanton Towers were a fortress that had closed its doors on its secrets, leaving her outside, like the boy in the poem who hobbled up too late. Everyone else had followed the Piper of Hamelin through the doorway of the mountain but he found it shut fast against him. She had rushed in here with the best of intentions, but had reached that closed doorway. Even the discovery of the stairway's route seemed to add to her frustration, for the simple reason that she still could not link it to Daphne. Admittedly that was completed only an hour or so ago, but she could see no way ahead that would help Mike.

The mere existence of another possible means of entry into the building ought to have some bearing on it, she told herself. For anyone with access to the keys to the smugglers' tunnel it would have been so simple to come into the cellar and up the steps to the orangery. That meant she was sure Andrew Mitchem had Mike in mind, but it could apply to any of the other staff, especially Ewan of course. She felt she was living in limbo, waiting for the magic link that would tie all these secrets together and produce the right answer – whatever that was.

As if in answer to that, she straightened up from stacking the chairs and saw Andrew Mitchem trudging across the lawn towards the orangery. Her heart sank. Not again. She'd thought he was leaving directly after they had parted as security was about to clamp down.

'Did I keep you too long?' he called over to her.

He looked tired, she thought, as he switched his trajectory and walked over to her. Where was the full-steam-ahead guy she'd been with earlier?

'I often stay late, and anyway it's not even seven o'clock yet,' she replied. A pause. 'Were you looking for Alison and Max?'

'Yes, where's the best place to find them without setting off the bells of hell?'

'Use the door phone at the family wing. They have supper around eight o'clock, so you've got an hour in hand.' He would probably know all this, Cara thought savagely, just as he would know that this was not the quickest route for him to have chosen. What was he playing at? Come to that, what was she?

'Are you about to leave, Cara? I'd like another word with you.'

Immediate warning bells. 'Something's happened?' she asked cautiously.

'No, I can't stop now. Could I call in at your home later?'

On guard. Did she want the intimacy of an invaded home again?

Best to get it over with. 'Yes, but I've an early rise tomorrow.' She immediately kicked herself. How on earth would he interpret that? Would he think she had assumed he was going to stay overnight? Too late if so, she couldn't pull back.

A fleeting grin. 'Point taken. I'll only be a short while.'

'Fine,' she replied. Well done, Cara, she thought crossly. I've stepped into the minefield all by myself.

Home, sweet home. However, when she got home it didn't look as welcoming as usual. No kicking off of shoes, looking at the post, checking emails, switching on TV. Instead it was a matter of skimming round, plumping cushions and general tidying up.

Andrew arrived about forty minutes later. Andrew? Is that how she was automatically thinking of him, she thought crossly. Why do that? Although he wasn't exceptionally tall – maybe 5 feet 10 inches, he seemed to dominate the cottage as he came in – even without hitting his head on the beams. She promptly dismissed that thought. He didn't accept her invitation to sit down at first, until she demanded he do so on the grounds that he was towering over her and they couldn't have a discussion. They were two wooden marionettes dancing around on strings.

'I needed to tell you something,' he began awkwardly, 'but I had to see Mrs Farran Pryde and Professor Max first.'

This wasn't going to be good news. 'Tell me the worst,' she said resignedly.

'We've released Michael Hanson.'

Different emotions shot through her. Disbelief, relief, bewilderment, doubt. Thankfulness. At last! But take care, she warned herself. There had to be a hitch. 'That's wonderful news,' she said cautiously, 'but could you arrest him again if you find more evidence?'

'Yes. His release doesn't mean he isn't still under suspicion.'

'Why not?' she asked indignantly. Of course. Nothing so simple. He was playing cat and mouse with her.

He looked embarrassed. 'I can't say more than I have.'

'But I can,' she said vehemently. 'It's because of the DNA, isn't it? As there are masses of reasons that his DNA would be found on her, you have to release him because you haven't found the real murderer.'

'Well reasoned, Cara.'

There was nothing to be said. She had to get her thoughts in order, aware that he was watching for her reaction. She couldn't oblige him on this. Whatever she said would achieve nothing.

'I should be going,' he said formally, rising to his feet.

She followed him to the door, shaken by his visit. Was it her imagination or was he actually at a loss as to what to say next, not the cocksure DCI she'd taken him for?

'Goodnight, Cara.' He stopped as he reached the door. 'If you find out anything more that might have a bearing on this case, however trivial it might seem, I need to know immediately.'

'But who else . . .' She stopped. It was merely a platitude on his part. Obviously, he couldn't answer.

He did in fact – in his own way. 'That, Cara, is the question.'

Another pause, then: 'You look tired,' she said impulsively.

'It's been a long day.'

And not a good one for him, she realized, despite their success over the stairway. 'Are you . . .' How to phrase this? 'Actively looking for someone else?'

She thought he wasn't going to answer as he stood on the doorstep. But again in his own way he did. 'Yes, and actively, but all options reserved.' A pause, then: 'Cara, when I was a kid, I heard a story about an old woman looking at a painting. She looked and looked and then she *saw*. I'm still waiting for the moment when that happens for me.' He stopped for a moment, then said, 'I don't like the way this case is going, Cara. I can't stop you hunting for this killer, but I can warn you. You're playing with fire.'

The news of Mike's release had spread quickly. Chiefly, Cara discovered, this was because Mike himself appeared on Saturday morning, a trifle hesitantly but nevertheless he was here again at the Towers. The whisper had gone round and when she heard it she rushed over to Mike's second-floor office. And there he was at his desk, rising to greet her.

'Welcome home, Mike.' Cara hugged him. 'So good to see you back here.'

'Thank Robert Broome for that.' It was clear from his drawn face that he was still feeling the pressure.

'Why?' Cara was instantly alert. What was this about? Andrew had said nothing about Robert being involved.

'It's quite a story.' Mike seemed eager to talk. 'It was obvious they were set on the DNA line, but I reckon their evidence was only that Daphne seemed to have been under the impression that I was coming to take her home, but if so I don't know why she would wait in the orangery. And anyway, she knew I was going home early.'

That was Rosalie's story too, Cara remembered.

'I suppose,' Mike continued, 'the police line is that after driving home I could have doubled back up the hillside to the smugglers' tunnel having pinched the keys, then nipped up the stairs to the orangery where by chance Daphne was standing right there for some reason I can't fathom . . .' His voice broke. 'So I murdered her for no apparent reason.'

'Poppy-cock.'

'So's the alternative they've probably dreamed up,' he said miserably, 'judging by their questioning. It's that somehow I scuttled back into the Towers after checking out at the gatehouse, hid up here in my office and popped down to the orangery when no one was looking. I've just heard about that secret stairway you've discovered, so maybe they'll re-arrest me thinking I used that.'

Her head was spinning. 'Hardly practical.'

'Especially since Robert might just have glimpsed me rushing past him to jump into the secret passage,' Mike continued gloomily. 'Anyway, he always goes down to the library at five o'clock and locks the Archive Room.'

'No wonder they had to discharge you. Do they want you to check in or are you completely free?' She remembered Andrew's caveat all too clearly.

He shrugged. 'I've no idea. But here I am. Waiting till they find out who really killed my wife.'

Daughters. Always loved. Always irritating just when you don't need it. For Cara that day was today. She had been longing to see Kate during her summer break, even if just for a few days, but now her own plans were truly busted. Pie in the sky. Facetime on the computer or phone calls were hardly the same as a good old natter and a hug. Kate's news, when she called late that evening, had come out of the blue. Instead of just a hello-and-this-is-the-time-my-train-arrives-at-Maidstone-so-pick-me-up-please, it was: 'Sorry, Mum, but I've scrapped that job I took in France. Indonesia's back on the schedule. I'll be away for a while, but I should be able to get down to see you for a day or two in late September.'

Great. Thanks, Kate. But all Cara could muster up was: 'Wonderful for you, darling,' and, 'Yes, of course I'll pay for your trip.'

'Thanks.'

The good thing about Kate, Cara reflected, was that she always realized when she had gone a step too far. That was quite something for a twenty-year-old who – if she remembered how she had felt at that age – had only one person right at the front of her mind. Herself. Now Kate was usually taking a real interest, which was decent of her, considering that most twenty-year-olds were not given to involving themselves in antiquated mothers' lives. True, murders at stately homes aren't that common. Kate, however, was too much like her mother, Cara feared. That was a relief because she wasn't confronted by memories of Kate's father, who had melted away quicker than ice cream in an oven when she informed him she was pregnant.

If she wasn't going to see Kate in person, she reasoned, she might as well tell her the whole story now and not wait until she was in Indonesia. Phone calls to the other side of the world were expensive – and rarely helpful.

Kate listened for a while, then interrupted: 'Have you checked out that new hidey-hole you found?'

'No. Closed for health and safety. We've been told it's been used in the not-too-distant past, but we don't know when. Ewan won't be running visitor tours up and down it yet.'

'Is Ewan that cute guy who looks after the events?'

'Fancy him, do you?' Cara retorted.

'Too old. He must be thirty at least. Is he still aiming to swing through the treetops like some ancient Tarzan?'

Cara laughed. 'Not quite. He has the bright idea of turning trees in the woodland into a children's area with tree houses and the like. So far Max hasn't been convinced, so Ewan's hell bent on his smugglers' tunnel.'

'Maybe that's how the murderer got in,' Kate commented. 'Who have you got lined up for that role?'

Cara sighed. 'This,' she said severely, 'is not a game. They're all my friends.' Or were, she thought sadly.

'Perhaps that's what Daphne believed.'

Ouch. Sore point.

'Who else is in the line-up for Miss Marple's consideration?' Kate continued. She listened quietly as Cara ran through her list, feeling more and more a traitor as she named each person.

'I think,' Kate said at last, 'that Robert Broome is the dodgy one.'

'You said he was rather a sweetie last time you were here,' Cara whipped back.

'Did I? I remember that he never looks people in the eye. Sure sign he's guilty. He's dodgy anyway.'

'He's just shy,' Cara said defensively.

'OK, have it your way,' Kate conceded. 'What about that old guy, Dan?'

'Possible,' Cara conceded. 'He pops up to La Galleria quite often.'

'Ah, La Galleria.' Kate giggled. 'The prized collection. Dear old Lavinia Fontana. Actually, she is quite wonderful. Planned her life brilliantly, thanks to her dad. Whoops! Sorry,' she carolled. 'Dads are forbidden territory. How would I know though?'

Beyond the pale, that one. 'You know all there is to know about your father,' Cara said crossly. 'Do you need to know every kiss and cuddle?' Tonight she was in no mood to brood on the past.

'OK. Point taken,' Kate said contritely. 'Back to Dan. I met him once. He's creepy too.'

Cara sighed. 'You only think that because he's in his fifties, which apparently goes side by side with creepiness for you.'

'He's far too jovial,' Kate decreed.

Cara battled with this. 'He's just defensive.'

'If you say so. Hang on,' Kate ordered. 'My pizza's ready. I'll be back but I need to turn the oven off.'

And this, Cara mused, was the daughter she had painstakingly encouraged to think in terms of healthy, home-cooked food.

Having ensured the safety of her supper, Kate returned with another idea: 'What about that Simon moron you mentioned? He was close to Daphne, wasn't he?'

'As close as Cain and Abel,' Cara agreed.

Kate crowed over this one. 'There's your murderer then. Now, you've ruled Rosalie out but there's this Keeley woman you told me about last time we spoke. What on earth would she see in an old man like Mike?'

'A reasonably well-off old man,' Cara observed, trying to see it from Kate's viewpoint, 'in the prime of sex life.'

Kate chuckled. 'You're getting the hang of it, Mum. Don't look at the romantic side, look at the basics.'

'I wish you'd take this more seriously, Kate,' Cara retorted. 'And anyway, the affair never took place. She's someone else's problem.'

'Sorry, Mum. I'm interested in Simon though. What's he like? I don't think I've ever met him.'

'He seems to me a slippery fish. But,' Cara added hastily, 'he's not on the Towers' staff. A grace and favour visitor when he likes, although totally lacking in grace. Bachelor, as far as I know. In his fifties.'

'You're fond of misfits.'

'Only ones I like, certainly not him,' Cara whipped back at her. 'Let me ask you something. Judging by what I've told you, who do *you* think murdered Daphne, as it's not Mike?'

'My answer: no idea,' Kate replied blithely. 'But if I had to pick someone I'd look at that Dan, plus I'd look deeper into that hidey-hole.'

'For that diagnosis,' Cara told her solemnly, 'I'll make you muffins for tea when you next deign to bless your home with your presence.' Then she remembered what Robert Broome had told her and added, 'On the day before her death, Daphne was raving with enthusiasm at some discovery she didn't explain, but the next day she was anxious and also very subdued. Unlike her.'

Silence while Kate pondered this. Then: 'Did Robert have any reason to strangle her? Anything to do with that secret stairway?'

'Hardly. He was annoyed at her disarranging his books and files, with which she'd obviously mucked around in her explorations, but no mention of the stairway. He was as surprised as we were when it was discovered.'

And yet, Cara realized, as she ended the call, what was so special about those Archive Room's files and books that Robert even mentioned them? Because, she supposed, that was just Robert all over.

Sunday had been a blessed day of peace – which Cara now defined as a day when she didn't have to worry about Daphne. She needed to concentrate on the Happy Huffkin and the Towers. Once upon a time Mondays had been one of her free days, but not at present. The Towers was not officially open but the staff had all opted to go in during the current circumstances and therefore the Happy Huffkin would cater for their needs. That needed preparation.

She had slept uneasily on Sunday night and had woken up today still sure that the stairway had something to do with the murder. Now that the good news had come about Mike, there was even more urgency to find out the truth or he might be re-arrested. She was quite sure that DCI Andrew Mitchem (no 'Andrew' now) was hard at work with the same thought in mind, although for different reasons.

Sammy was going to be late in today so, after she'd finished working out the statistics for the café's week ahead, she sat down at a window table in the folly to assemble her thoughts on the Towers. From where she was sitting she could see over the top of the orangery the brick side wall that she now knew shielded the stairway. It looked so obvious now and yet so natural.

It was the Archives Room itself that she kept focussing on. She tried to put herself in Sir Jeffry's shoes – which looked extremely uncomfortable, judging by what she had seen of his attire in the room that Alison devoted to eighteenth-century fashion. Sir Jeffry would have sat there at his study window overlooking the gardens, awaiting his next consignment of brandy up the secret stairway. No, that would surely come during the night. The idea of those smugglers coming up that spiral stairway, casks clasped to their bosoms, one of them at least carrying a lantern, was an appealing one – if one didn't have to do it.

On impulse, she glanced at her watch. She would have time to nip up to the Archives Room now. If Robert wasn't there, she could borrow the keys. Sure enough, when she reached it the door was locked, so it was back down again for the key.

Once inside, she studied the possible layout of the furniture in Sir Jeffry's day. Yes, that's just where he would have sat, whether back to the window or facing it, and maybe even at the present desk which looked old enough. Would he be able to see anyone popping up from that secret stairway? Yes, he certainly would. There would have been a journal, perhaps *The Monthly Review*, before him, ink, plumed pens and so on. She imagined him waiting for a delivery via the stairway. He would know when delivery day was and would be expecting friendly smugglers, perhaps in search of payment if that hadn't been settled at the cabin on the hillside. He might have locked or bolted the stairway at any other times. He would always keep an eye on it, certainly – just in case the Revenue or any other enemies rushed up it and out into his domain.

Cara shivered. That was enough scenarios. With Robert absent, this room was, she acknowledged, sending up far too many vibes – almost as though Daphne were still around, warning her of danger. Nonsense. Cara tried to shake off fear but the stillness and silence were beginning to get to her. There had to be something more here. On the wall to her left, was the portrait of Sir Jeffry himself. His wife's portrait had been banished to the annex under the arch where she couldn't keep her beady eyes on the intake of brandy. Where, Cara wondered, would the drinking glasses be kept? On the floor by the stairway entrance? Unlikely.

And then the door opened.

It wasn't Robert, it was Dan. Having marched in, he was barring the exit with his burly figure. Smiling, of course, but a trifle forced, so it seemed to her. Her imagination surely, but all the same she decided to tread carefully.

She pulled herself together. 'Hi,' she managed to greet him.

He nodded. 'Where's Robert?'

'On his way.' She had no idea whether that was the case, but it sounded confident.

'Are you here to poke around the stairway?' he asked flatly, moving towards her. Instinctively she drew back, feeling trapped at the table. Nonsense, she thought. This was Dan with whom she'd worked amicably for years. One part of her brain reasoned that fear was ridiculous, the other side battled with it. It was a draw.

'No, and I can't show it to you,' she managed to reply, 'because Health and Safety are still at it. Forbidden territory.' Light laugh. 'So I'm just off,' she added brightly, sliding out from behind the desk, 'but Robert will be along soon.'

'I'll tell him you wanted to see him,' Dan said casually.

Nothing to worry about. That was a relief. 'Thanks,' she replied, making her escape. This, she told herself, was ridiculous. She, Cara Shelley, scared of imaginary evils? They simply didn't exist. Dan was Dan. The man she'd always known, helpful and good company, if a bit on the starchy side. Nothing had changed – except of course for Daphne's murder, which she was doing her best to help solve and anyway the police were investigating it. No one would risk another crime while they were around. Nevertheless, she had to remember as doubt returned, the murderer was still at large. *That* was not a welcome thought.

Once in the corridor, she relaxed. A group of Keeley's cleaners
was making its way down the staircase to the first floor and she
hurried to join them, staying with them as they made their way
down the grand staircase where the portraits stared down at them
in disdain. Discretion had been the better part of valour, she
decided, and returning to the Happy Huffkin had never seemed
such a good idea. There it was, she thought thankfully as she
drew nearer – and there was Sammy plus only three occupied
tables.

Two hours and many customers later, however, Cara was left
with a nagging feeling that she had left her task in the Archives'
Room incomplete. There was more to be learned there, though
not with Dan present. At last she could wait no longer. Stupid
perhaps but, as the last table left, she decided to return to the
battlefield, that being the Archives Room at present, where hopefully if anyone were there it would be Robert. She was in luck.
He was.

'I dropped in earlier, and Dan was here. What did he want?'
she asked as casually as she could.

He looked surprised, so she deduced that Dan hadn't waited
to see him. 'I was interested,' she continued, 'in those files and
books of yours that Daphne disarranged. Were they anything
special?'

He looked even more surprised, as well he might. 'Everything
here is special,' he said severely. Then he relented. 'There were
two books which she carelessly left lying around in the annex,
a diary and some very precious letters, all lying tumbled in a
heap on the dresser shelf. Please do be careful, Cara,' he pleaded
as he followed her into the annex.

Andrew Mitchem had given her much the same advice,
although he wasn't concerned about the historical material but
about possible danger to her. She comforted herself that there
could be no danger from Robert. She'd known and liked him
since the day she opened the café.

Cara looked at the bookshelves, which were part of the old
wooden dresser and provided a flat space in front of them which
is where Daphne must have misbehaved with the files. The books
seemed innocuous enough, including a book on the Kentish
custom of Gavelkind, Lambarde's *A Perambulation of Kent*, and

an ancient leather-bound volume which might be Sir Reginald's diary of his military career. They looked in impeccable order now and it was hard to see what might have attracted Daphne, although the reprint of Sir Hugh Plat's *Delightes for Ladies* written in 1609 certainly attracted Cara.

'Did Daphne ask to borrow any of these books?' she asked. 'Or to take away the files?'

'Only staff are permitted to remove anything from this office and then only with my permission,' Robert informed her smugly. 'I offered to arrange an appointment for her to continue studying but she wasn't interested in that. She was a very strange woman.'

'So, what did interest her about them?'

'I'm truly not sure, save that everything about Tanton Towers enthralled her, naturally enough. I'm sure she was fascinated by these books on Kent. Those in the annex are here because in theory they should get less handling. Except by Daphne,' he added crossly. 'The covers are in excellent condition and most interesting in that they—'

A sudden thought made Cara cut across him as she stared at the bookshelves. 'Was she looking *at* the books or behind them?'

'I can't say,' he replied stiffly. 'There's nothing behind the shelving but the wall panelling.'

Panelling? That rang bells. 'Can I look . . .' She put out her hand purposefully towards the books.

'No!' Robert squealed, but it was too late. She was already busy pulling them down.

'Please do *not* do that,' he cried in great distress. 'I'll have to report this to Max,' he added miserably as she took no notice but feverishly continued dragging books from the shelves.

'*Look!*' Cara still paid no attention to him. Victory! The shelves had no backing of their own and she could see more panelling behind them, more carved roses. Just like the hidey-hole in the dining room. Just suppose . . . She studied them carefully. The stems of those roses, were they really stems or something else? Was that a crack or was she imagining it? It ran all the way down the panel too . . .

'*Please* be careful,' came the voice behind her, not squealing now, but sharp. That wasn't Robert's usual style – but she had no time for that now. What was before her was taking all her attention. Pressing, turning, trying to move that panelling this way and that. There had to be a way. But nothing worked, nothing moved, nothing even looked hopeful.

Tears of frustration filled her eyes and were running down her cheeks. Ridiculous. This was just Towers' mania, dreaming up scenarios. One of those roses looked slightly bigger than the other, but so what? It was all hand carving; no machines used in the carpentry of this gem. She thumped it more forcefully than she'd meant to – and felt it give under her clenched fist.

A noise that she remembered all too well. *It was happening again.* Inch by inch. The door was moving and not one but two whole panels were sliding open, revealing all too clearly what was within.

An initial screech from Robert was cut short as Cara stared disbelievingly into the dark interior. There were no more shouts from Robert and she was silent. They could both see what lay in the musty-smelling depths of this hole.

It was a skeleton.

FIFTEEN

'I didn't know. I didn't *know*!' Robert yelled over and over again.

By this time they were in Max's office, having left the Archives Room locked with a No Entry sign on the door. When she first came to Tanton, Cara remembered, the annex had still been used for storage. She'd assumed correctly that it had always been part of Sir Jeffry's study and that its furniture and fittings had remained where they were. Even the portraits on its walls still hung there hopefully awaiting a brighter time ahead. Now they had it, she thought grimly, though whether Sir Jeffry and his second wife appreciated it was in doubt – especially as the first wife's portrait was opposite the hidey-hole with the lady staring out at them looking very disgruntled, as though this situation was nothing to do with her.

Cara's stomach was still turning over, and she suspected that Alison and Max felt much the same, as they were all unusually quiet while they waited for the police's arrival. For once there were none left on the premises, and attendance had been very patchy in the last few days. When Max had telephoned about their awful discovery, the very mention of Tanton Towers had meant not a routine police officer to inspect a skeleton but the transfer of his call to a detective inspector, and then onwards up the chain. That would mean DCI Mitchem, of course. This was no ordinary skeleton. This was a Tanton skeleton.

Such crazy thoughts continued to rush through her mind as she struggled with what they had seen. From the brief glimpse of it, at first she'd assumed that the death of this victim could be laid at Sir Jeffry's door, but that had given way to the sickening realization that from what she saw of the skeleton's decaying clothes it did not look as though they dated from the eighteenth century. No tee-shirts and jeans in Sir Jeffry's era.

Max remained quiet, but Alison broke the silence by stating

the obvious after Robert finally ceased his agitated wails of innocence. 'It can't be too old.'

Robert abruptly stood up and rushed out of the room. No need to wonder why. He was going to be sick.

The more awful the possible explanations for that skeleton's presence seemed, the more Cara knew she had to blurt out what was on her mind.

'Robert told me about Daphne's shocked appearance the day before she died. Could she have found *it*?'

Alison reacted immediately. 'Yes.' Then she changed her mind. 'No. She'd have screamed out for help, not kept quiet.'

Max broke his silence. 'Not necessarily,' he said, as Robert returned, ashen-faced. 'Shock brings odd reactions.'

'I believe that Daphne did find it here,' Robert said miserably. 'I thought she was just pulling books off the shelves to read but she might have tugged them out for access.'

'That would suggest she did know or had suspected the hidey-hole was there or, worse, that the skeleton was there too,' Max pointed out.

'You and I didn't know it was there,' Alison said plaintively, 'and we live here, so how could she have known?'

'I didn't know either,' Robert bleated again. 'And I'm the historian. Daphne would surely have told me if she knew about this hidey-hole.'

Cara summoned up what emotional strength she had left. 'Suppose the skeleton is quite recent,' she suggested. 'Were there any days when the house was open for visitors when you weren't here, Robert?'

He shook his head. 'Of course not. I am always here, and I ensure it's locked when I leave. It's just not *fair*!' he burst out. 'I'm always here. I didn't *know*.'

'Then it's likely this atrocity happened before you moved up to this floor, Robert, although that skeleton has to have been put there by someone who knew – or knows – the Towers,' Alison said flatly.

'Which means in all probability he died here too,' Cara added. Should she have said 'he or she'? No, the remains of the clothes definitely looked fairly male. She forced herself to face the inevitable. The police would arrive shortly and questioning would begin. Robert looked very shaken, but that was natural enough if he genuinely had no idea about that hidey-hole and its contents.

Max had been meditating. 'To state the obvious, it was murder,' he said out of the blue. 'No idiot would climb in just to look around, even if it was only a storage place at that time.'

'Yet another hidey-hole down to Sir Jeffry,' Alison said wearily. 'He must have spent hours designing them,' she said bitterly. 'Are there any more, I wonder? The casks could be whizzed up the stairway and into their own little hidey-hole just so that he could have fun.'

'It isn't fun for me,' Robert said forlornly.

'Taking it that the hidey-hole is old but that skeleton is from fairly modern times,' Max said, 'it can't be very recent or you, Robert – to put it politely – would have suffered from the smell for a long time.' He rose to his feet. 'I can hear the house bell. The police must have arrived.'

The clap of doom. Cara steeled herself.

'I'll come down too, Max,' Alison said, going to join him. 'Cara,' she added apologetically, 'do you feel up to whipping up coffee for the troops?'

'This isn't a social event,' Max pointed out soberly.

'Didn't Alexander Pope write that coffee makes the politician wise?' Alison countered crossly.

'He concluded with,' Max shot back at her, '"and see through all things with his half-shut eyes." We, my darling, are not politicians.'

Cara hastened to the rescue. 'I'll serve cappuccinos. Especially good for police officers.'

Not only for police officers. They were all going to need cappuccinos.

'Trouble, eh?' Sammy cast one look at her face as Cara reached the café.

The police had already installed themselves and she had had to stop to make an initial statement. There had been no sign of Andrew Mitchem.

Sammy cocked an eye at her. 'Skeleton in the closet, eh?'

Cara grimaced. 'Word gets around.'

'Whole body? In bits? Smell, did it?'

'Charming,' Cara muttered. 'It was whole and no smell. Would you like a detailed description inch by inch?'

Sammy ignored this. 'What's up, Cara? Serious?' He peered at her keenly.

Cara managed a grin. 'It's not one of Sir Jeffry's antiques, but it wasn't put there yesterday either.'

'That inspector. Good man. He'll sort it.'

That hadn't occurred to her. He would probably be in charge, as the cases might be linked. Why should they be, she wondered. Only because of Daphne's odd behaviour on the Tuesday, she decided. Silence was out of character for her but that skeleton was neither very recent or very old.

'I suppose you're right, Sammy. I'm not doing too well in trying to solve the case.'

'Not doing well himself.'

Cara grinned, then sobered up. 'Thank you, oh sage. Of course, the skeleton might be older than I first thought – even if it was a tee-shirt I thought I saw, they go back quite a long way.' Knowing Daphne, she wouldn't have examined the skeleton closely, she thought, but surely she wouldn't be keeping the news to herself. She didn't run to Robert, but had she talked to Dan? If so, why not Alison or Max?

'He's here,' Sammy remarked dourly.

She turned to see the now familiar figure of Andrew Mitchem walking over to her, nodding at Sammy. What did he want, she wondered wearily. This would be an official visit. An interview or would she get away with a nice cup of tea?

'I need to talk to you, Miss Shelley,' he began formally. 'I've seen your statement to my colleague. You found the skeleton.'

Question answered. 'Through an idea I had about Daphne's messing about with books and files by those shelves,' she told him, trying not to sound belligerent. He had a perfect right to question her – just as she needed to try to explain why she had been crazy enough to start hunting there.

'My officers are looking into it,' was all he replied. He sounded stiff and if she hadn't known better she would have said he was ill at ease. He then stayed silent until she could bear it no longer.

'Cappuccino?' she enquired politely, waving him to a table.

'Please.'

Not so formal then. There was a pause while she went inside the café for the coffee but on her reappearance he promptly resumed.

'My grandfather used to pick hops somewhere around here. He was put in charge of hordes that came down from London to pick them every year. He sorted out the huts they lived in and kept them under his eye for good or bad. The smell got to him in the end. And to my father. Wouldn't touch beer after that. I know you're not licensed but can you ever serve it here?'

'Very rarely and only through arrangement with the Towers for any big events they put on.' Cara was impressed. It had been a long and personal speech and not from a high and mighty DCI. 'Any possibility this skeleton could be linked to your case?' she continued casually.

Silence. The DCI was back.

'I interpret that as a "don't know" or a "yes", then,' Cara continued, but she had to push further. 'If Daphne did discover both that skeleton and the stairway, she must have wondered whose skeleton it was, once she'd recovered from the shock. Why did she keep silent about it?'

More silence from him too. Nevertheless, she might be getting somewhere. 'Whoever the skeleton is, someone in Tanton Towers must have been involved,' she said bravely.

This he did answer. 'No comment.'

Good. That meant she was on the right track. 'And in modern times because of the clothing? Within the last twenty years or so?'

Back to silence.

'*If* it becomes important, could it be narrowed down to within ten years, perhaps?' Cara held her breath.

Silence.

Cara congratulated herself. Well, even that was progress. 'That implies that whoever killed Daphne might also have been behind that skeleton's death. But if she found it,' she belatedly added, 'that means she or someone else must have closed up the hidey-hole. That doesn't seem likely.'

There was still no reply, but she did not need one. It had been a daring leap but she had had a soft landing. She could go no further. With (presumably) herself and Sammy ruled out, Dan,

Ewan, Robert, Simon, Rosalie and, she supposed, ridiculous though it was, Alison and Max, might be under suspicion. Volunteers too? Outside staff? And the biggest question of all: whose was that skeleton?

That skeleton. Robert Broome realized he was staring into space at the Archives Room window. His mind was occupied with only one thing. That skeleton. He was, he considered, bravely remaining at his post while police marched to and fro through *his* place of work to the hidey-hole in the annex. The mysterious stairway to the cellar was also still troubling him, with health and safety people trampling everywhere.

His secure haven was no longer safe, for the dragons of the recent discoveries were breathing fire. This new hidey-hole with its awful secret coming so close on the heels of the stairway discovery signified that the unknown had truly burst upon him. He had thought all that was behind him, but it wasn't. It ought to have been, because if they established that skeleton had been there for over three years he would be reasonably safe from suspicion. His office had been on the next floor down. Anyone could have put the skeleton there because it had merely been a storage room.

Once upon a time the answer to any problem worth considering could be found in his records, whether it was to do with Sir Jeffry's magnificent creation of Tanton Towers or on any events or damage wreaked on it over the years. It was his fortunate job to ensure that Tanton Towers' history was preserved and accessible. Its sheer stability stood steadfast as a symbol that life's problems could be vanquished. In this room he had so often felt that Sir Jeffry was watching over him, beaming with satisfaction at what he, Robert, was achieving. Now it was under threat, despite all the steps he had taken. His kingdom needed protection but now everybody pretended to know as much as he did, even though this was *his* domain.

He had been badly hit with the shock of the police marching in. If he chose, he could just hand in his notice, but he wouldn't do that of course because it would look so suspicious and the police would seize on it now they had released Mike. Besides, in a way this was what he had been working for. He was the protector of Tanton Towers' heritage. He was An Authority. He wasn't like Dan – who had laid so many eggs in different baskets that he wasn't truly an authority on anything in this house. Dan had been nice enough to work with – unless you crossed him. Anyway, the death of the victim in the hidey-hole couldn't easily be laid at his own door, Robert thought thankfully. The Archives Room had operated downstairs and he had only joined the Towers' team five years ago. More recently than Dan.

That skeleton. Dan pondered how he could best exploit this unfortunate situation. It would be difficult as the skeleton had not been identified and nor could he even give hints of its identity until the police sanctioned it. There might be family involved or official records. There might be all sorts of ramifications that could have unfortunate consequences if it was proved to be linked to Daphne Hanson's murder. How could the police have evidence to do that? This skeleton could have been there for years and years. Even with the clothes, DNA, dental records and so on, they would need a starting point to identify it. No, any publicity stories at present would have to steer clear of making any connection, especially now that Mike had been released.

That sounded bad, of course, but it was only sensible that he should be the media voice for Alison and Max as he had been over Daphne's death. This new drama was just asking for him to step in. A murder like that spoke for itself and he had just stepped in easily as the media contact, but a skeleton needed more work. *Historical* work. He could make a good story out of it even though it seemed from the gossip that it had not been there that long. He needed to kick off immediately though, or Ewan would hog the limelight looking the picture of a youthful eager entrepreneur in the making. Ewan would never make it, though. Dan comforted himself that Ewan didn't have the expertise that all his own years' seniority and scholarship had given him. But there was Cara . . .

That skeleton. Yes, he could build on that, Ewan decided. Its discovery had been a shock, but he'd make the most of the situation. The newly discovered hidey-hole would be part of the tour, once the police had finished and the skeleton was gone. The real one, of course. He could have a replica popped in there, if he could cajole Alison and Max into it. That would be a brilliant idea to draw the crowds. No disrespect of course, and it depended on what the outcome of the police and forensic investigation team came up with. How could they discover the identity of the skeleton when no one knew who he was and could trace the family? It could be one of the volunteers. Anything to hurry the investigation along though, with the open day getting so danger-ously close. There must be something he could do about the situation in the meantime. After all, history flows on in ancient houses as everywhere and children loved a ghoulish story from the past – maybe he could hijack a ghost or two as well. Daphne's? No, he thought reluctantly. Too soon for that. Robert Broome wouldn't like visitors traipsing into the Archives Room, but he'd already spotted a way in which that could be managed.

He couldn't invent a story involving Daphne's death with the skeleton in case it was identifiable. DNA was a risk to any stories now, and one way or another the future looked uncertain. The main thing was to look confident. How better then to declare the smugglers' tunnel open on 16th August on the same day as the two new hidey-holes. He had plans for the first one and indeed for showing them off together. *Yes!* That was a fantastic idea. The skeleton (or a replica) could be a tour de force at the end of the tunnel tour for those who were brave enough – he could hear himself saying those dramatic words as he led his flock down into the cellars (and show them where Daphne had died too). And now there were two more hidey-holes, one of them with the results of yet another murder. What a tour that was going to be, eh?

Highly pleased with himself, he wondered what that creep Simon Harris was making of all this for his history of Tanton. Poor old Daphne had missed out on running the smugglers' tunnel visits. Now the last thing he wanted was for the skeleton to be identified, which would slow down the fuss over that and endanger the open day.

That skeleton. Simon was glowing with eager anticipation of what would lie ahead. The discovery of the skeleton had been a shock but in the long run was definitely a help. While everyone was concentrating on that, he himself could forge ahead with his history with a clear path now that Daphne was out of the way. His plans for an audio version would go side by side with it. Poor old Daphne would have been beside herself if she'd known about that skeleton, but as it was, he, Simon Harris, would benefit. He would deliver a credible story, not one jazzed up as everyone else must be planning. Things were working out very nicely for him and the future lay ahead like a golden path – if Cara didn't get in his way.

That skeleton. Alison was limp with exhaustion after Rosalie had left. Rosalie had given her the latest figures as Mike was not yet fully back to work. It might be good news financially for Tanton but the sheer pressure of all those extra visitors to Tanton on top of Daphne's murder was having its effect both on her and on Max, who was burying himself in La Galleria. At least Lavinia did not present a problem as the skeleton had. Alison was dismayed to realize that she had no idea whose the skeleton might be – but surely, as owners of Tanton Towers, she and Max ought to have some notion. It had happened in their home and she felt powerless to take up this problem and run with it. How could that have come about?

The only slightly positive side was that it began to make sense of all this recent talk of fakes and theft, which the discovery of that stairway down to the cellar had made just about credible. Recent usage of that stairway made it theoretically possible there could have been fakes in the past, though it required a big stretch of the imagination. Given that security in those days was hardly to be compared with modern methods, it was possible. And, she realized, the stairway also added a theoretical chance of more modern fakes. It was time that Max called in an expert to check La Galleria's paintings.

She tracked Max down in La Galleria (of course), where he had drawn up one of the chairs to scrutinize the portrait of Elizabeth I and decided to be ruthless about interrupting this vital work. 'Did DCI Mitchem say how long the forensic team is going to take?' she asked him.

'Weeks probably,' he said absently. 'But it doesn't affect us, does it? We've already thrashed the subject to death and we've no idea who it could be.'

Alison was silent. Obviously Max didn't want to have to face
the stark fact that the unknown victim had been placed in the
hidey-hole perhaps before the time that La Galleria was established up here. A storage room as it then was would have been
an ideal place to hide such a secret. Poor Sir Jeffry. He would
never have dreamed that his study could become a morbid tourist
attraction.

She braced herself for this more immediate problem. There
was no avoiding the fact that she and Max had to discuss it. 'It
does affect us, Max. Either we close down for a while, or we
carry on. That means more publicity, more visitors – all of whom
will be demanding to see the skeleton in the hidey-hole. Poor
Robert is really upset. On top of the turret stairway, this one is
too much. That's three hidey-holes, none of which we knew
about. We're hardly good custodians, are we? And what about
the staff? Ewan must be agonizing over the open day. Robert is
still going around assuring everyone he didn't know anything
about it, and even Dan's upset.'

'Calm down, darling,' Max merely replied. 'He might be upset
because he *did* know about it.'

This really riled her. 'No, Max,' she said sharply. 'We agreed
not to suspect anyone here of murder until we *know* for sure
who's responsible. I'm afraid Robert might give in his notice.'

'I doubt that. He's committed to the Towers.'

'I'm not sure it works that way,' Alison replied drily. 'The
ones who are committed are probably the ones who see personal
advantage in what's been happening here.'

'Cynical.' Max paused, then said, 'What's going on here,
Alison? Have we been wrong all along about what the Towers
means to everyone – to *us*?'

She could feel tears coming and fought them away. 'No, Max.
We're losing our way though. Maybe Cara will find it for us.'
She had meant that as a light-hearted pleasantry, but then it struck
her that she might well be right.

SIXTEEN

'How much longer?' Cara agonized. It had been two weeks since the dreadful discovery in the Archives Room annex and still the shock had not worn off. The police had clamped down on publicity, but somehow the news had wormed its way out and the strain was beginning to tell on them all. Alison had been in favour of the Towers closing temporarily despite the fact that it was now July and the holiday season was close upon them. Max, supported by Mike as the accountant, had been firmly against closing, so, silently, had Cara, and even more strongly so was Ewan because of his open day plans.

Ewan's pitch was: 'Historical horrors such as this are educational. Seeing where they took place is important to smooth the leap from history to the present day.'

'Splendid,' Alison had snapped. 'Suppose you explain that to Rosalie and Keeley who have had to deal with the surge through our doors. I grant you that Simon Harris is on your side, but that's because of the publicity for the Twerps.'

And, Cara thought to herself, the added excitement of the skeleton drew public attention to the Towers, although so far the Archives Room had remained out of bounds for visitors. As predicted, there were a great many of them.

'Really?' Max had been surprised. 'Would Simon think that way?'

'Oh yes. And,' Alison had informed him bitterly, 'Ewan's on your side too. It's only six weeks away and this skeleton is the wrong kind of publicity. Not good.'

Max had frowned. 'Closing down, even for a short while, will draw too much attention to the reason and suggest we have something to hide.'

'We have!' Alison snarled.

Cara had restrained herself from entering the fray. Wisdom comes with age, she told herself. Today, two weeks later, she

had as usual hopefully opened the Happy Huffkin even for the
trickle of business that the staff provided on a Tuesday – and
even in the shower that the weather gods had unthoughtfully
sent. Tomorrow the pandemonium would begin again, but she
suddenly realized that something unusual must be happening,
because she could see Alison once again rushing across the lawn.

'There's news?' Cara called out.

Alison was waving something in the air as she dashed up the
steps, sinking into the first chair that she could reach inside the
folly.

'I need an espresso first,' Alison meanly told her.

'Right away, ma'am.' Cara rushed to the kitchen. Sammy
wasn't here today as Tuesdays were set aside for his beloved
bowls game unless there was a dire necessity for his presence.
Bowls were his overriding passion after the Happy Huffkin, but
sometimes the folly won out.

'There,' Cara said, plonking first the espresso then herself at
the table, as an unsubtle hint that she wasn't going to move until
she had heard the news. 'A free cookie too,' she pointed out.

'Thank you.' Alison took a deep breath, a few sips of coffee
and then gave her the news, clasping the letter in her other hand.
'First, we can open the scene of the skeleton discovery tomorrow,
if we want to, and Max does. I suppose I agree.'

Tomorrow? Would that mean even more visitors? Cara had a
moment's panic. Could she cope without Sammy's presence?
She suspected that Alison had more to tell her so there were
more important issues at stake.

Alison read her expression correctly and said encouragingly,
'You'll do fine, Cara, as you always do. The news is that the
skeleton's male, fortyish, height about 5 feet 10 inches, well-
preserved teeth. It had been there between four and eight years.'

'So it's relatively recent.' Cara was unexpectedly dismayed,
realizing that she had been hoping against hope that the skeleton
would be older and therefore have no relevance to their current
crisis.

'Yes. That's from the DCI's very own letter. That's why I've
come to you, oh Great Detective. They've some DNA, thankfully,
but without a few ideas on who the man was, that isn't worth a
lot. Max and I are stumped. The only people with anything to

do with the Towers who have died suddenly or disappeared couldn't possibly be that skeleton.'

'I haven't worked here long enough to help there,' Cara said regretfully, 'but I don't recall any missing persons being talked about in my time here.' What had she expected? A magical solution?

'Your name came up and I think DCI Mitchem would welcome any direct input from you. I can see his point. You're one of us but you're detached.'

That was one way of looking at it, Cara rather reluctantly agreed. Moreover, she hadn't been here long enough, not like others of the current staff – and of course even Alison and Max might in theory be suspects. 'Does he know yet how the man died? If it was a man,' she added belatedly. They'd assumed it was, given that brief look at the clothing.

'That's the gory bit. I wrote it down.' Alison consulted a notebook. 'Yes to the sex. A small bone was fractured – as with Daphne the hyoid at the root of the tongue.' A silence, then she added diffidently, 'The police think he was killed manually.'

If Cara's heart didn't actually miss a beat, it certainly jumped. 'Like Daphne?' she managed to repeat. Images of what she had seen overwhelmed her yet again.

'It could be coincidence,' Alison added hurriedly.

'Agreed.' Cara made a determined effort. 'I suppose the clothes fitted that time frame.'

'Yes. The shoes were lying there separately as if they were tossed in after him. Did you see them? I didn't look very hard,' Alison added apologetically.

'Nor me,' Cara said wryly.

'He seems to be hoping that between us all at the Towers we can identify him. I suppose it's probable. It could hardly be a stranger dragged in here to be murdered.'

'His killer certainly couldn't have been a stranger,' Cara said bluntly.

Alison winced. 'I'm afraid not.'

Cara thought about this. 'Four to eight years. I've been here for only three years. Happy ones,' she added jerkily.

'And we render our thanks in the form of two murders,' Alison said sorrowfully.

'The skeleton's definitely being classified as murder?'

'Yes,' Alison replied. 'Suicides don't involve self-strangulation.' She broke off, then burst out: 'What's happened here, Cara? It seems as though all Max and I hold dear about Tanton is being swept away as if it was a mirage that didn't exist.'

'It did exist and it will again,' Cara vowed, 'when we get these murders solved.'

'You mean *if* we do,' Alison said bitterly.

'*When* we do.' This was brave talk, Cara realized, but she meant it, even though she was already getting the shivers. 'You realize there's now another motive for Daphne's death? *If* she saw that skeleton, suppose she made a shrewd guess as to whose it was – and therefore who might have killed him?'

Alison looked appalled. 'I hadn't got that far. It's a big jump but the DCI might be thinking that way too. No wonder he's still on the skeleton trail.'

Cara braced herself. 'Who of the present staff was working then? And who has left? Or,' it occurred to her, 'since we don't know exactly when it happened or what time of day, it might have been a volunteer who killed him. Or, perhaps, another similar semi-staff member – such as one of the Twerps.' This was sounding all too familiar. They were up against the same hurdles as with Daphne's death.

Alison groaned. 'You're right, of course. As for the staff, Dan was here part-time for the last seven years, and Ewan's been here six or so. I take it we're leaving women out, frail creatures that we are,' she added.

'Yes, if merely because of the weight of lifting a body into that hole. That could mean there could be more than one person involved in it. Do we exclude Robert?' Cara asked cautiously. 'He's been here five years, hasn't he?'

She would have loved to exclude him, but he had the best opportunity – or did he, she wondered. Robert wasn't working on that floor when he first came. Anyway, it didn't fit. He had seemed more concerned with Daphne's annoying habits than with her opening that hidey-hole – though he certainly disapproved of her meddling in his annex.

Back to Daphne then. A problem. Had she opened that hidey-hole or not? She would have screamed the place down if she had and not closed it if she saw the contents. If she hadn't seen it, however, why was she so silent when Robert returned?

'Yes,' Alison said. 'He's been with us five years full-time. Before that he worked from home part-time. Keeley came well after you did, Cara, but Rosalie has been here much longer.'

'And Simon?' Cara asked. 'He's always had the freedom of the house?'

Alison grimaced. 'Like Mike and Dan, he's been around for a long time, over five years anyway. Simon's always been interested in our history and wandering around for years, even before the Twerps started dancing here.'

'What about people who worked here then and have now left?' Cara asked again, getting desperate for any facts to cling on to.

'I'll check the records. I know I ought to have some ideas, but I don't,' Alison said despondently. 'I can't bring myself to realize that the Towers has been nurturing one if not more vipers in its bosom. I suppose,' she asked hopefully, 'the skeleton couldn't be just an errant visitor who got killed by mistake by his companion who then panicked?'

'One who knew that a storage room on the top floor had a hidey-hole? 'Cara enquired politely.

Alison managed a grin. 'No, I realize that doesn't sound too likely, but I'm getting to the point that I'm scared of finding out that Max is a multi-murderer,' she joked.

'Rest assured you won't,' Cara replied. He and Alison could be wiped off that list even if they could theoretically be suspects, as she herself had been, for the simple reason that neither of them would have entered with such enthusiasm into all her hidey-hole hunts if they had murdered and hidden one of their staff in one. 'Not unless a gang ran off with all his Lavinia Fontana masterpieces,' she continued, then had another thought. 'Could our killer or even the skeleton be someone on the staff who isn't working here any longer?'

Alison thought for a moment. 'There was an accountant called Peter Amos from whom Mike took over about six or seven years ago and there was a PR lady before Ewan swept in about the same time. They were both freelance so they both disappeared from the scene quickly. Mike had been working in insurance, so it was a good match for him to come here. His predecessor had riled everyone up, demanding concrete proof of every penny spent.'

'Laudable in theory, not in practice,' Cara commented, thinking uncomfortably of her own methods of record keeping.

'Quite. Mike's arrival of course led to Daphne's Twerps coming here regularly. Daphne started her prowling somewhat later. She was always entranced by the smugglers' connection. Then there was Robert. His predecessor, Tim Hargreaves, died on holiday in the Pyrenees. We wrote the family a letter of condolence. Robert had only worked part-time until then. Before Ewan, we had a bright spark doing publicity. I can't remember the details about that lady. Anyway, she left us.'

The devil's in the detail, so it's said. Cara ruminated on this after Alison's departure, the detail in this case being that Daphne could have been fixated on the Towers' romantic history right from her and Mike's arrival, even if she didn't begin her prowling immediately. A detail but it made a difference. Andrew Mitchem – she realized with mild surprise that she was now thinking of him by name not rank all too frequently – had professed an interest in her opinions. Would he thank her if she had ideas of her own about this skeleton? Probably not. Would that stop her? No. She was fired up now and would honour Andrew Mitchem with a visit. Definitely at work. Much too personal otherwise.

Charing Police HQ. An appointment with His Majesty. Cara fidgeted. As the time passed, sitting in the entrance hall of this purpose-built station waiting for Andrew Mitchem to summon her, she felt as though she were in handcuffs awaiting sentence.

Finally, he appeared as if from nowhere. 'Thank you for coming.' He was gazing at her with those intense eyes that made her think those handcuffs were hidden behind his back about to clamp on her. 'Shall we go to my office?'

Standing close to him in the lift, she began to regret this mission. Or, it occurred to her, was she merely regretting that she was clad in her old jeans and tee-shirt while he was dressed up in posh trousers and jacket? At least there was no tie.

'That skeleton,' she began, once established in his surprisingly small office at the rear of the building. 'Are you following up on the former staff at the Towers?'

'Try me.'

'Mike Hanson's predecessor?'

'Alive and well.'

'And their publicity lady?'

'Upward bound in her career.'

Not looking good. 'Robert Broome's predecessor who died in the Pyrenees?' Cara asked.

'So far we can't track down any family for DNA.'

'There must be a path to him somewhere.'

No reply. So that was that. Cara knew how to make an exit – and after five or so minutes of polite chatter she did so. It was frustrating though, to say the least. Was she being hood-winked into silence? Nothing so simple, she decided. What about that Pyrenees man whose family couldn't be traced? Everybody must have family members somewhere if one went far enough back in time. After all, she thought, look at all the people who claim to be descended from Elizabeth I. She was a strong lady who wouldn't let a few enemies stand in her way. Perhaps Lavinia felt the same and that's why she had chosen Lizzie to paint.

Get back on track, Cara, she told herself as she drove back to the Towers. She'd had enough of being at a dead end in this story. The words 'dead end' were a challenge in themselves. The whole Serious Crime Directorate had failed to turn up trumps for this poor man who had apparently died on his annual holiday, so she conceded her chances seemed low. But why should that stop her?

Somewhere in the Towers there must be a clue to his family and Alison would probably hold it if only she could recognize it. She must have known the family name because . . . Cara clutched at her memory. Hadn't Alison said something about a 'letter of condolence'? Didn't she also mention the word 'family'? His wife? She was family, and if he had been single then there might have been an ex-wife or children for the solicitors involved to track down. Cara's hopes rose. They almost soared. If only Alison could find a copy of that letter or an address or *something* to check out this possibility, it would at the very least tick another box.

Alison, an hour or two later when Cara had managed to track

her down, was none too encouraging. 'It would have been a handwritten letter,' she pointed out. 'We wouldn't have kept a copy.'

'You might have an address on your computer or at least in one of your office business files,' Cara said hopefully.

'It was a long time ago,' Alison protested. 'Even if there aren't paper records, there's probably something online. Computers store.'

'I'll check, Cara.' Alison glanced at Cara's expression and obviously got the message. 'Now,' she added in resignation.

Cara grinned. 'Just tell me,' she began en route to Alison's office, 'what happened to this Tim Hargreaves?'

'He died in an accident in France.'

'Yes, but was he buried there?' Cara persisted.

'So we were told. And I don't remember going to a funeral.'

'Who told you?' Cara asked patiently.

Alison pondered this, while Cara sat impatiently with fingers crossed so tightly they hurt. 'He seemed to live alone in a cottage in the village,' Alison eventually said. 'I think it must have been the travel agent he'd booked with who told us the news and that the funeral had already taken place in France. We were all horrified, because not only was Tim a first-class historian, but we all liked him. Robert had been working with him part-time so he took over the Archives Room right away. Max was rather disappointed because Robert isn't a Lavinia Fontana fan as Tim conveniently was. Tim knew his stuff where art was concerned, so he put up with Max's obsession.'

'The letter of condolence,' Cara said patiently, 'who did you send it to?'

'It's all coming back to me now,' Alison said thankfully. 'I asked the travel agent about his family, but they couldn't help, so I asked the village post office if they knew of any relatives. There was some unpaid salary to which his estate would be entitled. They gave me an address – a sister's, I think – to which post was being forwarded. So that's what we used.'

'And would you still have it?' Cara scarcely dared hope.

Alison awarded her a sweet smile. 'I can look. Her name wasn't Hargreaves, it was Mrs something else. And that's coming back to me too. It sounded vaguely Cornish somehow. Pol something. Yes, Pollard. That was it.' A pause. 'Shall I hunt for the address now?' Another sweet smile.

Cara graciously accepted the offer.

'Mrs Pollard?'

The door opened. At last Cara felt she was getting somewhere. Here was a lady who might, just might, provide the information that could possibly lead somewhere. Number 12 Hunter Street in this Kentish seaside village of Winton near Deal proved to be a small Victorian cottage perched at the end of a row which, with luck on her side, might house a living relative of Timothy Hargreaves.

Cara was greeted with a pleased smile of satisfaction. Mrs Pollard looked a comfortable sixty or so with the air of one who knew what she wanted and had it. No fashion model, no squeezed waistlines, no make-up and a happy smile. 'Come in. You'll be the lady from Tanton Towers, so you can't be after anything I've got lying around.' A jolly laugh. 'Come along then. Follow me, Mrs Shelley.'

Cara dutifully obeyed, noting the automatic Mrs awarded to her, and was led to a small living room where she was duly guided to a comfortable sofa which seemed to eye her up and decide she would do. No stiff cushions to fight her off.

'Come about my poor brother, have you? Cup of tea?' Mrs Pollard enquired.

'Thank you,' Cara said sedately. She was not a tea drinker, but if ever a house and owner decreed that tea was a passport to approval, this was it.

She was duly presented with a bone china cup and saucer five minutes later. 'I'm keeping it warm for him,' she was told.

Cara stiffened. Where was this leading? 'The tea?' she cautiously enquired, and was relieved to hear a cackle.

'Good gracious no,' Mrs Pollard replied. 'This cottage, I meant. Timmy rented a place in Tanton so to my way of thinking he'll have nowhere to go when he's back here. And he'll be back all right one day. After all, his seven years aren't up yet.'

Cara was thrown again. 'Seven years?'

'Can't be presumed dead before then. You see, Mrs Shelley, he has a lot to live for. He loves his job. A real history lover he is. And artist too. He and Mr Max have lots of laughs and quarrels over that collection Mr Max is so fond of. Tim knows a lot about art, he does. "They're fakes," Timmy told me last time I saw him. "Mr Max won't have it though." Timmy was quite sure. "You can always tell a fake – you just study it and sniff,'" he said. She beamed.

'Sniff?' Cara had never noticed Max sniffing, but maybe the sniffing was the metaphorical sort. It was time that she took charge of the conversation or she'd be lost in this weird interview. 'His presumed loss while away from home on that holiday must have been a big shock for you.' You're getting too stilted, Cara told herself. Calm down.

Mrs Pollard looked blank. 'What holiday would that be?'

Whoops. Here we go again. 'In the French mountains, where he died,' Cara said, carefully.

'When was this?' Mrs Pollard's face began to crumple, to Cara's alarm.

'About five years or so ago. Max was informed by the holiday company that your brother had died in an accident and his funeral had been held in France because no relatives could be found. Then Mr and Mrs Farran Pryde managed to trace you. They sent you a letter.'

Mrs Pollard breathed a sigh of relief. 'That's right. I remember that. They said what a good worker he'd been but they never said anything about funerals or holidays or I'd have remembered. I thought they were just sorry he'd decided to go off somewhere. That's because he's wayward, is Tim. Obstinate. If he wants to travel somewhere, he will.'

But he hadn't. Cara was increasingly sure of that. He had never left Tanton.

Mrs Pollard began to brighten up. 'But you mark my words, he'll be back all right. He's just missing, is my Tim.'

SEVENTEEN

Almost certainly that skeleton now had a name, Cara thought triumphantly. The idea of an absent Tim Hargreaves still travelling the globe was surely untenable, and the DNA would surely be a match now that Tim Hargreaves' sister had been traced. While they were waiting for that, there must be something she could do, she thought impatiently. But there wasn't – not without ignoring Andrew Mitchem's instructions. He had taken the news without comment, save for a courteous 'thank you', adding, 'You can talk freely to Mr and Mrs Farran Pryde but no one else yet, not even Mr Broome.'

That was reasonable, she reluctantly supposed. There would have to be official confirmation of the identification but the first stage was done and dusted, subject to DNA. It had been a blow to both Alison and Max because they had liked Tim Hargreaves and because his horrible death on their property was appalling. Thankfully they too realized that the net might now be closing in on Daphne's murderer as well as that of his killer, and there was surely a chance that they were linked. If so, the next outstanding question would be obvious: Why did both Daphne and poor Tim Hargreaves meet such an awful fate?

Cara pondered her next step. At least she wasn't forbidden to *think*. Tim's death was in the past, and not one that might endanger the safely of others today. Or was it, she thought uneasily. Had its discovery opened up a can of very evil worms? No matter whether it had or not, that next step would be to talk to Sammy, even though that meant disobeying His Majesty King Andrew's edict. After all, Sammy was not only an outsider, as she was, but as he had worked for Tanton for some years before the days of the Happy Huffkin, he might be a useful source of information where Tim Hargreaves was concerned.

'Do you remember Tim?' she asked him, having broken the news to him.

At first he merely nodded, as though he had suspected this all along – as indeed he might have done. Then he relented after examining the serving plate he was placing with great care with its fellows on the kitchen work top. Cara waited. This usually worked.

'Dogged,' he announced first to her bewilderment. 'Blooming puppy. Hung on. Something in mouth, shake it. Won't let go. Like old sock,' he added. 'Grrrrh.'

Another long speech for Sammy, but she'd press on. 'If Tim Hargreaves was your metaphorical puppy, could he have had something in his mouth about the Towers' history?'

Sammy ignored her. 'A loner was Tim.'

Looking hopeful. 'Could he have known about the turret stairway?' she asked. If he had then she could be getting somewhere.

'Can't say.'

'Women in his life?' she asked in frustration. 'Real ones or the ones in La Galleria? I'm told he liked art.'

Silence. Then he nodded. 'Liked pictures, he did.'

Theories galore galloped through her mind. 'Lavinia Fontana's?'

Silence, then another nod.

Well, that was something. 'His sister says he liked going off on his travels without notifying anyone.'

'Wouldn't know.'

She sighed. 'Anything else you remember?' she asked hopefully. 'Was he friendly with anyone in particular? Robert, I suppose, even though Robert didn't work here full-time.'

Sammy stopped his plate-laying. 'Maybe. Pally with Mr Dickson.'

She didn't want to push her luck, but she couldn't stop now. 'Why would he or Robert have a reason to kill him?'

'Wouldn't know,' he said grumpily. Another silence, then: 'Not one for art is Mr Broome. Tells you when Good Queen Bess kicked the bucket. With Mr Hargreaves it was how it was painted and why. And whether it's a fake.'

Cara stared at him in disbelief. Was this taciturn Sammy speaking? Targeting Lavinia Fontana? And that magic word 'fake' again. She would have another shot at this. 'Do you mean that portrait in La Galleria that Max is so fond of?'

'Could be.'

'It's an oddity, so Ewan points out on his tours,' Cara said. 'Alison told me the lifespans of Lavinia Fontana and Good Queen Bess overlapped. In theory that portrait could have been drawn from life; in practice they would never have met.'

She had lost Sammy's attention. It was time to put the huffkins in the oven, and a busy July afternoon lay ahead with visitors due to pour in in two hours' time. While she was performing her part in the familiar routine, she was busy thinking. Tim Hargreaves had been an art enthusiast, Daphne had been devoted to exciting stories in the Towers' history, so what was the link between the murders? Surely there had to be one, otherwise the coincidence was too great. Suppose both Daphne and Tim had found fakes in Max's beloved collection? Tim perhaps, but not Daphne surely. Far more likely that she had made the gruesome discovery of Tim's skeleton by chance, as Cara had done herself, and that had led to her own death. Cara shivered. That was a terrifying thought.

She mustered up her courage to take her thinking onwards. She didn't even know that Daphne *had* seen inside the hidey-hole. What evidence was there about that or indeed on whether she had found the stairway? If the latter, it could have been the reason that Daphne was snooping around the Archives Room to look for storage places for Sir Jeffry's liquor just as they had. The only firm evidence was Robert's statement that Daphne told him she had made an exciting discovery and that she was very upset when he had seen her the day before she died. Hardly the level of evidence that Andrew Mitchem would accept. Nevertheless, the strong possibility was that Tim Hargreaves' death had something to do with La Galleria and its precious contents and that Daphne's death had followed as a result of the discovery of his skeleton. Could that all stem back to the Lavinia Fontana collection and fakes?

'*Fakes?*' Dan stared at her. 'I've been through all this before. No way.'

'But if Tim was pursuing that line, you'd have known about it, wouldn't you?' Cara asked. She wouldn't give up just because he was blocking everything she asked.

'Not necessarily. He wasn't that kind of guy.' Dan seemed to be paying more attention to the arrangement of some papers on his desk than to her.

Good, he was clearly rattled. Cara switched tactics. 'Did you know Tim Hargreaves well? Did he just go off travelling without warning?'

The answer came in a rush. 'I wouldn't know. He'd have arranged it with Alison. He wouldn't go away for that long without giving notice. He used to go away for conferences and so on. I remember there wasn't a funeral. Robert took over and that was that.'

That was indeed that. An air of defiance had entered his voice. No more to be done. She was about to leave, however, when he said airily, 'He spent a lot of time up there in La Galleria not long before he went off on that holiday to France. He said he had something to show me, but he wasn't sure about it. That might have been about fakes. He'd have been wrong, of course.'

He smiled.

Fakes. She needed Alison's input before tackling Max, Cara realized. The suggestion of fakes had reared its head before and had been dismissed and the current security systems seemed to make recent fakes less likely. There had always been the practical difficulties of switching originals with fakes and removing relatively large framed paintings from the second floor without being noticed, but now the stairway suggested a more feasible and safer route.

Problem: if so, Cara fumed, why would it be necessary to replace them with fakes? Answer: to prevent the trail being picked up too quickly. Or because, Cara realized with sinking heart, the thief was in their midst. Certainly no paintings or drawings seemed to have gone missing from the collection and therefore installing fakes would have been essential, despite the chances of discovery being high. Even five years ago, which was when Tim disappeared, hauling them up and down would be risky to say the least, whether by the stairway or not.

A sudden thought, remembering her talk with Dan about fakes. Could Tim Hargreaves himself have been involved in such a plot? Steady on, Cara told herself. She was thinking herself into cloud cuckoo land. Even if Tim Hargreaves was the thief and had discovered the stairway, that theory didn't work. Tim had been murdered. Could the smugglers' tunnel have been used and he discovered that? Experts had confirmed that the stairway had been in recent use and so this theory became more likely as an exit route combined with the tunnel.

A thief from outside could have used that and then emerged into the Archives Room and along to La Galleria, Cara thought hopefully. Then a chill ran through her. Only, she realized, if the thief either had access to the keys of the house and tunnel, which meant surely that he or she was either on the staff or in cahoots with one of them.

Back to square one, Cara. She braced herself. What was outstandingly obvious was that there was now another motive for Daphne's death, and a terrifyingly compelling one. Once that DNA match had been confirmed, the secret would be out and Tim's murderer and Daphne's too were probably still amongst their ranks. And here she was, away with the fairies, having abstruse theories about faked paintings. She would sort this out with Alison *now*.

Murmuring apologies to Sammy, she tracked Alison down in the garden, persuading her with a coffee and a piece of Sammy's very special shortbread at the Happy Huffkin.

'What are you bribing me for?' Alison asked suspiciously, as Cara sat down at the table with what she hoped was a meaningful look.

'Another chat about Lavinia Fontana.'

'*What?* Now that, Cara, is unfair. I have to listen to that blessed woman being lauded to the skies every day, so why . . .' Alison must have read her expression correctly, because she changed course abruptly. 'Tell me the worst.'

'Tim Hargreaves. I expect Andrew Mitchem has discussed him with you.'

Alison relaxed. 'Yes. He hopes to have the DNA match or otherwise confirmed tomorrow. It's sad news, Cara, but thank you. We all liked Tim so, although we knew he was dead, the manner of his going is just ghastly. Especially when it's obvious that whoever killed him was close to us.'

Into action, Cara ordered herself. A lot might depend on this.

'I gather Tim liked art, so did he approve of the Fontana collection?'

'Adored it,' Alison said promptly. 'He was always chatting to Max about it. There were one or two in particular—'

'Good Queen Bess?' Cara interrupted. So far, so good. Her hopes rose.

'Yes, but there are the two we looked at when we went round La Galleria together. There's the one that makes it look as though Lavinia is putting herself forward as another Emmeline Pankhurst, demanding women's right to vote, and there's the portrait of that young man either setting out to rule the world or destroy it.'

Cara remembered both clearly. 'Are all the staff keen on Lavinia? Does it go with the job?'

Alison looked at her searchingly. 'You mean those who were here in Tim Hargreaves' time? If so, Dan was here then, Ewan, and Robert of course part-time. Rosalie but not Keeley. Simon Harris was also around and Daphne plus the Twerps and Mike too.'

'How involved was Daphne with her history hunt in Tim's time here? Could she have been looking for hidey-holes back then?'

'I doubt it very much. It's only recently she seems to have been talking about them. Before that it was always the smugglers' tunnel. She shared Ewan's enthusiasm for opening it up to the public. It might even have been she who promoted the idea.' Alison paused. 'There's going to be another staff meeting later today, so you should come.'

'Are you and Max happy about Ewan's open day?' Cara ventured to ask after thanking her. As an outsider, one of the few problems about her being so close to Tanton Towers and to Alison and Max was that she was fearful of overstepping the invisible demarcation line, even in such dire circumstances as these.

Alison pulled a face. 'I wouldn't say happy. It seems sneaky to make capital out of a tragedy and even more so now that Tim's skeleton has been found. But we've agreed to at least discuss the stairway openings in due course, plus I suppose this new horror hidey-hole. Not yet though. Poor Robert would have a fit if a tour party suddenly popped their heads into his beloved working space, and no wonder.'

'Like Sir Jeffry,' Cara commented, 'when his wife so inopportunely popped up in ghostly form. It's no wonder he kept a stock of brandy to keep his spirits up – so to speak. Sorry about the pun.'

'Odd you should say that,' Alison said. 'Daphne had an interesting thought on that. She noticed that Sir Jeffry kept his portrait of his first wife in his study's annex after he planned to marry his second wife. She was convinced he went for a snifter on the wedding day, turned around and saw the portrait and in a drunken stupor mistook it for a ghost.'

'*Daphne* thought that?' Cara cried out, as the import of this dawned upon her. 'Perhaps she *looked* for the hidey-hole then.'

'The portrait couldn't have been tucked away in it.'

'No, but it was hanging there opposite it.' Think, think, *think.* 'Suppose Daphne had pulled out the books and documents to read at some point,' Cara began carefully, 'and that led her to believe there might be hidey-holes somewhere around in the Towers. On the day we know she was so upset, she noticed the portrait of the first wife glaring behind her on the walls, remembered the story of the drunken Sir Jeffry seeing her on his second wedding day and wondered what had brought him to this particular spot. Could it be brandy and his hidey-hole? She tried the panelling – and found as I did that one knob was just a little out of kilter with the others. She pressed it and there was Tim Hargreaves.'

'It still doesn't answer the question of why she didn't scream the place down,' Alison pointed out. 'She might have even guessed whose remains they were, because she'd known him.'

Cara thought rapidly. 'Perhaps it was because this was a Tanton secret and she loved secrets. Even if she'd known him, she might have wanted to tell you first. But someone killed her.'

'A day or so later,' Alison said. 'And she didn't tell us.'

She was right, Cara realized, deflated. Perhaps this was leading nowhere. There was no proof that Daphne had opened the hidey-hole, no proof that her murder was connected to Tim Hargreaves and no proof that the two murders were connected. And yet . . . and yet . . .

Alison drew a deep breath. 'So what now? We can't take this

further until we officially know for sure it's Tim – and even then we're only working on supposition.'

Cara summoned up her energy. There had to be a way through this. 'Right now,' she said firmly, 'the spotlight's on La Galleria.'

'And fakes? Max isn't going to like this,' Alison said gloomily.

'I'll tell him then,' Cara offered nobly. This could be the start of a whole new battle.

'Fakes?' Max was bewildered. 'How can there be? I would have noticed.'

'You'd see only the paintings you love,' Cara replied, treading as carefully as she could. 'You wouldn't examine them closely each time.'

At least Max seemed to be taking this seriously, Cara thought with relief. Alison, she noted, had kept very quiet. Any fakes there would have to be fairly recent if they were linked to Tim or Daphne's death.

'We took over the Towers twenty years ago,' Alison said gloomily at last, 'and I don't think there could already have been unidentified fakes here. Max's grandfather had it all checked out as faking is a centuries-old gambit. What we're talking about now are the fakes that might have replaced originals in recent years. What do you think, Max?'

Max deliberated but at last he said, 'No. I can't accept there are *any* fakes here. Take Fontana's portrait of Queen Elizabeth I for instance.'

Cara's heart sank. He was on his bandwagon once again. The painting that had no flaws and was perfection itself.

'I look at that every day,' Max continued. 'I look at the frame, even its back sometimes, which is an art form of its own, with its history of sale and ownership. And then I look at the portrait. Although I accept that there is no obvious way in which Fontana and Elizabeth could have met for a live sitting, its provenance is clear because during her fruitful years in Bologna both Flemish painter Denys Calvaert and the Carracci family had training academies in the town and Calvaert had even been an apprentice with Lavinia's father. No doubt Lavinia was inspired by one of their portraits of the queen, studied the face, appreciated its hidden qualities and produced her own masterpiece. It is *not* a fake.'

'Forget Elizabeth, Max,' Alison at last managed to intervene. 'What about other possible fakes?'

'There is none.'

'Max, there's no point in using balance scales in an argument, if one side of it is pinioned to the ground,' his wife whipped back at him.

'Very well. I agree the idea of a fake being planted here many years ago is worth consideration,' Max replied grudgingly. 'Not in our time, however. Sold as fakes to my ancestors, perhaps, but the idea of thieves crawling up hidden steps into a room at some distance from the gallery, getting through the security system to La Galleria in today's world and replacing the genuine Fontana with an inferior copy is ridiculous. Even had a faker's two-way journey been negotiated successfully, I would have noticed the difference,' he repeated.

Alison pounced. 'But what if that happened before La Galleria was established? Three years ago you kept Queen Elizabeth downstairs, but most of the collection was stored up here.'

'Still impossible.'

'If Tim Hargreaves had discovered a fake,' Cara pointed out, 'that would have been before you had the new super security system in. And there might not have been any fakes smuggled in after his death because there would be a corpse to think about – assuming that's why he was murdered.'

'Or,' Alison added brightly, 'his death could have cleared the way for a super-fake.'

Max glared at his wife. 'Thank you, darling, but no. Without evidence, these are all mere theories.'

Time to intervene again, Cara thought. How to attack the situation? Suppose she was wrong? Could her theory beat this blank wall? Walls can either be knocked down or climbed over. Which to tackle? Alison was looking at her, willing her on – or so Cara hoped.

She would knock this wall down. 'As she met all these artists in Rome and Bologna,' she began, 'wouldn't at least one of them have painted her?' Silence. Cara ploughed on. 'That wouldn't be a fake. And couldn't she have painted one or two of them?'

Silence while Max considered this. 'The latter is possible, particularly in Bologna. There are many self-portraits by her but

as for her painting others . . .' He stopped for a moment for some
more consideration. 'There is of course that splendid one of the
wild young unknown man in our collection – though I prefer
Elizabeth. He might have been a fellow artist. Might that be a
fake, as you put it? With self-portraits that is a different matter,
of course. As Lavinia does not attract money in its millions it is
hard to see why any of those should be thought to be fakes.'

Dead end. Well, she'd begun, Cara thought, so she might as
well go on even if she had to put her foot in it big time. 'Leaving
the unknown man out of it, the portraits you have here both of
herself and others are all definitely by her, as are her religious
paintings?'

'Of course.'

Then Alison intervened. 'What about the self-portrait you once
called the Inner Self? That's somewhat different to the others; it
conveys a new sense of her character.'

Inner Self? Cara was aware she was getting out of her depth.

'Lavinia had an ongoing battle with the constant need to cede
to the superiority of men while believing in equal rights for
women. It has the inner sense of conflict,' Max explained, 'of a
Caravaggio.'

'Could it *be* by Caravaggio?' Cara asked in desperation.

Instant silence. Max looked startled and even Alison was taken
aback. 'It's true that it is reminiscent of his style,' Max finally
replied, 'but I feel the portrait lacks an overall message. How
therefore could it possibly be by anyone other than Lavinia struggling to convey her own conflict? Lavinia has chosen to paint
herself looking at the viewer with her easel and brush prominent
and in the background a symbolic tree in full bloom perhaps on
a windy day. It is true that the depth and sense of drama are
unusual, but they're effective.'

Cara could scarcely believe it. It seemed as though they had
taken two steps forward, and only one back. At least Max was
considering the possibility of something amiss in his collection.
Could she be winning?

Alison must have sensed that too. 'What about that wild young
man? Do you feel the same about that?'

Max's hackles were raised in defence. 'There is nothing at all
amiss with that. Pure Fontana, just a different approach. Are you

suggesting that that young man could have been Caravaggio himself?' Pause.

Max himself seemed startled at what he had said, Cara thought. Perhaps justifiably so if he'd by any chance hit upon the truth. She knew very little about art prices but she did know that works by well-known artists like Caravaggio brought in an awful lot of money.

'Nonsense,' Max then said briskly. 'It is most certainly not one of Caravaggio's self-portraits and, as his life in Rome was a notoriously wild one, Lavinia's and his paths would not have crossed. It's true that in theory my ancestor Thomas who bought the painting might have concealed the subject's identity as Caravaggio's reputation was then extremely low, but a fake is out of the question even if it does lack a certain lustre.'

Max looked at them both thoughtfully and then continued, 'We all have off days so perhaps . . .' Pause. 'I'll call the experts in just to satisfy you that there are no fakes in my collection. That art auction house Blink & Marlowe is still going from my ancestors' time. Are you satisfied? I'll tell them it's urgent.'

'Thank you,' Cara said meekly, quietly rejoicing. There were a lot of ifs about the fake theory but it was a path to follow. She still had to work out how possible it would have been to use the spiral stairway for entry, even the smugglers' tunnel perhaps, and what the security systems were like in Tim Hargreaves' time – if that proved relevant, of course. And how long would such a theft take? It would have been no easy task to gain entry, switch originals with fakes and exit safely again.

There was a yawning gap in the theory though. Photographs. Any recent thefts would involve careful photography not just of the painting but of its frame. Either a double journey would be necessary or more likely the person who would provide the keys and information about the entry route might also have to provide first-class photographs of the paintings at the very least. Her heart sank. A master planner would have been required for this operation, which would have to be someone on the staff, past or present.

This wasn't going to be just another meeting. Cara braced herself. It was – unusually – in the family wing. There was a

sizeable study there which Max rarely used, preferring the
delights of working near La Galleria. It was at the far end of
the wing overlooking the gardens and in the background the
estate stretching beyond it. He and Alison had circulated the
information that the skeleton was indeed that of Tim Hargreaves,
but in practice the afternoon meeting was dedicated mainly to
the open day. An odd combination, it seemed to Cara, to fanfare
the opening of the tunnel together with a murder. Both issues
had to be tackled. All health and safety issues over the tunnel
(and even the stairway) had now been satisfactorily settled and
the pathway to the open day was therefore clear.

Cara arrived in good time for the meeting to find that only
Ewan was as yet present.

'Still hoping to solve our murders?' he asked lightly.

'We all are, I hope,' she tried to reply cheerfully. Was there a
note of anxiety in his voice? She lectured herself not to see bogies
where there were none. There was a bunch of keys on the table
in front of Ewan and she seized the opportunity. 'Are they the
tunnel keys?' she asked.

'Good guess. Yes.'

'Would the tunnel have been accessible five years ago, even
if it was officially closed?'

She held her breath. Was it her imagination, or was Ewan
suddenly tense? 'Sure, Miss Marple. You're as bad as DCI
Mitchem.' He laughed – or did his best to do so. 'I can't see
why on earth any of us would have wanted to use it though.
Workmen of course excepted. But give me a break, Cara. If
you're still thinking that one of us crept along the tunnel to
kill Daphne, you're way behind the times – and if it was used
when that chap Hargreaves was killed there's no earthly way
of proving it now.' A note of satisfaction in his voice, she
detected.

The rest of the staff were now arriving, with Alison and Max
in the lead. Mike was with them to her relief, but thankfully the
emphasis this time was clearly going to be on the open day, with
its special opening on a Tuesday, and not on Daphne's death.
Cara relaxed as the meeting got under way, mentally sorting out
the Happy Huffkin's needs for the open day. Ice creams? Use
those special mugs with smugglers depicted on them that she'd

ordered? She was barely taking in what was going on when Ewan addressed her:

'Are you happy about our plans, Cara? Or are you bent on the possibility of a ghostly forger of Renaissance art wandering out with a Lavinia Fontana tucked under his arm.' He laughed dismissively.

Careful, she warned herself. Hit the right note here especially as all eyes were fixed on her. 'Why not?' she asked lightly. 'It's happened elsewhere. Wasn't there a Munch lifted from somewhere and of course the Mona Lisa herself vanished for several years.'

'True enough. Art theft and fraud are all too common and always have been,' Max replied.

'But are our security systems tight enough both in the house and tunnel?' Mike queried. 'They no sooner get put in nowadays than the villains work out how to silence them. And that would apply to the tunnel too.'

Here we go again, Cara thought. It wasn't her field, but surely it was too late to start worrying about that with the open day so close.

Dan picked up on this. 'The police are taking a great interest in that, though whether they're considering two independent murder cases or linked ones is a moot point.'

'Either way it leads back to that stairway,' Ewan said.

'But not La Galleria,' Max calmly pointed out. 'Security was upgraded three years ago and extra systems put in. In theory someone in the house already could turn it off, but even that would flash up a brief alarm.'

'What about the cellars?' Cara asked.

'Ah, you're really worried about that stairway, aren't you?' Ewan replied, managing to imply Cara was going overboard. 'That's being dealt with. The cellars are alarmed, so is the orangery, both at its exit and where the steps lead down to the cellar.'

'And the tunnel?' Cara persisted.

Ewan grinned. 'The new system fitted at both ends was installed a few days ago and it's still independent of the house, so any naughty forgers or thieves creeping along there would be able to have a nice picnic in the tunnel but get no further. They'd have to work a lot harder to get to the stairway. I'll show you if you like, Cara. I'm going down there myself at five o'clock. We can stroll along the tunnel together.'

He was smiling at her. Why did that give her goosebumps?

EIGHTEEN

Cara shivered. The goosebumps were still in place and waiting in this cellar was no fun at all. The sun might be shining outside but its rays certainly weren't reaching down here where the electric lighting was no substitute. Ewan had said he'd be along in half an hour but forty minutes had already passed.

What on earth was she here for? Having theories was good, but proving them was a different matter, especially as the Happy Huffkin needed her attention. Furthermore, did she really want to walk along this tunnel with Ewan? He was, she was uncomfortably reminded, one of the few people who could have been responsible for Daphne's death and possibly Tim Hargreaves' too. At least, she comforted herself, her theory about possible fakes could therefore also be a key to both murders. Daphne might have been killed for having discovered Tim Hargreaves' skeleton, but if so the question of fakes might have nothing to do with either death.

Another shiver. Where was Ewan? It seemed to her it was getting colder with every minute. She consulted her watch and saw that forty minutes had turned into nearly sixty. At least the door into the tunnel was already unlocked and a peep inside revealed that the lighting was on inside it. Was that odd? Not really. No Lavinia Fontana forgers seemed to be crawling along it, so she must have made a mistake. Ewan must be waiting at the woodland end of the tunnel and would be getting impatient. Stupid of her. He might already be coming along the tunnel to meet her, having realized what had happened. Next step: she might as well nip along to meet him.

She pulled the door open and it retaliated with a squeaky groan. She jammed it against closure and then surveyed what lay in front of her. The tunnel sloped gently downwards until it turned beyond sight. The first step was the worst because she was heading for the unknown, but she cheered up as she made

her way along the gravelled track. The walls were now decorated
with prints of times gone by, famous smugglers, clashes with the
Revenue, bottles of brandy and every so often a print of Sir Jeffry
enjoying the fruits of his law-breaking. True, the presentation
was masking the cold stone walls which were a testament to the
tunnel's age, but the lights were clearly marking the way. That
meant Ewan must be expecting her even if it did feel as if she
was walking into the unknown.

'Ewan!' she yelled.

No reply. How long was this tunnel, she wondered. Two or
three hundred yards, perhaps? Faced with a suddenly darkening
scene before her as the ground dipped away, her doubts grew
again. Where was Ewan? Should she turn back? For all her
attempts to fight it, the silence around her, the roof close above
her and the chill of the damp walls were beginning to have their
effect. She couldn't get to the end of this awful place soon enough,
now fully aware that she was underground on her own and a
long way from the Towers.

She tried to imagine the smugglers creeping along this tunnel,
with only their lanterns lighting their way. A dim memory of her
mother hurrying in with a small night light when she was a child
who was bawling with fright in the dark came back to her. She
quickly shut it out. Her mother had long since disappeared from
her life after the divorce and so had her father. Looking back on
it, it was as if both had walked off in their differing directions
forgetting about their child stuck in the middle. OK, she had
loved living with her grandparents, but she still remembered how
that eight-year-old Cara had felt, wondering what she had done
wrong as both mummy and daddy had left her alone.

Darkness had lain ahead then and it did now as she picked
her way carefully along the tunnel. Suppose it collapsed in front
of her? It wouldn't, of course, because it had been through every
official safety check ever dreamed up and shortly hordes of people
would be trampling along it quite happily.

That was a comforting thought, but it failed to alter the fact
that tonight she was on her own. Still no sign of Ewan. He must
still be waiting at the far end. She turned a bend in the tunnel
and to her relief she saw not more walls closing in on her but
blissful daylight.

An open door! She ran towards it. Thank goodness for freedom.
'Ewan!' she cried out.

No reply. Tension grew again. Then, yes, a muffled sound from
the woodland outside, this time definitely a 'hello'. She stumbled
out into the fresh air with relief.

'Ewan!'

There was still no reply. Nobody there. Only the woodland
trees, bushes and a felled trunk or two turned into makeshift
seating greeted her. And then as she went towards it she saw him
lying there, flat out, face down in the muddy earth. It was Ewan.
Motionless. Silent.

So who had replied to her? Terror welled up inside her as she
fell to her knees to see what was wrong. It hadn't been Ewan
who had cried out to her. There was someone else here, someone
who from his very silence was almost certainly a murderer.

But it wasn't.

It was only Mike coming towards her to help her as she stag-
gered to her feet in relief. It didn't last. This wasn't the Mike
she knew. His face was distorted in hatred.

'You had to interfere, didn't you, Cara.' He was wrenching
her arm, pulling her closer, then he dropped the arm. Those hands
were coming to her face, her throat.

Then everything was black.

'Cara!' Someone was shouting, but she could do nothing. Her
lips wouldn't move and something was wrong with her face.
'*Cara!*'

With difficulty she opened her eyes to focus on whoever was
supporting her on the ground. She knew that voice.

It was Detective Chief Inspector Andrew Mitchem's.

'*Cara!*'

NINETEEN

'**W**here's Mike?'
They were the only words she could whisper as she emerged from hospital two days later to be greeted by Alison and Max. That meant home after the whirlwind.

'Typical,' Alison said fondly, tucking a warm coat around her (completely unnecessarily) as she helped her into their car. 'If you really need to know, that murderous skunk will be safely charged with first-degree murder and attempted murder. Any other urgent questions?' she asked fondly.

'Ewan?' she croaked. She'd worked it out now. Ewan was innocent, attacked as she had been.

'Recovering in hospital. Severe stunning but no permanent damage. Anything else?'

Another croak. 'Cottage?' She fastened on the one thing that made sense at the moment: she hadn't told her neighbour to take in the food delivery she was expecting.

'Sammy's looking after it. You need TLC, tender loving care, so you're coming to Tanton Towers for a day or two.'

Coming to Tanton Towers. What a wonderful phrase. Cara smiled but then she thought of the other burning question, throat hurting or not.

'Andrew Mitchem – how there?' A bunch of flowers from him had arrived, but no more, and those were the only words she could croak out. Tucked away in the clinical world of hospitals, outside life had been suspended for forty-eight hours and economy on words was becoming unavoidable. But she had to find out how he managed to be there for her.

'That will wait,' Alison told her.

'But . . .' Cara stopped. Perhaps they were right. She'd wait too. Her eyes closed as Max drove in through the familiar gates of the Towers. Everything would be all right now. She didn't understand how or why, but she knew that. After all, she was at Tanton Towers.

Her day or two at Tanton seemed to have turned into three. The throat was no longer a problem as it was merely sore, but the dizziness in her head was. Today she had woken up clear-headed to a glorious new world. She was at the Towers.

This must have been obvious as Alison nodded instant approval as she appeared for breakfast. 'Today?' Cara asked huskily. It was weird being in the family wing, eating breakfast with them and still not knowing what had happened. After all, she was part of the drama.

'Yes. After breakfast,' Max declared.

'Ewan?' she asked.

'At home, due back in a few days.'

Cara did her best to concentrate on the milky porridge, but was thankful when they adjourned to the familiar living room. The chiffon scarf round her neck was still welcome protection.

'I bet everyone here already knows the story, don't they?' she managed to whisper. She was on tenterhooks. What were the staff up to – her friends – while she'd been in hospital? Staff without *him*, of course. She shuddered even thinking about Mike.

'We're the darlings of the media and everyone here is making a fortune out of TV and articles and goodness knows what,' Alison informed her. 'Everyone wants the story. Tanton Towers, together with the Farran Prydes, is on the map.'

'With your approval?' Cara asked, taken aback. Personal publicity was not Max's forte either for himself or for his staff.

'Absolutely,' Alison said. 'With poor Ewan's open day postponed for a week, we have to move with the times. We're becoming experts at this publicity game.'

'Be warned. It's centred on you at present, Cara,' Max added. 'Attack at Tanton Towers leads to re-arrest of Michael Hanson. Sammy's in his element giving interviews.'

This Cara doubted. His idea of an interview was answering with a yes or no. 'How about telling me what's happened please?' she asked humbly. Never rush Max.

'In what order?' Max enquired.

'Andrew Mitchem,' Cara promptly answered. 'He saved my life. How did he come to be there, or know that I would be somewhere in the middle of the woods?'

'He was always on Mike's trail,' Max told her soberly. 'Hence he felt responsible because although he knew it could be asking for trouble to leave Mike at large, he thought he could handle it. Thankfully he came over to us when he found Sammy alone at the Happy Huffkin and, finding you not here, he was worried to say the least. Ewan had informed the world at our meeting about your proposed tour of the tunnel with him, so Mike just told him you'd decided to change the rendezvous point. Ewan believed him.'

'But why attack me?' Cara howled – or at least in her mind she howled. Sore throats didn't permit that.

'Unfortunately for you, you were delving too deeply and Mike was all too well aware of that,' Max told her. 'Two murders already; you would have been the third.'

'But thankfully, you weren't,' Alison said softly, taking her hand into hers.

Cara felt tears forming, and perhaps seeing that, Alison took up the story again. 'Poor Keeley is annoyed with herself because she was friendly with him and knew Mike had worked in art and antiques insurance. We were all aware of that, of course, but she had gathered at some point that he was in touch with specialized auction houses. DCI Mitchem has told us he master-minded or initiated the exchange of at least those two originals with fakes before La Galleria was established, but they were then in storage up there rather than downstairs with Max. He had his beloved Queen Bess downstairs, didn't you, darling?' She laughed.

Max beamed. 'A most interesting point about one of the two paintings which I now appreciate are fakes, Cara. We still like them, fakes or not, though I fear the originals are lost to us along with the money they would have fetched. Lavinia's self-portrait seated in the studio with the tree in full bloom outside is, according to John Hubert – the expert from Blink & Marlowe, who inspected La Galleria yesterday – probably not by Lavinia but by . . .' He paused.

Another laugh from Alison. 'Tell her the worst, Max.'

'An artist called Caravaggio,' Max told her somewhat shamefacedly.

'*What?*' Cara reeled in shock. Her accidental stab in the dark had been right.

'And that means, I'm afraid,' Alison said, 'that we are not going to be blessed with the millions that would have brought in. Both paintings are going through various tests but John Hubert is sure they're fakes and that somewhere in the world new owners are gloating over the originals. Not confirmed yet, but we are resigned to it. Mike of course would have profited nicely from it. It was his plan and the police think that the Towers wasn't the only house to suffer from them.'

Max had been pondering the matter. 'I'm in agreement with Alison,' he declared. (A rare occurrence, Cara thought fondly.) 'The other suspected fake is indeed Lavinia's portrait of that rebellious young man who is, I now concede, almost certainly Caravaggio himself, and probably painted by Lavinia in Rome, despite Caravaggio's notoriety there a few years before his death. Still to be proven is whether these two canvases were switched quite recently for the originals or much earlier or possibly were bought by one of my ancestors. However, John Hubert is all but sure – tests will tell – that they were stolen, relatively recently; he estimated about five years ago.'

'Which probably coincides with Tim Hargreaves' death,' Alison added.

Cara began to relax. This was – in an odd way – good news. Modern fakes. She had at least been on the right lines. What about Max's favourite portrait though?

'Good Queen Bess?' she struggled to ask.

Max glared. 'You see how wise I was to keep her close by me before La Galleria was born. Being on the first floor, it escaped, or undoubtedly it too would have been a victim.'

Alison laughed. 'We both win on that one,' she said. 'John thinks it is a true Fontana but the quality is poor owing to its not being drawn from life, just as we thought. He agrees it was – subject to more checks – probably based on the work of a Flemish artist who'd visited England, perhaps even Denys Calvaert as Max believes.'

'Of course it's a genuine Fontana,' Max insisted in self-defence.

'Despite the possible fakes that John's looking into, the others are all true Lavinia,' he added defiantly.

Alison took up the story. 'We don't know what precisely the most recent usage of the stairway was for but if it's confirmed that the fakes were switched about five years ago, there's no doubt that Mike supplied the keys to use the stairway even if he didn't do the dastardly deed itself.'

Cara mustered all her strength. The vital question was not yet answered. Thefts could wait. 'Mike. Charged Daphne's murder? Tim Hargreaves?' she croaked.

'Yes,' Alison replied. 'We're going to see your Mrs Pollard with DCI Mitchem to tell her as much of the story as we think she'll take at present. She'll hear and see a lot when it comes to the trial, I'm afraid. We've been checking dates and records together with Robert Broome. Poor Tim's death had not been part of Mike's plan, and Mike must have killed him on the day he was due to leave for that tour. The police have tracked down the holiday he was thought to be taking in the Pyrenees, and he was down as a no-show. The phone calls to us purporting to be the travel agent involved were obviously bogus. Robert had only worked part-time before the thefts took place and any visits would have been to the first-floor office. He wouldn't have been near the pungent decaying corpse there and by the time the Archives Room moved upstairs it would no longer have been detectable.'

Cara managed another croak. 'Why kill Tim?'

'Mike has been oddly loquacious about that,' Max told her, 'and the police have given us permission to tell you but only you.'

'He was burbling away while he was being arrested,' Alison added.

'Tim loved art, as you know,' Max explained. 'We don't know whether he had discovered the stairway or not, but he had clearly realized that those two Caravaggio paintings were fake and deduced that Mike was involved with their theft and their being whisked away with his help, so in all probability he had known about the stairway, even if Daphne didn't. Robert has discovered that it was not only used to convey Sir Jeffry's casks of brandy but also at other times, including the First World War when this was a hospital for the duration. We don't know if Daphne was aware of that or how she discovered the hidey-hole.'

Daphne. She'd been right. That's what had upset Daphne so much. Cara braced herself for a big speech. 'Daphne find hidey-hole, skeleton?' she managed. 'Why not scream? Why shut again?'

'Simple,' Alison said. 'We think it was like this. She was beginning to put two and two together. She kept quiet about the skeleton because she wanted to talk it over with Mike first, not realizing he was mixed up in the story. Robert wasn't in the office, so she just slammed the hole shut again. She might even have had an idea about who the skeleton was. It's probable that the great big discovery she told everyone she was expecting to make was not the stairway but the hidey-hole in the annex. The discovery of the skeleton changed everything.

'When she blurted it all out to Mike that evening, he insisted on her keeping it a secret,' Alison continued, 'but it sealed her fate. He suggested meeting her in the orangery which was a nice handy place for them both to reach.'

'He came through the smugglers' tunnel and up the steps to the orangery intending to kill her?' Cara was getting into her element.

Alison laughed. 'Sorry to disappoint you. No. The answer's much simpler, but it was his downfall. Not too pleasant for us either.'

Where was this leading? Cara's mind was beginning to whirl now.

'We think Mike drove home,' Alison told her, 'just as he told us all. He left the car at home, walked back to the footpath off Church Road through the estate, avoiding the public car park, and emerged at the tradesmen's back gate. He then just sauntered up the path past the end of the family wing and the servants' wing to the far door of the orangery near which Daphne was waiting for him.'

'*What?*' Cara shrieked, throat aching from the effort. 'Suppose he was seen?'

'That was the trick. He took a chance and wasn't seen. But suppose he had been spotted? He could make up any number of reasons for his having returned unexpectedly and though it would mean postponing his attack on Daphne, he had a fall-back plan on hand. As it was, he had a choice after killing her: he could go back the way he had come or take the tunnel, the safer route. He chose the latter, because security was not yet kicking into action and he had access to the keys.'

'Why take that risk?' Cara asked.

'He was the only person on the staff who could get away with it. He was her husband, his office was in that building, his wife had been dancing there – and he was the only person who had a seemingly impeccable alibi.'

Tomorrow, Tuesday the 23rd, would be the postponed open day with Ewan back in command. Dan was revelling in his role as chief informant to visitors about art theft; Ewan was as happy as a lark (though Cara had never understood why larks should be happier than other birds); Robert had cautiously resumed his place in the office, having been assured that no more hidey-holes would be revealed there; Sammy was hard at work with huffkins and she had been flying around trying to help. And best of all, Daphne could now be laid to gentle rest.

Only one thing was amiss. DCI Andrew Mitchem had not yet visited her so that she could thank him for saving her life. This had to be done, but short of storming into his office there was nothing she could do about it. The silence had continued.

Until now.

With the last gulp of milky hot chocolate to soothe her throat, she turned off the television, ready to call it a day. Then the doorbell rang. Always the unexpected. It was of course Andrew Mitchem.

'Come in,' she stuttered, taken aback to see him as she pulled the door open.

'Perhaps not tonight.' He thrust a bunch of red roses towards her.

'But I have to thank you for the ones you sent to the hospital – and for my life,' she added helplessly as she took hold of the flowers. Damn. Why was she so tongue-tied? 'We need to talk. I can't just send you a thank-you postcard,' she added defensively.

'No,' he agreed, standing there like a yeoman of the guard.

Silence. 'Did you expect me to faint in your arms?' she blurted out.

'I can think of more interesting things to do there.'

An enormous heffalump pit opened up before her. This was a statement of intent. Result? She couldn't step forward, but wouldn't step back. What to say, what to do? She wasn't there yet. This wasn't fair. It wasn't time. She didn't know.

'I'm not a huffkin. I take longer to bake,' she managed. It wasn't good, but it would do.

'I'll wait.'

She watched as he turned and walked back along the path and through the gate. Then she closed the door, well pleased.